"Come o

Jake coaxed softly, his grin devilish. "How are we going to convince people we're lovers if you jump every time I approach?"

Reggie licked her lips, then abruptly stopped as his eyes followed the motion. "I believe I said I'd pose as your business associate," she managed to get out, her chin coming up.

He reached out and very lightly touched her cheek. She flinched instantly, and for a moment his dark eyes glinted with seriousness. Just as abruptly, the seriousness was gone and he was simply teasing her once more. "Honey, you're a beautiful woman. No one who knows me would ever believe I'd let you remain just an associate."

Dear Reader,

It's summertime, and the livin' may or may not be easy—but the reading is great. Just check out Naomi Horton's *Wild Blood*, the first in her new WILD HEARTS miniseries. In Jett Kendrick you'll find a hero to take to heart and never let go, and you'll understand why memories of their brief, long-ago loving have stayed with Kathy Patterson for sixteen years. Now she's back in Burnt River, back in Jett's life—and about to discover a secret that will change *three* lives forever.

We feature two more great miniseries this month, too. Cathryn Clare's ASSIGNMENT: ROMANCE brings you *The Baby Assignment*, the exciting conclusion to the Cotter brothers' search for love, while Alicia Scott's THE GUINESS GANG continues with *The One Who Almost Got Away*, featuring brother Jake Guiness. And there's still more great reading you won't want to miss. Patricia Coughlin's *Borrowed Bride* features a bride who's kidnapped—right out from under the groom's nose. Of course, it's her kidnapper who turns out to be Mr. Right. And by the way, both Alicia and Patricia had earlier books that were made into CBS TV movies last year. In *Unbroken Vows*, Frances Williams sends her hero and heroine on a search for the heroine's ex-fiancé, a man hero David Reid is increasingly uninterested in finding. Finally, check out Kay David's *Hero in Hiding*, featuring aptly named Mercy Hamilton and enigmatic Rio Barrigan, a man who is far more than he seems.

Then join us again next month and every month, as we bring you more of the best romantic reading around—only in Silhouette Intimate Moments.

Yours,

Leslie Wainger,
Senior Editor and Editorial Coordinator

Please address questions and book requests to:
Silhouette Reader Service
U.S.: 3010 Walden Ave., P.O. Box 1325, Buffalo, NY 14269
Canadian: P.O. Box 609, Fort Erie, Ont. L2A 5X3

THE ONE WHO ALMOST GOT AWAY

ALICIA SCOTT

Published by Silhouette Books
America's Publisher of Contemporary Romance

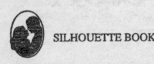

SILHOUETTE BOOKS

ISBN 0-373-07723-8

THE ONE WHO ALMOST GOT AWAY

Copyright © 1996 by Lisa Baumgartner

Books by Alicia Scott

ALICIA SCOTT

recently escaped the corporate world to pursue her writing full-time. According to the former consultant, "I've been a writer for as long as I can remember. For me, it's the perfect job, and you can't beat the dress code." Born in Hawaii, she grew up in Oregon before moving to Massachusetts. Now an avid traveler, she spends her time chasing after two feisty felines, watching Val Kilmer movies and eating chocolate when she's not running around the globe.

She is currently at work on her latest project in Boston, where she awaits the discovery of true love or ownership of a chocolate shop—whichever comes first.

To the New England Chapter of RWA, because everyone offered me not just knowledge, experience and expertise, but also friendship. And particularly to Terry Pino and Betsy Eliot, whose energy, creativity and generosity never cease to amaze me. I'm so glad I moved to Boston and met you all.

Prologue

The black-clad figure flitted out from behind the first old oak. Ducking low, he raced along the ground, a lithe shadow skimming over the earth. He flattened himself against the next tree just as the security camera rotated again.

Jake Guiness checked the glowing dial of his watch and counted off the seconds until the camera arched back in the other direction. Thirty seconds. Not much time, but he could do it, he told himself. He shook his head.

"Should've gotten crisscrossing cameras, Donnar, old boy," he muttered. Whistling lightly to himself, he uncoiled the thick rope hanging from his shoulder. In black jeans and a black turtleneck, he was clad far differently than his usual double-breasted suit. He was also a long way from the Guiness Corporation boardroom. He smiled in satisfaction, tying the end of the rope to a three-pronged anchor. "Perfect," he complimented himself. "If the global market gets much tougher, I really could become a full-time thief. Certainly it's more entertaining than combatting fifty years of communist thinking in Eastern Europe."

He glanced back around the tree to find the camera. It turned toward him, an oval eye in the darkness. Jake ducked down and began counting off the seconds once more.

The tree was only ten feet from the stone wall encompassing the house. At least Donnar's security company had had the good sense to cut off the lower branches; Jake would make sure he reported that back to his friend. Leaving the tree at all, however, had been a mistake. One Jake was about to reveal.

The instant the security camera started back toward the old stone wall, Jake darted out and swung the anchored end of the rope up over the base of the first tree branch. He pulled the rope tight, and the metal ends of the anchor dug into hundred-year-old bark. A moment later, Jake flattened himself against the tree, letting the security camera drift past.

As the mechanized eye looped back, he grabbed his rope with gloved hands and using mountain-climber's boots for leverage, he scrambled thirty feet up the trunk to the thick branch. He glanced at his watch again. Twenty-eight seconds. Close, but all those afternoons in the gym were finally paying off. He sat down on the gnarled old branch, safe from the camera, and contemplated his options while catching his breath.

The two-foot thick stone wall was generously sprinkled with jagged daggers of glass. A nice touch, Jake conceded, though totally irrelevant now that he could swing down into the yard from the tree branch, avoiding the top of the wall altogether. At this point he was more concerned about the two Dobermans prowling the interior boundaries of the stone bastion.

No guard managed the dogs, he noted; Donnar always had been cheap. Jake pulled the dog whistle out of his pocket and hung it around his neck. Then, just to be safe, he clenched the tip of the metal whistle loosely between his teeth. The dogs disappeared temporarily around the corner, and Jake executed Part B of his plan.

He rolled up his rope, then flung it over the wall into the yard. If everything had been perfect, the thick branch would have extended deep into the yard. Instead the tip of the branch ended right where the wall began. That made his task trickier, but not impossible. Of course, the fact that he was thirty feet in the air added a nice touch of danger.

"Self-made millionaire goes splat in best friend's yard," Jake muttered. "Nah."

He wrapped the top of the rope loosely around his hand, doling out ten feet of slack. Then, he crouched at the end of the thick branch and leapt backward into open air. For a thrilling moment, he flew back ten feet, the rope skimming briskly through his gloved palm. Then *bamm,* his weight carried him forward, and he came down hard against the top interior of the wall. He relaxed his knees, absorbing the shock of impact, and found himself eye level to the shards of glass rimming the thick top. He allowed himself one triumphant grin, then quickly scaled down the inside wall, the thick rope rasping through his leather gloves. He'd barely hit soft, grassy ground when the Dobermans came darting around the corner.

Teeth bared, small ears flat against their sleek skulls, the dogs raced toward him like black bullets. Beneath the ski mask, Jake felt the sweat bead on his brow. One thousand one, one thousand two—

He blew the whistle, hard and long. The dogs stumbled, breaking stride and tumbling down with low whimpers. Mercilessly Jake blew the whistle again, darting quickly to the rolling shapes. He pulled out the two muzzles he'd brought and quickly slid them onto the sleek snouts. His glove-encased fingers weren't exactly nimble, and he almost swore twice before he realized he couldn't afford the wasted breath. One of the Dobermans recovered enough to swipe at his wrist, and he almost lost the dog whistle altogether with his exclamation of surprise. Finally, he slid in the last buckle, securing the dog. Unfastening leashes from around his waist, he attached them to the dog collars and led both dogs around the corner.

His hands still shook from the adrenaline.

The way Jake remembered it, only the main doors and first story sliding glass doors were monitored by cameras. He tied the dogs to the wrought-iron bars protecting a lower window and brushed his hands off. The two Dobermans lunged for him, but the window bars held.

All right, he was in. And still in one piece, he added silently. He grinned in the night, his teeth a huge, white flash of Guiness arrogance and charm.

Jake began to whistle again, glancing around the dark, shadowed yard, contemplating his next move. He stared at the dark stone mansion for a minute longer, then realized he was running out of time.

Knowing Donnar, he'd turned the basement into the gallery.

Jake found an ivy trellis and used it to pull himself up to the second floor patio. There, he balanced on the stone railing and explored the bottom of the third-story window with a small pen flashlight. It didn't appear to be wired.

Jake retrieved the glass cutter from his black leather pack and slowly cut out the pane. Wire clippers eliminated the screen. Reaching in with a gloved hand, he found the metal slide pins that controlled the windows. What a pain.

No longer so carefully balanced, he reached in with both hands, squeezed the inside latches of the window inward and awkwardly pushed the window up. Stretching onto his tiptoes he got the window three quarters of the way up. Taking a deep breath, he carefully eased himself down to flat footing. God, he *was* going to get himself killed. And all as a favor to a friend.

He shook his head, then stared at the open window once more. He gripped the sides, praying that the casing was solid, then wedged his metal-pronged shoe into a mortar crack. He heaved himself up, and like a gasping fish, wiggled through the window. After a precarious moment, he fell headfirst onto the floor of the room.

"Not graceful," he muttered as he sat up and shook his masked head, "but effective."

From here on out, it was a piece of cake.

No one was in the mansion; Donnar was in the Congo, while his wife and daughter entertained themselves in Paris. Always cutting corners, Donnar didn't maintain a house staff when he was away, and the dogs were taken care of by the security company that monitored the cameras from their headquarters. Even if Jake had been spotted on one of the cameras, he knew it would take ten minutes for someone to arrive on the scene, ample time for a messy hit-and-run. Jake preferred the more subtle approach simply because he liked the challenge.

He wandered downstairs at a leisurely pace, more than satisfied with himself and his venture thus far. When he reached the front doors, he pulled out an aerosol can of hairspray and lightly sprayed the air. Sure enough, three lasers reflected back in the tiny particles. So, Jake mused, if he'd broken in through the front doors, he would have triggered the laser-activated alarm. Nice touch, Donnar, but how many thieves use the front door?

Jake shook his head again. Good thing he was proactively finding all the flaws in his friend's security system. Better him, at least, than the real Highwayman who was currently wreaking havoc on private art collections all along the East Coast. That clever fiend had pulled off four major heists in the past three months, snatching major art works and leaving behind a single red rose and verse of flowery prose, thus earning his dashing nickname and igniting the romantic fantasies of half the women on the Eastern seaboard.

Jake found the thick metal double doors leading to the basement and tested the air with his handy hairspray. Three more lasers.

Hmm. Slightly trickier this time.

He could probably pick the lock without activating the laser-triggered alarm. Then he could dash in and out, triggering the alarm but still having ten minutes to complete the heist before the security company or police arrived. He figured he could steal something and disappear in that time.

But the approach lacked finesse; Jake wanted to actually beat the system, not simply outrun it.

Maybe he could wiggle beneath it. He sprayed the air again and checked the height of the bottom laser beam. Too low to the ground for a man to slide underneath. Then another thought hit him, and he fired his aerosol can one more time. Beneath the lowest bar and above the highest bar were out of the question, but *between* the bottom and middle bar had possibilities.

One clean dive would do it, followed by a simple drop roll down the stairs.

Next to impossible.

He liked it.

Grinning already, he whistled to himself as he played with the combination lock on the double doors, his hands steady and fluid as they worked the combination between the two laser beams. Birth dates yielded nothing, nor did social security numbers. He tried Donnar's favorite number. Nothing.

Jake stopped whistling and sat back on his heels, frowning.

"Donnar, you old goat," he whispered in the silent house. "Were you actually creative in picking your combination? Nah, you're never creative."

He rocked back and forth a few times, turning the matter over in his head. Combinations were never random; people picked things they could remember. All right, so what kind of things held meaning for Donnar? The international investor routinely made and lost fortunes hedging foreign currency rates. He was passionate for his Jaguar and one-hundred-year-old Scotch. He dressed well, buying only personally tailored clothes, and he'd recently taken up safari-style hunting.

Not much to work with. Oh, what the hell, Jake thought as he rose again to carefully reach through the invisible bars and spin the combination lock. He tried Donnar's shirt measurements, having recently accompanied his friend on one of his many shopping binges. The metal wheel whizzed around with a smooth whir, then clicked.

"Donnar, Donnar, Donnar," Jake chastised in the dark. "You vain old devil."

He swung open the thick doors carefully, revealing a small boon. Rather than opening over a spiraling staircase, the heavy metal doors lorded over a red-carpeted minifoyer. The foyer boasted a side table with an impressive flower arrangement in a Ming vase. The twenty-by-twenty foot space ended with a graceful, downward sweeping staircase. Jake could stop his forward roll by then. Piece of cake. He just had to make sure he didn't somersault into the vase. Stealing a token momento was one thing, breaking a Ming vase would most likely incite Donnar to shoot to kill.

Stepping back a few feet, Jake sprayed the air one last time, pinpointing the three laser beams and shaking his head at his own daring.

"Here goes nothing," he whispered. He dived headfirst through the three-foot space, his lean, muscular body arching through the darkness. Tuck and roll accomplished, and he found himself suddenly sitting up in the middle of the nicely padded foyer, Ming vase to his immediate right, staircase dead ahead.

"God, I'm good."

He began whistling wholeheartedly, turned on his flashlight and sauntered down the graceful, spiraling stairs to his friend's private art collection.

He turned on the light of the windowless museum. God, Donnar had an eclectic collection. Van Goghs hung on the wall, as well as two minor Rembrandts. There were two Picassos, three Dalis, plus one Mayan statue and a single gold doubloon. Donnar didn't pursue an interest; he snapped up bargain opportunities as investments.

Jake saw the small collection of Oceanic sculpture and knew he'd found his trophy. He selected a small, amply rounded woman's figure decorated by bright, bold colors. He smiled to himself.

"Pocket-size," he said with a sigh. He cut a hole through the glass and removed his prize.

Leaving the museum, he walked out the front door, no longer caring if the security guards sitting eight miles away saw him or not. He waved at the camera, even holding up his statue for posterity, then trotted across the yard to his rope.

Tucking the statue carefully into the pack around his waist, he grabbed the rope and climbed back up the wall. Piece of cake, he told himself again. Donnar was going to have a cow when he realized how many holes his "new and improved" security system still had. Jake could already see his friend's face.

He lowered himself down from the tree, realizing at the last moment he didn't know how to get the embedded anchor out of the tree trunk. He shrugged, slicing the rope with his pocket knife instead. He didn't want anyone else taking advantage of his hard work and blatant ingenuity.

He was walking away when he realized the night seemed much quieter than he remembered.

He stilled, and all of a sudden he knew he wasn't alone. His muscles tensed, his ears straining. What the . . . ?

The unmistakable sound of a cocked gun cut through the silence. "FBI," came a clear voice. "Hands over your head. Now."

Bewildered, Jake slowly raised his hands. The night seemed to part, and a woman flanked by two other agents stepped into the clearing. Her 9-mm gun never wavered from his chest.

"We got you this time, Highwayman," the suit-clad woman said triumphantly. With one hand, she reached over and snatched the ski mask off his face.

Jake looked into her bright green eyes and suddenly began to laugh.

Chapter 1

"Look," Jake began, "there's been a very simple misunderstanding here. I'm not the Highwayman."

The agent's gun slowly lowered, but her emerald eyes did not relent. Her short-cropped hair lay flat against her head, framing those magnificent eyes with spiky fringes. He would bet the navy blue pantsuit was Ann Taylor; the clean tailored lines fit her to a tee. Jake grinned at her.

"It's a federal offense to lie to an agent," she stated grimly.

He started, shocked by her unrelenting austerity. For one moment his hands wavered above his head. Her gun came back up sharply. "Hands in the air!" she promptly barked.

Jake spared a glance to the two agents behind her, but they also had their weapons out. He took a deep breath and sought to control the rapidly disintegrating situation.

"I know how this looks," he said, trying valiantly to keep the grin on his face. "But I'm Jake Guiness. I can buy any piece of art I want. I don't have to steal it."

"I know who you are," the woman replied tersely. Her eyes darted to the other two men, and Jake thought she looked a bit nervous. Then she steadied the gun in her hands, and he kept his eyes on it instead.

"Do you have any ID?" he asked quietly.

Regina O'Doul stared at him for a full minute. Of all the arrogance. She'd caught him stealing, and he wanted to see *her* identification? Her bright green eyes narrowed dangerously. "Agent Reggie O'Doul," she snapped. "Wesley?" The other agent obligingly reached into his suit jacket and flashed his credentials. "Jake Guiness," she said clearly, "you're under arrest."

He looked startled, but no more startled than she felt. She hadn't really expected it to come to this. She'd known it was possible; after all, her job was to arrest people. But this was her first real arrest, and as she reached to the small of her back for the handcuffs, she could feel her hands begin to shake.

Was she supposed to Mirandize him now? Suddenly the Academy and the lessons of Hogan's Alley—the FBI's simulated version of reality—seemed so far away. She glanced at her two fellow agents, but they were watching her with expectant eyes. She'd taken—no, demanded—the lead in this case, and they were giving it to her. Just enough rope to hang herself, she thought grimly, pulling out the handcuffs.

She was taking him into custody, and, therefore, should read him his rights. At least that was the way she remembered it. "You have the right to remain silent," she began, pulling his arms behind his back.

Jake didn't protest but shook his head like a dazed man while she read him his rights. Under arrest? He was under arrest as a thief? He looked down at his black turtleneck and black jeans, and all of a sudden he wanted to laugh again.

"Look," he tried for the third time as the beautiful agent led him to a car parked at the edge of the property, "can't you listen to me for just one moment?"

"Anything you say can be held against you in a court of law," she reminded him. She had a husky voice to match her sultry eyes. Under any other circumstances, he would have bought Reggie O'Doul a very nice bottle of wine and maybe a single perfect orchid. At this point, however, he didn't want to be accused of bribery.

"I know, I know," he said as they arrived at the car. At the last moment he stopped walking, jolting her arm with his sudden resistance. Her eyes narrowed, her hand already reaching for the 9-mm. "Hang on just one moment," he said hastily. He grinned at her. "I know you're doing your job. And I'm sure I look as guilty as hell. Maybe it's the clothes. But this whole 'burglary' wasn't real. Donnar asked me to test his new system, just like I recently tested my own, to ensure—you guessed it—that the systems would stand up against the Highwayman. The *real* Highwayman."

"And where is Donnar Ivansson now?" she asked him coolly.

He smiled weakly. "The Congo."

Her pointed look said it all. "Rather convenient, isn't it, that Mr. Ivansson is out of the country."

He took a deep breath and felt his frustration spiral dangerously close to anger. Jake Guiness didn't get angry; anger was a purposeless emotion. He drew another deep breath and when he trusted himself again, he pasted a tight smile on his face. "Well, Regina, it would've defeated the purpose to break in when Donnar was home."

"Agent." She corrected him. "Agent O'Doul." She held open the car door. "And do you really expect me to believe that you broke into 'your friend's' home without any sort of contingency plan in case you were caught?"

Jake scowled. "I wasn't going to get caught."

She arched a knowing brow.

"So I'm arrogant! That's not a crime!"

"Maybe not, Mr. Guiness, but breaking and entering is."

"Oh, for God's sake," he exclaimed, "my brother works for the Bureau!"

"And I've heard Mitch Guiness does fine work," she assured him. She took his elbow and guided him into the back seat. She leaned down and looked at him with steady eyes.

"It would be better if you cooperated, Mr. Guiness. Better for you and your brother."

For the first time, she saw him stiffen. Suddenly his eyes weren't grinning and incredulous anymore. The brown depths had become quite serious and quite dangerous. She found herself automatically pulling back, then cursed herself for the weakness.

"Don't you threaten Mitch," Jake Guiness told her quite softly. "You've made a mistake, Agent O'Doul. Given the circumstances, I can be understanding to a point. Don't push me beyond that."

Her own eyes suddenly snapped green fire, her Irish temper rising despite her best efforts. Just as she was about to deliver a snapping retort, Wesley stepped between them.

"We understand, Mr. Guiness," Wesley said pleasantly enough. The agent turned and gave her a wry smile. "Let's get him back to headquarters, Reggie. You can annihilate him there."

She nodded, taking a deep breath of her own, and accepted the car keys from Wesley. She had an exemplary record—except for her temper. She had to remember to keep it under control.

She'd just made the arrest of her life, she reminded herself as she climbed into the car. One way or another, Jake Guiness was the key to the Highwayman. And if she could just unlock that puzzle, she would never have to listen to whispers of her being Frank O'Doul's daughter ever again.

She had a long time to contemplate that as they drove to the Hoover Building in D.C.

Jake was still grinning, but his cheeks now hurt from the effort. He sat in a small locked room with a two-way mirror, his hands finally free but with no place to go. In front of him stood a table, and behind the table sat Agent O'Doul with another man she'd introduced as Special Agent Ron Buchanan. In the end, Jake had called both his lawyer and Mitch. It was only a matter of time before they arrived.

Jake was trying very hard to cooperate because he was not an international art thief. For crying out loud, he worked eighty-hour weeks as it was. Where the hell would he find time to moonlight as a cat burglar?

"Where were you the night of March 8?" Reggie O'Doul asked *again*.

Jake shook his head. "If I'm going to keep sitting here, I want interesting questions at least."

"And I want the truth," she snapped back.

Jake looked at her. "You know, I've encountered pit bulls with less persistence."

"Just answer the question," Special Agent Buchanan intervened.

"I have answered the question," Jake replied slowly. "I've answered the question three times now, and it's a stupid question to begin with. I'm sure you've checked with airlines, hotels and numerous associates who've already told you I was in London at the time. If you want credit for having done your homework, I give you both a gold star."

Reggie O'Doul's cheeks began to color again. He liked the way her cheeks flushed and her eyes brightened when she got mad. Then she would abruptly tilt her head to the side as if she was listening to some internal voice. Next would come the deep breathing exercises. So far, the only entertainment he'd had was realizing the breaths were becoming shorter and shorter while accomplishing less and less. Still, he gave her credit for trying. His older brother Garret would have already blackened his eye by now.

"Is there something you'd like to say, Agent O'Doul?" he asked pleasantly. God, her cheeks were red. Her head tilted to the side, the overhead lights catching the brown strands of her hair and setting them on fire. He liked redheads.

"So you admit you were present for all four of the burglaries?" She gritted out the question.

He nodded agreeably. "Definitely. But then—" he leaned forward with just a hint of seriousness "—I can name for you twenty-five people off the top of my head who were present at all four occasions. Come on, each burglary happened after a major social event, charity ball, whatever. The usual guests were all in attendance. Can I have a drink of water?''

She smiled, a tight smile. He smiled back, a broad smile. She got up, poured him a glass of water and carried it over to him. The pantsuit flowed over her, highlighting long legs. He bet she was a natural athlete. He glanced down at her hands, now holding the cup out: blunt-cut nails, long fingers, probably some calluses. He accepted the cup while casually brushing his fingers across the back of hers. She practically dropped the water in his lap.

"Basketball," he said after a long sip. She looked at him suspiciously.

"What?"

"I bet you play basketball. Can you beat all your associates? I bet you're good."

She looked flustered, but Buchanan smiled. "She's very good," he said.

Reggie shot her superior a heated look, but he waved it away. "Mr. Guiness has been cooperating," the older man said. He gestured for her to return to her chair. "You've done well, O'Doul. Now I think it's time to get down to business."

She nodded reluctantly, taking her seat. After looking askance at Buchanan, she leaned forward. "We have you on tape, Mr. Guiness," she said quite seriously.

Jake nodded. "Yeah, I know. But as I told you, the break-in wasn't real."

"And the photos, Mr. Guiness? How do you explain the photos?"

For the first time, he appeared genuinely shocked. Reggie stood, pulling two photographs out of the manila file on the table. She walked to the front of the table, leaning against it almost casually as she held the photographs in front of him.

He stared at the grainy, black-and-white images of himself unrolling a canvas. His first thought was that it couldn't be him, since he'd never seen the painting before in his life. His second thought was that he definitely needed his lawyer.

"That Vermeer was stolen from the Isabella Stewart Gardner Museum of Boston in March 1990—before the Highwayman even began, or perhaps that was really his first job. There are less than forty Vermeers in the entire world, Mr. Guiness, and only one belongs to a private collector—Queen Elizabeth II. Did you really think you could hang on to such a piece without anyone finding out?"

Jake looked back at the photographs. God, that really was *The Concert* in his hands; he recognized it from the newspaper articles on the theft. *But he'd never* personally *seen that canvas before in his life!*

The door opened abruptly, and Mitch Guiness walked in wearing one of those formal blue suits he despised so much. Jake had never been more grateful to see his oldest brother.

"Mitch! Thank God. Would you look at these photographs?"

Mitch gave Jake a reassuring look, then calmly shook hands with both of the agents. Mitch turned to Buchanan, nodding his head.

"Buchanan, it's nice to see you again. I don't suppose I could see you outside for a moment?"

"I made the arrest," Agent O'Doul said. Mitch tactfully inclined his head toward her.

"Then perhaps all three of us could discuss this."

Agent O'Doul opened her mouth as if to object, but the older agent spoke up immediately. "Of course, Mitch."

Jake found himself releasing his pent-up breath. He'd disliked resorting to calling Mitch, but Mitch worked for the Bureau as an independent specialist for the Witness Protection Program. If anyone could figure out what was going on, Mitch could. Besides, Reggie O'Doul had already implied Mitch was involved due to his relationship with him. Given that, Jake wanted Mitch to know what was going on up-front. His brother had a phenomenal record in the Witness Protection Program. Surely that meant something to them.

Still, when Mitch walked in alone forty-five minutes later, his brown eyes held open concern.

"What the hell is going on?" Jake demanded at once.

"Please tell me you haven't taken up art theft."

"Oh, for crying out loud—"

"All right, all right." Mitch held up his hands. "But the question had to be asked. Jake, I know Agent O'Doul probably isn't your favorite person right now, but she certainly did her homework. If I were her, I would have arrested you, too."

For a moment, Jake simply stared at his brother as if he'd lost his mind.

"Mitch, do you even know how much money I have these days?"

"One hundred and fifty million," Mitch replied. "Reggie showed me your portfolio. And boy, that new ceramics factory in Poland is costing you a fortune."

"Start-ups take time," Jake said, annoyed.

Mitch nodded, but continued to watch his brother with assessing eyes. "You know you have a history of pranks."

"Hey, I returned the Quaker mascot uniform to Penn . . . with only a few minor adjustments."

"You follow the art world."

"So does half of New York."

"You were present for all four burglaries."

"Again, so was half of New York. Did she at least show you the guest lists for those parties?"

"Yeah, but of the twenty or so people who were present for all the thefts, only a handful are fit enough to double as a cat burglar. You make a great suspect, Jake, and that's not even counting tonight's little incident."

"Just contact Donnar. He'll clear the whole thing up."

"We're trying to. I'm afraid cellular phones don't reach the Congo yet. Even then, Jake, there's the matter of the photos."

Jake just shook his head. "Mitch, I swear to you I have no idea what's going on. Hell, I just replaced my security system in Virginia because of this Highwayman fellow. That's about all I know."

Mitch sighed and contemplated his brother with steady brown eyes. "They sent me in here so I could ask you straight out. If you don't admit to anything, they're going to get really bored listening to our conversation."

Slowly Jake grinned. "Is that so? So what do you think of Regina O'Doul anyway? Doesn't she have the biggest pair of—"

The door abruptly opened, and Agent O'Doul walked in looking ominous. Jake grinned at her, feeling better than he had all night. "Eyes," he finished innocently. "You have the biggest pair of green eyes that I've ever seen."

"Mr. Guiness, you are in serious trouble."

Jake looked back at Mitch, then sighed. "I don't think I should say anything more until my lawyer arrives."

Mitch looked at Reggie. "Show him the pictures again, O'Doul. I think you've made your point."

Reggie seemed disappointed, but she held up the black-and-whites once more. "Do you see anything unusual in these photographs, Mr. Guiness?"

Jake looked at her skeptically, then turned back to the pictures. After a moment, his forehead wrinkled into a frown. Something didn't seem quite right. Abruptly his forehead cleared, and he sat back with a jolt.

"There's no shadow!"

"I told you he was the smart one in the family," Mitch commented from the table.

Reggie looked at them both with annoyance. "You're right," she admitted reluctantly to Jake. "In the picture, the light is directly behind your head, yet no shadow falls upon the canvas. Do you want to know how I got these pictures?"

Jake obediently nodded.

"They came in the mail, accompanied by a note saying to keep an eye on you. Of course, we were already doing that given your presence at each of the burglaries." Her green eyes briefly skimmed down his lean, muscled figure while a hint of color tinged her cheeks. "You are one of the few people fit enough to execute such crimes."

"I am fit," he agreed jovially.

She cleared her throat and glared at him. "I'd like to arrest you," she said abruptly. "Frankly I'd like to throw the book at you. You had opportunity, you have the ability and you fit my profile to a tee. The only problem is the damn photos." She stared down at them with disgust. "Obviously someone wants you arrested. Someone wants you arrested so badly that they tampered with these pictures."

Jake looked at her with keen interest now, the wheels of his mind turning. "And that person has the Vermeer, or at least knows where it is." Reggie nodded. "You think that person is the real Highwayman, don't you?" he concluded. Again she nodded. Abruptly his eyes narrowed. "Then why am I the one locked up?" he said explosively.

"Because it was easier to believe you were just being framed before I personally caught you stealing a Melanesic statue from Donnar Ivansson's house!"

"But that was a favor for a friend!"

"Maybe you consider Isabella Stewart Gardner an old friend."

For a moment, Jake almost lost his temper. He hadn't been this close since the day he'd discovered one of his internal audit managers was stealing from him. He took a deep breath and grinned even though it hurt his cheeks.

"What the hell, Reggie? I can't be both the real Highwayman and the person framed for being the Highwayman. How long have you had me followed anyway? And just when were you going to tell me that the photos were faked? Don't I have a right to know what's going on?"

She glowered at him, but didn't refute his point. "All right," she clipped briskly. "We started noting your activities after the first break-in. We started following you after the third break-in. Shortly thereafter, I received the photos, determined they were faked and decided to increase the level of surveillance on you. One way or the other, you're connected to the thefts. Maybe you're the actual thief. Maybe you're the mastermind behind the thefts. And maybe, just maybe, you're somehow a victim. Either way, I intend to find out what your connection is to this case."

"And how do you propose to do that? By keeping me locked in a room until I crack under the weight of your stale, boring questions?" His voice was deliberately dry.

It had the desired effect of darkening her cheeks once more. The hot-tempered Regina took a few more steadying breaths. "We have questions we still need answered. To do that, we need access to certain people, certain circumstances. And while we do that, we have no intention of letting you out of our sight."

"Uh-oh," Jake said, his mind rapidly filling in the blanks.

She smiled at him with saccharin sweetness. "We have a proposal for you, Mr. Guiness. You can be released into my protective custody." Both of Jake's eyebrows fired up in shock. "You will not be allowed out of my sight. In fact, you will introduce me to your friends as your associate, and I will accompany you to all social functions, including next week's Children's Charity Ball at the Kendall estate—"

"You think that will be the Highwayman's next target?" Jake interrupted.

She simply gazed at him coolly. "Our research indicates it's a better than likely chance. We need access to that party, Mr. Guiness. Plus, with you under close watch by the FBI, hopefully the real Highwayman will think his plan is working and grow sloppy. Do we have a deal?"

"Gee, Reggie, I'm rather flattered and all, but aren't you forgetting that I have a business to run? I can't just take off to play undercover agent."

"Perhaps I didn't make myself clear." She leaned forward, her green eyes emerald hard. "Cooperate, Jake, or I will book you with theft right now for your actions at Ivansson's house. Got it?"

"You didn't win Miss Congeniality in college, did you, Reggie?"

"Jake," Mitch intervened smoothly. "Think about it for a moment. Someone wants to frame you as the Highwayman. That person knows a lot about you, and that person is the real Highwayman. Don't you want to know who's doctoring photos to get you arrested? Isn't that a little more pressing than your latest business deal?"

Jake's lips thinned in consternation. His oldest brother did have a rather good point. But given the fragile state of the new factory he'd just opened in Poland, he honestly did not have time for this. On the other hand, he was the only one in the room with a black ski mask and a stolen art statue in his pocket, not to mention that he was now starring in doctored photos. And to think, just this morning he was wondering if life wasn't becoming too dull.

That would teach him.

He contemplated Mitch for a minute, then Reggie.

"So you'd pose as my lover?" he quizzed, his quick mind beginning to identify the opportunities.

"Associate," she said.

He waved his hand. "Like anyone would believe that. Ten days, huh?" His lips twisted wickedly. Oh, the possibilities.

"Mr. Guiness, you are still a suspect!" she informed him in her sternest voice. "This isn't some jaded slumber party. You will not be allowed out of my sight whatsoever until we have absolute confirmation from Donnar that you entered his home with his permission."

"Of course," he agreed readily. His grin almost reached his ears. "So to briefly recap events thus far, you think I might be an art thief, thus I'm sentenced to endless days and nights in the company of a beautiful woman—"

"Federal agent," she snarled.

"Sure. No offense meant. I will try to take my punishment like a man."

Reggie O'Doul's face turned a becoming shade of scarlet, and her hands balled into fists with such force he thought it was a small miracle she didn't wallop him in the stomach. Life was becoming more entertaining all the time.

"Jake's all right," Mitch interjected soothingly, giving Reggie a sympathetic smile. "In fact, if he ever comes on too strong, just give Garret Guiness a call. He'll have Jake straightened out for you in no time."

"I can take care of myself," Reggie said, but she did look grateful. For a moment, she looked from brother to brother and hesitated. "I have some 302s to fill out," she said at last, her gaze resting on Mitch. "I suppose Mr. Guiness—"

"Jake."

She hesitated again. "Jake can be allowed out of the room as long as he's in your custody. Maybe you can take him to the cafeteria for coffee. But at this point, I don't want him out of the building. Buchanan will want to speak to us both again. You understand?"

Mitch nodded, accepting his charge. "When you're ready, you can find us in the cafeteria."

She nodded, then turned to Jake one last time, her green eyes hard and unrelenting. "Understand, Mr. Guiness, that as long as you cooperate, I'm willing to work with you. No one wants to catch the Highwayman as much as I do. And understand that if you are the real thief, nothing will bring me as much pleasure as personally putting you behind bars. Your brother has interfered on your behalf. From here on out, everything you do reflects upon him. Don't do anything you'd both regret."

She smiled at him tightly, and as Jake's mouth opened with a firing retort, she simply stepped out of the room.

"My God," Jake said with a sigh of half-admiration, half-annoyance, "she really does know what buttons to push." He looked back at his brother, then shook his head again at not being able to get in the last word for only about the second time in his life.

"She's a good agent," Mitch said seriously. "Her investigation of you was very thorough. And to her credit, she's the one who first determined the photographs were fake."

"Yeah, well, even I figured that out." Jake rose for the first time and slowly stretched out his back. It had been a long night, and he had the beginnings of a headache.

"Cut her some slack," Mitch said softly. "She just transferred from the admin side to criminal investigations. She probably thinks she has a lot to prove."

Jake gave his brother an assessing glance. "Sounds like she's pretty junior to be leading an international art theft investigation."

Mitch nodded. "Most of the art squad is located in New York. But it appears Agent O'Doul spent her time in criminal justice information nagging Quantico's training division for information on serial killer profiling. She's adapted the criteria and applied it to other serial crimes, producing a profile of the Highwayman as her case study. Buchanan, who's in charge of the investigation, is quite impressed."

Jake considered this information, finally rolling his neck to ease his tight shoulders. He felt dead tired. He still hadn't adjusted time zones from his Poland trip, and things had been beyond hectic these days. How much had he slept last night? Two hours? Maybe three. He shook out his arms.

So he was officially suspected of being an international art thief. At least the Highwayman had an impeccable reputation. And then there was Regina O'Doul. He'd always had a weakness for redheads. He looked at Mitch for a long time, then grinned slowly. "She's gorgeous," he said, not needing to mention a name.

Leaning against the table, Mitch shook his head at his younger brother. "Just remember, Jake. FBI agents are authorized to shoot to kill."

Jake looked startled then started to laugh. "And you're letting me be released under her supervision? Thanks, Mitch. Thanks a lot."

Mitch grinned at his brother, and for a moment the two could have been twins. "Somehow, you're not the one I'm worried about, Mr. Harvard. Now then, your phone call pulled me away from a very important meeting with the rest of our siblings on what to do for Mom and Dad's forty-fifth wedding anniversary. Plus, you yanked me away from my new sons and beautiful wife. I think the least you can do is buy me a cup of coffee. And then I'll tell you what we decided you were going to contribute for Mom and Dad's anniversary gift. Of course, I didn't know your net worth at the time...."

"Uh-oh," Jake said quite cheerily. He followed Mitch to the door. "You know," he commented thoughtfully, "I honestly think she doesn't like me." He seemed rather pleased with the idea.

Mitch looked at his brother's face and shook his head knowingly. "Jake, those women are the most dangerous kind."

Jake looked surprised. "What do you mean?"

"The only woman I met who didn't like me at first sight, I married."

"Oh," Jake said. He seemed to consider this, then vehemently shook his head. "Nah. I'm the smart one, remember?"

"Sure brother. Sure."

Walking down the corridor from Buchanan's office to her own, Reggie could still feel her palms sweating. For the umpteenth time that morning, she resisted the urge to wipe her hands on her crepe pants. Things were going okay, she reminded herself again. Working undercover with Jake Guiness was actually the perfect opportunity. With his access to the elite, she could really push the investigation forward.

She could feel the importance of the case in each knot in her shoulders.

God, maybe she was in over her head.

Fiercely she forced the thought away. A lot of people were waiting for her to fail. The few times she'd visited the Boston office, she'd seen them standing in the halls, watching her walk by. *"There goes Frank O'Doul's daughter. Real shame about him. But 'ya gotta wonder..."*

She took a deep breath and stepped into her office, lined with stacks of paper. Her entire life, she'd wanted to be an FBI agent. She came from the classic Irish cop family; all her uncles and cousins were Boston cops, but she'd wanted to be an agent. Fidelity, bravery and integrity, that's what her shield read. She'd worked so damn hard for that shield. Only one in twenty people were accepted into the Academy, and she'd graduated the top of her class.

Right after her father's arrest, when things were particularly tough, she would think back to the first day of classes, sitting at the long table with twenty-eight classmates, a card with her name in front of her as well as a blue spiral notebook with FBI emblazoned on the cover. She and her classmates had sat through the introductions, nervous and professional in their suits. Then at the end of the introductions they had stood as one, holding up their right hands: *"I do solemnly swear that I will support and defend the Constitution of the United States against all enemies, foreign and domestic..."*

She'd taken the vow with as much emotion as a bride. Her father had told her it would be like that, and the day she'd taken the oath, she'd taken it for both of them, at least so she'd thought. Certainly, when she'd graduated from the Academy he'd been in the front row, handsome in his police officer's dress uniform, clapping and screaming, "That's my daughter! That's my girl!"

Now, she sat down at her desk, looking at the neat piles that comprised her office, and wished she wasn't thinking about him.

Frank O'Doul had been a hard man. He'd raised her as a son, because he'd been too proud to have a daughter. And the day she'd stood there while they sentenced him for corruption, he'd looked only at her, mouthing the words "O'Douls don't cry."

That was Frank, father to the bitter end. Had he truly believed his own behavior as a cop wouldn't reflect on her? She'd had the Office of Professional Responsibility investigating her for a year after his conviction. And promising young agents generally didn't start in the admin side of the Bureau.

She pushed the thought away, surprised, as she was always surprised, by how much the memory still hurt. Frank O'Doul had died in prison fourteen months ago. She no longer lived his life, or paid for his choices. Now she was on her own, finally working in criminal investigations and reminding herself on the rough nights that O'Douls didn't cry.

Buchanan, serving as the case agent, was entrusting her with so much, letting her take the lead when there were fourteen other agents also working the case. After finally getting her chance, she couldn't bear to let him down. She'd told him as much in his office when he'd questioned her.

"Are you sure you can handle this, Reggie? Going undercover isn't easy."

"It's not like I'm posing as a drug runner. And you and Mitch both seem convinced that Jake is innocent."

"There's all kinds of danger in the world, Regina O'Doul. From what I've read, Jake is a real ladies' man."

She'd arched a fine auburn brow at that. "All good things must come to an end," she'd snapped back.

Buchanan had laughed. "I think we should wire you just so we can hear the conversations. Think he knows what he's in for?"

She recalled the way Jake Guiness's eyes had skimmed appreciatively over her figure and felt her cheeks flush a fiery red. "Probably not," she growled.

Buchanan had leaned forward. "Be careful, Reggie," he'd said softly. "We'll keep you under surveillance, and I know you can take care of yourself better than most agents, but Jake keeps very different circles than an Irish cop. And beneath that grin, he's a very sharp man. Don't underestimate him like you think he's underestimating you."

"I can handle him," she'd said stiffly.

Finally Buchanan had smiled at her and sat back. "I guess you can," he'd said. "Well, by your own report, the Highwayman is most likely to strike again during the Children's Charity Ball next week. Jake's already RSVP'd his attendance, so you should be all set. In the meantime, until we actually get a hold of Donnar Ivansson, I don't want him out of your sight. For God's sake, we do have one legitimate tape of the man stealing. Mitch's brother or not, that's highly irregular!''

She'd nodded, allowing herself a small smile. She'd seen the tape herself when she brought Jake to headquarters. As part of her research, she'd watched tapes of burglars caught doing a lot of stupid things on camera, but never had she seen a thief actually wave and hold up his prize. For raw arrogance, Jake Guiness took the cake.

''Will that be all?'' she'd asked at last.

Buchanan had nodded, and she'd headed for the door. At the last minute, he'd stopped her.

''And, O'Doul,'' he'd said after her. ''Remember Hoover's dictum—'Don't embarrass the Bureau.'''

She'd granted a curt nod at the time, but now, sitting back in the sanctity of her own office, she puzzled over his choice of words. Hoover's name wasn't invoked too often anymore; they were now the new FBI.

It really was a strange thing for him to have said.

Chapter 2

Jake Guiness didn't look dangerous when he slept. His thick black hair splayed against the window, and when she drove over a particularly rough bump, his head bounced against the glass in a way that made her want to reach over and protect him. A silly, leftover maternal instinct, Reggie assured herself.

Still, she found her gaze wandering from the road and over to him more and more. He'd fallen asleep the minute he'd gotten into the car. Now, his arms were folded across his chest, pulling his thin black turtleneck tight. She could see the outline of well-formed pectorals and biceps. The man obviously worked out, his body lean and nicely sculpted. She found her eyes drifting down to his thighs, encased in black denim, and she jerked her attention back to the road. Her hands maintained a near-death grip on the wheel.

She took a deep breath and exhaled slowly.

She didn't react to men sexually—at least not generally. Her whole life she'd been one of the guys, running around with her male cousins, shooting hoops with the neighborhood boys. She competed with men, fought for toeholds in their world because she'd never understood her own. She hadn't even had a boyfriend until she'd gone to Boston College for her psych degree. There, she'd met Brian, a track star, and while she taught him how to play *H-O-R-S-E,* he'd taught her much more interesting games. Sometimes, if she worked too late or didn't sleep enough, she could still remember the taste of him on her lips and the feel of him thrusting into her, sweaty and knowing.

Her knuckles turned white on the wheel, and she released her breath with a pent-up shudder. Those days seemed so far away, there were times she wondered if they'd happened at all. Surely the driven Regina O'Doul had never been in love. Surely she'd never stood in front of the mirror on a Friday night applying a sparing coat of mascara because *he* was coming over, her thighs already trembling with the anticipation.

Her father had never liked Brian. He was the one who pointed out what a distraction a relationship was. The day she'd been recruited into the Academy, the day she'd walked away from Brian, Frank had slapped her on the shoulder and told her she'd done well.

To look at things now, maybe her father had been right. She was the worker, the agent to the core. Special Agents in Charge already knew they could call her to get things done, nights, weekends, it didn't matter. She had that edge. As her father had always told her, she was tough.

She smiled with self-mockery, looking out at the winding strip of back road leading to the Virginia suburbs. Yeah, the great Regina O'Doul.

She knew everything about competing and nothing about anything else.

Her eyes drifted over to Jake and lingered. She imagined he was very good with women. He had that knowing spark in his eyes, that way of caressing a woman with his eyes as if he alone understood. That grin of his had probably toppled a reserve or two. If not the smile, then his low voice with its undertone of the South. He didn't drawl, but his North Carolina upbringing hovered beneath the tones, a sonorous hint of hot, humid days and torrid, rainy nights. She bet he tasted of fresh ground coffee and single malt whiskey.

Her stomach tightened uncontrollably, hunger spiking through her, shaky and unexpected. She quickly shifted her gaze to the wheel, flexing her fingers.

She'd been working too hard, that was all. There was so much to prove that at nights she went home and simply stared at the ceiling, unable to sleep. She could do this, she would repeat to herself over and over again, her jaw tight.

But sometimes she simply saw the last game of the NCAA championships, herself driving to the hoop. She'd been powering up for the game winning basket, when suddenly Chelsey Harper had appeared out of nowhere, hammering the ball from her hands. The University of Connecticut Huskies had stolen the ball, scoring the winning two points with thirty seconds on the clock. The Boston College Eagles never found their way to the hoop again, though Reggie had tried. With every fiber of her being, she had tried. Worse, when the last blare of the game horn boomed through the thick mugginess of sweat, she'd looked over to see her father already turning away.

He'd never said anything about the game when she finally caught a ride home with a friend. He didn't say anything at all for nearly two days. What could he say, other than how badly she'd failed?

She shook the thought away, hating herself for remembering. Her father had had his own problems. She just hadn't known about them at the time.

The number of pine trees along the road suddenly lessened, and abruptly the new condo facility appeared. Gratefully she made the turn, her mind already reverting to work. She should sleep soon, and the last of the melancholy would leave her. Once more, her eyes drifted to Jake Guiness. She hadn't figured out yet how she was supposed to sleep and keep an eye on him.

She pulled into her parking space and rubbed the bridge of her nose. The minute she turned off the engine, he stirred.

"Are we in the Bahamas yet?" he murmured, his voice gravelly. He looked over at her with heavy-lidded eyes, his black hair tousled around him. Slowly he grinned and the hunger in her stomach ignited into a slow burn.

"I just need to get my things," she said tersely. "Then we'll be on our way to your place."

He ran a hand through his hair, smiling lazily. "Sure thing, sweetheart."

"I'm not your sweetheart."

"How about honey bunch or sugar pie? You look like a darlin' to me." His brown eyes swept over her face like warm velvet, lingering on her full lips.

"Reggie will do just fine," she said, but a certain breathlessness took the force out of the words.

Jake Guiness looked at her and shook his head. "You're supposed to be my lover. Don't you think Reggie's a bit formal for lovers?"

She began to search for the door handle in earnest. His words strung her nerves so tight she could hear ringing in her ears. "Reggie's fine," she whispered and popped the door open as if she were a woman gasping for breath. She scrambled out without looking back. He followed at a leisurely pace.

The air was crisp with fall, the maple trees sparking the gray sky with streaks of amber, crimson and gold. She loved this time of year, when winter nipped the air and landscapes boasted brilliant colors. She was rarely home when there was still enough light out to appreciate the grounds. She took the time to do so now, focusing on the fiery maples against the distant pine, while brushing her hands over her suit.

There were eight buildings on the premises, three more under construction. Each building housed two two-story condos. The tall, thin structures reminded her of Boston's brownstones—maybe that was why she'd bought her condo last year. The structures weren't made of stone, but were actually pale painted wood with various trims of blue, green and brown. Brick accents around the bay windows added charm, however, and the hardwood floors were lovely.

She could feel Jake's eyes resting upon her, so she began walking up the sidewalk to her door. She was still fumbling for the key when a huge black cat suddenly sprang from the low bushes.

"Mrrrow," the cat announced, thick padded paws the size of saucers instantly pressing against the closed door.

"My God, it's a tank," Jake breathed behind her.

Fifteen pounds of cat turned at the noise and eyed the newcomer with suspicious golden eyes and flattened ears. A growl of warning rumbled from its throat.

"Tom doesn't care for strangers," Regina said simply and opened the door. Tom bounded in while Jake whistled in appreciation.

"What are you feeding him?"

"Nothing," she replied, stepping into the entryway. "He's not really mine. He just shows up, that's all." She shrugged, looking around with a nervous eye. The two bedroom condo was more than adequate for a single person, and the hardwood floors gleamed with fresh polish. But compared to the places Jake Guiness hung out, her condo was probably a walk-in closet. She moved forward gingerly and suddenly wished she hadn't brought him to her home.

An agent's salary was very respectable, especially if one didn't have kids or other dependents. In the last five years, it had enabled her to buy the condo, as well as nice clothes and a new car. And she had a feeling all of it appeared provincial to a man like Jake Guiness. She glanced at him sideways as she moved into the large living room which dominated the first floor.

With one hand, she gestured haphazardly to the open space, filled with too few pieces of furniture and too many stacks of paper.

"It isn't much," she said at last.

"I like the bay windows," Jake told her, his grin warm and reassuring. "And I've always been a sucker for oak floors."

She nodded, feeling better and hating the fact that she'd needed his reassurance. "If you want, you can just wait down here. I'll only be a minute."

Tom reappeared, leaning heavily against her leg while he contemplated Jake with golden eyes.

"And the cat?" Jake asked. He bent down and held out a hand. The black monster simply stared at him flatly, his battle-scarred ears alert and suspicious. Jake grinned broadly. "What a stud."

Reggie shook her head and walked away to set her brief-case by the coffee table. "Would you like something to drink?" she asked, her eyes momentarily skimming over the books she had stacked on the surface.

"Coffee would be great," Jake said. She nodded, figuring she could use some herself. Her low heels clipping against the hardwood floor, she walked into the kitchen. She could feel Jake's eyes following her, and when she suddenly heard the sound of his steps on the floor, she didn't know whether to remain casual or to run.

He caught up with her as she pulled the coffee beans out of the freezer. The kitchen area was modern but small, containing an eat-in bar versus an area for a kitchen table. She'd hoped he would settle at the bar, but of course he walked into the square kitchen area, leaning against the front of the counter.

"What kind of coffee?" he asked.

"Hazelnut."

"Cream or sugar?"

"Black."

"Morning drinker, recreational, or serious?"

She looked at him with amusement. "Serious."

He nodded. "Me, too." He crossed his arms again, which pulled the turtleneck tight. She hastily looked away, concentrating on pouring the coffee beans into the grinder. She pushed down on the lid and filled the kitchen with the high-pitched rasp of grinding coffee. The noise, familiar and routine, settled her nerves.

"I bet you taste great with a touch of hazelnut on your lips."

She practically dropped the grinder, her hands suddenly nerveless as her green eyes rounded in shock. From the counter, Jake simply grinned at her, his eyes knowing and arrogant.

Very slowly, he uncrossed his arms and stepped toward her. She instinctively flattened herself against the far counter, her breath caught in her throat like a trapped bird.

"Come on, sweetheart," Jake coaxed softly, his grin devilish. "How are we going to convince people we're lovers if you jump every time I approach?"

She licked her lips, then abruptly stopped as his eyes followed the motion. "I believe I said I'd pose as your business associate," she managed to get out, her chin coming up.

He reached out and very lightly touched her cheek. She flinched instantly, and for a moment his dark eyes glinted with seriousness. Just as abruptly, the seriousness was gone and he was simply teasing her once more. "Honey, you're a beautiful woman. No one who knows me would ever believe I'd let you remain just an associate."

She turned away, stepping out of his reach. He stopped her with a mere touch on her arm. "Why so nervous, Reggie?" he whispered intensely. "People will assume we're lovers. Why call attention to ourselves with denial? It would definitely be more prudent to simply act as they expect us to act." He leaned a little closer, pinning her with those warm, beguiling eyes. "Haven't you heard that practice makes perfect?"

Her eyes caressed his full lips unconsciously, noting the sensuous shape, the knowing grin. At five foot ten, her gaze naturally came to rest on his lips, making it harder to look away. Worse, it meant he was one of those rare men who required her to look up to make eye contact. Her hands fisted at her sides, her chin setting stubbornly. "I work best under pressure," she stated clearly. "Let's just leave it at that."

She pushed away seriously this time, and he let her go. She ignored the flash of disappointment in his eyes and consciously suppressed the disappointment in her own. She grabbed a filter and poured the freshly ground coffee into the cone. After a moment, she felt him step away and lean against the counter once more. His eyes on her back, however, remained sharp.

"Do you really think I'm a thief?" he asked abruptly, all traces of teasing gone from his voice.

Her hands stilled on the coffeepot, then resumed their motion. "I have you on tape," she said.

"Why would I steal?" he prodded. "I'm very successful in my own right."

She turned, looking at him with serious green eyes. "The challenge," she said. "The arrogance. You like to do things other people say can't be done. You like to push the boundaries."

"You determined all this while spying on me?"

"That is my job."

"That's cheating," he murmured, leaning back against the counter, "to spy on me, and not let me spy back. I think I have some catching up to do."

She instantly stiffened, her eyes opening wide with alarm. He grinned at her, amused by her response. "Oh, yeah," he drawled slowly, "I really am looking forward to this next week."

Her cheeks flushed bright red, her head tilting to the side while she drew in so many rapid breaths the world grew momentarily fuzzy. Never in her life had she met someone so damn insufferable. Her hands clenched at her sides. She wanted . . . she wanted to . . . oh hell, she just wanted this to end.

She pushed herself away from the counter and stalked furiously back to the entryway. She wasn't surprised to hear him follow.

Lips thinned into a narrow line, she told herself she didn't care and climbed the stairs to her bedroom. She walked in angrily, opening the closet door and jerking out a canvas bag for clothes. She looked at the clothes hanging before her and began to rip a selected few from their hangers.

Jake walked around the room behind her, seemingly oblivious to her mood.

She had good taste, he conceded as he looked around. The furniture, at least what he could see of it beneath more piles of paper, was an eclectic mixture of pine and wrought iron. Her dresser was a huge old bureau, stained the color of sand with a faded blue trim. Next to her bed, a round table with a chipped marble top sat on a curved, wrought-iron pedestal. A tall armoire, painted a faded blue, stood against the opposite wall by the closet. Her bed boasted a gracefully curved wrought-iron headboard, flowing into elaborate curls he wouldn't have associated with her. On the other hand, the caramel-colored comforter with a burgundy paisley skirt was very Reggie. He wandered over, brushing a hand over the thick pile of pillows at the headboard. He could see the faint indent from all the nights she'd obviously leaned against the pillows to read. He rested his hand in the curve, and for a moment, could almost see her lounging there, short auburn hair flaming from the lamplight, graceful neck bent as she read through wire rim glasses. He bet she slept in an old college T-shirt, long, curved legs sprawled seductively against the sand-colored comforter.

He swallowed thickly and reminded himself to breathe. It had been a while since he'd wanted a woman as much as he wanted this one. And not just because she was beautiful, but because she looked at him with wary green eyes that seemed intent on keeping their distance.

She'd been right downstairs after all; he did like challenges.

He blocked out the image of her half-naked body on the bed and picked up one of the several reports littering her nightstand. Casually he flipped it open to a page.

Kemper: I could screw your head off and place it on the
table to greet the guard.

Jake hastily closed the report. "Not exactly good dreams
material," he said, holding up the report. Reggie glanced up
from the closet, squinting at the document he held in his
hand. He held the interview notes from Edward Kemper III
who had killed his mother, grandparents and six other people. She hadn't slept the night she'd read those notes from
Quantico. And she'd kept the lights on for nights afterward.

Slowly she set down the canvas bag, crossed the room and
took the confidential report from Jake's hands.

"You shouldn't be reading that," she said.

"Don't worry," he told her, looking at her with genuine
interest. "I don't think I want to. Are the rest of the books
and files around here as pleasant?"

She hesitated a moment, struck once again by how she
had to arch her neck just a fraction to meet his eyes. Slowly,
hoping it appeared casual, she took a step back. "When I
was little," she said at last, her voice brisk as she returned
to her packing, "my mom used to tell me the story of Billy
Goats Gruff. For the longest time, I was convinced trolls
were the worst evil in the world, lurking in closets and under beds to snatch unsuspecting little girls. Now I understand that mankind is far worse."

Jake simply stared at her, for once in his life not knowing what to say. "And you make this your life's work?" he
asked seriously.

She nodded, crossing over to her dresser. "It's not pleasant stuff," she said as she opened the drawers. "But it's real.
You can't bury your head in the sand and pretend it doesn't
exist, and you certainly can't flip on a light switch to make
it go away. There are real monsters in the world, and the
profiling techniques developed by John Douglas, Howard
Teten, Patrick Mullaney and others have gone a long way
toward unveiling those monsters. It's incredible if you think
about it."

Jake nodded, impressed. His brothers had all chosen paths pursuing those monsters in one realm or the other. He'd been the academic one, however, the Harvard man. He operated in walnut-paneled boardrooms with prime rib dinners where other gray-suited individuals argued strategy and industry trends. They worried about the survival of their businesses, not themselves.

"And you used this profiling technique for the Highwayman?" he said, turning to watch her with measuring eyes.

"As much as I can," she said, straightening and meeting his gaze for the first time. "See, applying the profiling for nonsex crimes is a totally new ball game. With sex crimes, much of profiling is based on the mental abnormalities. For example, the first major criterion is psychopath versus schizophrenic. We're profiling the disease really, because the killer is a victim of that disease. He will kill again not because of rationality or logic, but because he has to. On the other hand, a thief is acting on external motivation. Maybe he steals because of the challenge—" she looked at him pointedly "—maybe for the money. Either way, the thief is fundamentally different than the serial killer."

"It sounds to me then, like you *can't* apply the profiling to nonsex crimes."

"But I think we can." She leaned against her dresser, the canvas bag completely forgotten as one foot tapped out her thoughts. One half of her mind warned that maybe she shouldn't be discussing her work with a possible criminal. The other half understood that she wasn't giving away a secret formula. "Some descriptors still apply, you see. For example, another category is organized versus unorganized. The organized killer is generally the psychopath. He's very smart and is socially and sexually competent. He's controlled and thorough with his crime—no rash actions. Later, he'll follow his crime in the media. He believes he's the best. At the other extreme is the disorganized killer, the schizophrenic. He has only average intelligence, lives alone and is not socially adept. He'll act spontaneously, and generally against someone he knows. He may be young and in-experienced, sloppy.

"Most thefts I think fall into this category of disorga-nized. The 145 Mayan and Mixtec treasure filched from the National Museum of Anthropology in Mexico City in 1985 was stolen by two dropouts who had no idea what they'd even taken. Then there's the 1994 theft of the Richard Gray Gallery in Chicago where the thieves simply smashed the windows and grabbed a Picasso while the silent alarm rang. In fact, most break-ins aren't that sophisticated or spectac-ular."

"Except the Highwayman," Jake finished for her.

She nodded quite seriously. "The break-ins are subtle and sophisticated, obviously done by someone with above av-erage intelligence. The knowledge of electronics and secu-rity devices suggests an engineering background, and the method of entry indicates someone who is physically fit. He has intimate knowledge of the theft sites and likes to linger long enough to place a red rose and write some torrid verse."

"I didn't leave a red rose or 'torrid verse' behind at Don-nar's," Jake interjected.

"Maybe you didn't have time," she retorted coolly. "At any rate, I bet the Highwayman is following the media cov-erage with a vengeance. He's the first serious international thief we've had, and he definitely thinks he's the best."

That made their job a little easier, but she wasn't about to tell Jake that. In fact, they had agents staking out the past break-in sights right now, taping and monitoring everyone who visited. They'd caught serial killers by staking out the crime scene or burial site before. Particularly on the anni-versary of the event, the organized killer liked to come back and crow.

"What about a caterer or someone working the party?" Jake asked. "They'd have knowledge of the locations, bet-ter than most guests I'd think."

She looked at him in surprise, begrudging respect light-ing her eyes. "Actually I did look into that," she admitted. "The same catering company and two limo companies have been present at all four crimes. But of the duplicative personnel, no one fits the profile.''

"But I do,'' he said and grinned at her.

She looked at him steadily. ''Mid-thirties to late-forties, physically fit, well dressed, well educated, superiority complex and somehow connected with law enforcement. You fit.''

He sank back against the pillows. ''What do you mean, superiority complex?'' He tried to look injured, but she ignored him. In fact, after that rousing indictment of his character, her attention seemed to have reverted to her packing—except for the tight set of her square jaw and the faint pounding of the pulse on her throat. God, she looked determined. ''But I have no motive,'' he pointed out, his brown eyes searching.

''Maybe you're Dr. No,'' she said. Her hand hovered over a pile of lacy underthings, a tribute to her foolish lingerie addiction. She risked a glance up only to find Jake staring at her with a crinkled brow.

''Dr. No?''

''After the Gardner theft,'' she said briskly, her hand slowly closing around a collection of lace, ''rumors circulated that a private collector bankrolled the theft. After all, you can't exactly sell a Vermeer on the open market. Everyone would recognize it. People wondered if an ambitious private collector had it stolen for an underground collection. Theft for the sake of owning. I don't really know. Except I have a doctored photo of you holding the Vermeer.''

''Wait a minute,'' he said abruptly, ''so we're talking at least two people.''

She stilled, looking at him through narrowed eyes. ''What do you mean?''

His eyes were narrowing in concentration, his gaze falling to the sand-colored comforter. She used the opportunity to grab a handful of lace and stuff it into her bag.

''Well think about it. There are really two sets of core competencies involved. One, theft skills. That's what you just rattled off, engineering knowledge, security system expertise, physical fitness. Second, however, you need the contacts, a market for world-famous pieces, perhaps even someone to bankroll the thefts. You know, a mastermind, a Dr. No.''

"True," she admitted reluctantly. In fact, from the very start the FBI had assumed there were multiple people involved. Stealing highly recognizable artwork would require the right contacts and inside knowledge of the locations. Jake had the rare honor of being suitable for either position—thief or mastermind. But overall, the FBI figured they would find at least two people, if not a whole international art theft ring. The first blow to that ring, however, would be capturing the actual Highwayman.

"Oh, geez," Jake said abruptly, and knocked his palm against his forehead. Reggie stared at him in shock. "Retirement," he said, as if that single word would explain the meaning of life.

She shook her head in puzzlement. "What?"

"Retirement," he repeated. "The Highwayman needs to retire. Think of it, four major thefts in the past few months. Let's say he's working as the personal henchman for a Dr. No. Surely this 'private collection' has got to be pretty well stocked by now. And the Highwayman is getting a lot of attention. Security systems are being beefed up, the FBI is hot on his tail. He needs an out, but you guys will pursue him and the mastermind until the fat lady sings. Therefore, he needs to get caught. Or more precisely, he needs *someone* to get caught."

She narrowed her eyes, contemplating his theory. Actually she'd entertained the idea before herself. "So you think he's framing you so someone will be held accountable?"

Jake nodded. "Why not?"

"Who would do something like that, Jake? Who knows you and your schedule that well?"

"They don't have to know me. The events get a lot of press. Joe Blow can read in the society paper that I've been at every party.''

She reached down and opened a new dresser drawer while she considered his words. She added a gray sweat suit to the bag and wondered if she wasn't sharing her room with the Highwayman right now. It was possible. At this point, anything and everything seemed possible.

She closed her dresser drawers and zipped up the bag. "Coffee's probably ready by now," she said.

Jake nodded, not paying much attention to the comment while he turned things over in his mind. Last night, he'd been excited and entertained at the prospect of successfully beating Donnar's new security system. Now, he found himself framed as the Highwayman by someone who obviously knew what he was doing. Jake was beginning to wish he was back in Poland, merely trying to undo fifty years of communist thinking and work ethic.

"I'm tired," he found himself saying out loud. He raked his hand through his hair and felt the exhaustion settle deeper.

Reggie stilled, watching him through narrowed eyes. She felt bone-tired herself, the night duty taking its toll. She glanced at the clock: two in the afternoon. She was a naturally light sleeper. Perhaps she could position herself on the couch by the front door, making sure to set the house alarm. If Jake woke up and so much as cracked open the door to leave, she would be on her feet and pointing her gun.

"Would you..." She had to clear her throat. "Do you want to maybe sleep here? Just for an hour or two? I have stuff to do downstairs."

Jake looked at her, his brown eyes taking on that glint she already knew too well. "I bet you could use some rest as well," he said shrewdly.

"I'm fine."

He grinned at her. "Come on, darlin', I'm not the big bad wolf, and I can see the shadows under those big green eyes." He patted her bed suggestively. "Lie down with me. We're supposed to be lovers, remember?"

"I'll go have a cup of coffee," she told him levelly.

He made a big show of fluffing the pillows. "Very soft," he said with a sideways glance. "Fluffy and comfortable and just waiting for your head to sink down, your eyes closing after a long night in the office . . ."

"You don't play fair, Jake Guiness. Now, if you'll excuse me, I'm going downstairs. I have work to do."

He shrugged dramatically, then did a decent job of looking forlorn. "It's your loss, sweetheart. I'm more than willing to lie here with you. I'll even promise not to touch, and I don't make that promise to just anyone."

She shook her head and stepped toward the door. "You're insufferable." She tossed the words out over her shoulder.

"Don't you at least want to change?" he called out after her. He was rewarded with her pause, and he leaned back against the pillows. "I can wait."

She turned and pinned him with her hard green gaze. "Let's get this straight. Our relationship is purely professional."

"Why, when it could be so much more fun?"

"You just don't quit, do you?"

"I'm not afraid to admit what I want."

"And I'm not afraid to tell you to go to hell," she snapped back. She pivoted and marched smartly down the stairs. He could hear her anger in each pounding footstep, then in the distant crash of dishes.

He smiled to himself, tucking his hands behind his head and settling back against the pillows.

"She wants me," he said, and closed his eyes with the grin still on his face.

Chapter 3

He found her an hour later, curled up on the couch with Tom tucked against her. The giant black cat looked up as Jake approached, blinking wary golden eyes, but Reggie remained sleeping. She had one arm under her head as a pillow, her blue crepe jacket thrown over her shoulders as a blanket. From his position in the middle of the living room, Jake could see the purple smudges of exhaustion beneath her eyes. Poor kid, he thought.

He stepped forward, but abruptly Tom raised a black paw. As Jake watched, the battle-scarred beast slowly flexed the silver-dollar-size pad, revealing each long claw with almost casual precision. The cat stopped his paw in midair and looked at Jake pointedly.

Jake shook his head and decided maybe he needed more sleep if he could read all that into a cat's actions. Cats groomed, they didn't stand guard. But Jake found himself turning around anyway and walked to the kitchen in bare feet. Cup o' Java sounded good.

He had some phone calls he needed to make to get through the next week. The joy of managing a holding company was that he didn't have to be directly involved. Each business the Guiness corporation owned had its own president managing its affairs. Jake directed strategy and charmed shareholders, and as he liked involvement, he generally provided his two-cents worth for major decisions. But his role was more the ringmaster of the circus than the performer. The Poland situation would be a little tricky, but he trusted Kramer to start implementing the new policies they'd already discussed.

Jake sighed and poured the coffee into the mug he'd found. He took a fortifying sip and returned to the living room. Keeping clear of the menacing Tom and sleeping Reggie, he entertained himself with investigating the stacks of papers that lined the walls and floors. He hadn't seen this robust a use of the stacked-file motif in decorating since his undergrad days at Harvard. Whatever else he thought of Regina O'Doul, she did take her job seriously.

Jake began to pick through the materials and did some intense thinking of his own.

The rich scent of hazelnut tickled her nose. Slowly, with only grudging compliance, her green eyes fluttered open. She could feel the solid heat of Tom curled up next to her stomach, taking up most of the couch as usual. As soon as she stirred, he automatically began to purr, a deep, throaty rumble that practically shook the cushions.

She winced and sought out the reassurance of the coffee. "Black, right?"

Her own blue clay mug appeared under her eyes, filled to the brim with wonderful black coffee. She blinked several more times, fighting through her gratitude to determine what was wrong with this picture. Abruptly she sat up, whipping out her gun in one smooth movement, and unseating Tom. "Don't move!" she cried.

Jake Guiness drolly raised an eyebrow. "All right. But the mug is burning my fingertips."

She stared at him for another thirty seconds, trying to collect thoughts that had only grown muddier from a scant hour and a half of sleep. Her bones felt heavy with exhaustion. She blinked several more times and drew in a ragged breath. She *never* slept that heavily! My God, what kind of guard duty was that? She shook her head in disgust.

"Reggie, are you going to accept the coffee or not?"

She eyed the mug warily, but finally lowered her weapon. "What's in it?"

"Arsenic," he said impatiently, and offered the mug again. "Come on, Reggie, I'm suspected of art theft, not murder."

Her scowl deepened. She glanced at the alarm box next to the door. It was still activated. If he had tried the front door, she definitely would have known. The realization gave her some consolation.

She replaced her gun in her shoulder holster, safety on, and took the coffee mug.

"How long have you been awake?" she asked finally, taking a deep sip of the brew. It scalded her tongue.

Jake shrugged, jamming his hands into the pockets of his jeans and eyeing her casually. "Not quite an hour. You know, I really would've shared the bed."

"I like the couch," she said stubbornly, then collected herself enough to add, "Besides, Tom wouldn't have shared the bed."

Jake laughed at that, a low, rich rumble that seemed to echo in her belly. "Somehow, I don't doubt that."

His eyes roamed leisurely up her body, lingering on her neck. At least that was what she thought before she looked down and realized her cream silk blouse now gaped open enough to reveal the lace trim of her bra. Abruptly she straightened, hastily yanking the blouse back into place with her free hand. Her eyes met his with stormy reprimand, but he just grinned more, and it was hard to be much sterner when she had to arch her head all the way back just to meet his gaze.

Lips tightening into a resolute line, she uncurled her feet and stood smartly. Unfortunately the blood rushed immediately from her head, undermining her show of force as she swayed like a kitten. Immediately Jake's hand cradled her arm, his fingers callused and warm on her bare skin.

"Take it easy," he murmured. "You haven't had much sleep." His eyes skimmed down her slender figure once more, but this time they were critical. "I bet you haven't eaten much, either."

She drew back quickly, unsettled by both his concern and his perceptiveness. "I'm fine," she said. "I just stood too fast." She took another sip of the coffee, glancing around her living room simply so she wouldn't have to meet his gaze. After a moment, she frowned. "You've been through my things!"

"Just exploring the library," Jake said easily. His brown eyes still searched her face. She looked pale beneath the tawny tones of her skin, and the black smudges beneath her eyes remained dark. He knew from personal experience that an hour's sleep was often worse than none, providing the body with just enough to know what it had been missing.

But Reggie wasn't paying attention to him. Instead she was looking past him to the pictures he'd uncovered on the wall.

"You don't have any right to go through my things," she said angrily. She moved past him before he could react, stopping midstride to set her coffee down on a table and hastily restack the reports that had hidden the trio of pictures. His brow furrowing, Jake followed her to the wall and the three pictures he'd been examining.

"Is that you?" he asked, pointing to a small, silver-framed black-and-white shot of a little girl. She appeared to be standing in the aisle of a church, long hair trailing down her back in fat curls while trounces of white lace cascaded from her waist to the floor. Her head tilted to the side, the little girl with ribbons in her hair smiled shyly.

Reggie frowned and tried to pile the stack high enough to cover the picture. Jake's hand stopped her.

She looked at him with level green eyes, though her cheeks were taking on that telltale flush of anger. "Of course that's me," she said tightly. "Do you mind?"

"You look like a little bride," he said softly, his eyes skimming her face. Why put up pictures if you didn't want anyone to see them?

"First Holy Communion," she explained curtly. "You really don't have the right to go through my things."

He arched a fine black brow. "This from the woman who's been following me for the past couple of weeks?"

"Hello, I'm an FBI agent. That was business."

"Well," he reasoned, "as you've stated, we're now in a professional relationship. This was business, too."

She drew in a deep breath and forced herself to exhale slowly. She was angry again, totally and completely angry in the way only an Irish woman could master. She felt the rage in each throbbing beat of her pulse, and her hands had curled into fists on the stacks of reports. She took another deep breath.

She'd promised to work on her temper. She'd promised to beat back the beast and become controlled and professional. Besides, Jake Guiness didn't know what the pictures meant to her, and by displaying too much emotion, she only made him wonder. It was better to be calm, dispassionate. Everyone had pictures on their walls.

He never had to know about the seven-year-old girl who'd knelt for her First Holy Communion, excited and beautiful because she was going to pray for her Mommy to come back. And he never had to know about the nine-year-old girl, who in a fit of rage had torn every page out of the Children's Bible she'd received that day because after two years of praying and counting her rosaries, her mother still hadn't returned.

She'd grown up since then, but not enough to forget the pain of the growing.

Jake's eyes were still on her face. She took a third deep breath and exhaled. She felt much calmer, like steel, really. She pointed to the second photo on her own. It portrayed a gruff-faced man with graying hair and deep laugh lines at the corners of his eyes. He wore a police uniform, the blue cap pulled down smartly on his forehead, the badge prominent on his chest.

"That's my father, Frank," she said.

"Law enforcement runs in your family, too?" Jake said quietly. She winced at the gentleness of his tone.

"Whole family," she confirmed, keeping her eyes on the photograph. She'd always thought her father looked handsome in blue. "Three uncles and six cousins. I call it the Irish complex. You become a cop, a firefighter or a priest. Of course, the O'Douls haven't produced a priest since 1920. On the other hand, my uncle Dave brews the best hooch you'll ever taste right in his bathtub."

Her light tone seemed to work, because Jake grinned at her, even if he was still standing too close. "The family reunions must be something else," he teased.

She smiled, a warmer smile than she'd intended. "Only if you don't mind listening to fifteen drunken Irishmen attempt to sing Irish ballads. I love my uncles dearly, but I don't think they can manage a single on-key tone among them."

Jake laughed. "No one in my family can sing, either, but at least we don't try. Then again, Mitch, Garret, Cagney and I once downed two cases of beer then raced to see who could still climb the oak tree in the backyard."

She looked at him sideways. His arm rested next to hers on top of the files and he was so close she could feel the heat of his body. "Who won?" she found herself asking. Unconsciously she licked her lips.

Jake leaned a little closer, meeting her gaze with warm, brown eyes. "I did, of course," he told her with a conspirator's smile. "I watched them all fall down and skin their hands, and decided to wait it out. After an hour or two, they fell asleep, and I sobered up enough to climb the tree. Garret wouldn't talk to me for days." His brown eyes appraised her with a wink. "I bet you climbed trees a lot yourself."

Wordlessly, her green eyes suddenly mesmerized by his brown ones, she nodded.

"I should introduce you to my sister, Liz," Jake continued. "You'd like her."

Reggie found herself nodding again, though she knew she would never meet Liz Keaton. Jake Guiness represented an assignment, nothing more, nothing less. All assignments came to an end. She just needed Jake to catch the Highwayman.

Unconsciously, she drew back and her eyes came to rest on the last picture. In it her mother wore short auburn curls and a yellow tent dress from the early seventies. She was stirring a pea green pot on the stove and laughing at something the camera holder had just said. The picture's color had yellowed with age, but Reggie could still make out emerald green eyes so much like her own.

"My mom," she volunteered, pointing at the last picture.

"I guessed as much," Jake said. "She looks just like you."

Reggie nodded. Relatives had been telling her that all her life. "She died when I was six or so." Old enough to know what had happened, not old enough to understand why.

"That must have been hard," Jake said quietly.

She nodded and unconsciously she touched the picture, her fingers lingering on the face that looked so much like her own. "My aunt Helen helped out a lot. She did my hair for First Communion, baked casseroles for us to eat. It wasn't so bad."

"It's good to have family."

She smiled. "Blood is thicker than water." Her hand remained on the photo, and for one minute she strained to compose her mother in her mind. Sometimes, the memories were hard to come by, more like fragrances than pictures. She knew her mother's smile, remembered the smell of basil and spices undertoned by vanilla.

"Every morning," she said softly, "my mother would kiss my father on the cheek as he pulled on his hat." Reggie's eyes narrowed, focusing the picture in her mind. "She'd say, 'Don't forget your lunch, Frank,' and he'd pick it up and smile at her. 'I'm going to stand guard,' he'd say with a smile—my father always smiled. 'See you at seven,' he'd say. And every night, he'd actually come home around nine, just in time to tuck me into bed. They'd both stand there in the doorway, then turn out the light. My line was, 'Still standing guard, Daddy?' so he could laugh and say, 'Still standing guard, pumpkin.' Then my mother would take him downstairs and reheat his dinner. I used to fall asleep, listening to the low murmur of their voices in the kitchen.''

Her voice drifted off. She and her father had continued the nighttime ritual even after her mother had died, though then she'd filled in her mother's lines as well. It had lasted until she was thirteen when she'd overheard Aunt Helen and Aunt Eleanor discussing the true cause of her mother's death. That night, when Frank had come home and stood in her doorway, she simply hadn't said anything. And the silence had drawn out like the gulf growing between them. Finally her father had turned and walked away. He never mentioned it, and the words were never spoken again. It wasn't until the funeral that she'd wondered how much she'd hurt him with that omission.

''I like your family,'' Jake said beside her. She jerked a little, so lost in her own rare reminiscences that she'd forgotten he was there. Suddenly she felt unbearably exposed. She began to restack the files with unnecessary haste. At least he didn't try to stop her. But his eyes remained on her face until she felt hunted.

''I should change,'' she said briskly when she was done. She couldn't quite look him in the eye. ''Then we can go to your place.''

He touched her cheek, and she flinched. Warily her green gaze crept up to find him looking at her with that unholy gleam in his eye. ''Want some help?'' he whispered and grinned wickedly.

Her cheeks flushed with outrage even as she felt the relief. It didn't matter that he was probably teasing her to break the mood. At least he was teasing her and she knew how to handle that.

She narrowed her eyes and frowned at him as forcefully as she could. "Well, I'd let you help," she said slowly, "but Tom wouldn't like it."

Jake found himself automatically glancing over to the couch, where the guard in question was resettled in a sunbeam, giving his paw a delicate bathing. Tom glanced up, his yellow eyes lazy and delirious with sun. Then he spoiled the picture by flexing the paw once more, hooked claws flashing out. The cat blinked and purred.

Jake shook his head. "I'd swear that beast is possessed."

In spite of herself, Reggie smiled. "I don't know where he came from," she confessed, "but he truly hates men. I find it rather charming."

The cat looked back down, resuming his bathing. Just as quickly, Jake's hand snaked out and wrapped around her waist. Even as her mouth opened to form a protest, he dragged her against him. Her eyes narrowed dangerously, her cheeks flushing with fire, but even then, her gaze fell upon his lips.

"Quick, while he's not looking," Jake whispered, then he dipped his head down and captured her lips.

He teased her lower lip with slow and deliberate nips. A sophisticated man, he revealed his experience with every tantalizing touch of his tongue, outlining her lips, caressing the corners. He dipped his tongue in for the tiniest taste, finding her tongue as if he were a thief snatching a prize, then just as quickly darted away.

He let her go so abruptly, she nearly fell.

"Hazelnut. Exquisite," he pronounced. He grinned arrogantly, and she felt the first tendrils of outrage. Her stomach clenched with raw desire while her mouth still hungered for more. And he could simply grin at her that way?

Her hands curled tightly at her sides, her short nails scoring the tender flesh of her palms. The insufferable, son of a...

Like lightning, she snatched a fistful of his black shirt, wrapping the thin cotton around her capable hands.

Her green eyes darkened dangerously, her jaw taking on a telltale set. For one moment, she simply looked at him with narrow, burning eyes, so close he could feel the short hiss of her enraged breath.

Abruptly she dragged his head down. If he'd kissed her with polish, then she found his lips with rage. Her lips slanted across his openly, finding his mouth like a tornado. Her high, curved breasts flattened against his chest, her strong arms wrapping around his neck. She kissed him hungrily, her tongue delving deep into his mouth, stroking the warm, moist interior, reveling in the taste of coffee and desire. His body went instantly hard, and he reached for her waist.

Savagely she pushed out of his grasp. She could see the shock and raw hunger in his eyes, and it filled her with satisfaction even as her heart nearly thundered out of her chest. If he thought he could just finesse his way through her control, he had another thing coming. She raked him up and down with all the disdain she could muster.

"I'm not one of your toys," she told him in a low voice, her breath still labored. "I give as good as I get, Jake Guiness. Maybe in the future you ought to consider that."

His eyes turned molten, his hands reaching out for her, but she evaded him. Turning rapidly and with as much aplomb as her flushed features could handle, she marched up the stairs.

Jake watched her go with his hands still clutching at air. It took him another thirty seconds just to draw oxygen into his lungs. Slowly his hands drifted to his sides, but his gaze remained on the empty staircase with reluctant admiration.

"Wow," he said.

She didn't look at him when she came back downstairs with bag in hand, her anger still simmering. She was furious at him for kissing her, and furious at herself for returning the kiss. Damn it, in her whole life no one had treated her the way he treated her. Why couldn't he be intimidated by her as every other man she'd ever met?

She took a deep breath, tossing him the keys without really looking.

"You can drive," she stated tightly. "You know where you're going."

Jake simply nodded, though she could feel his warm eyes appraising her. As her anger only entertained him more, she drew in another deep breath. "I'm ready."

She held open the door and called to Tom who obediently jumped off the couch. After giving Jake one last disdainful look, the giant cat sauntered out the door.

"Don't you need to leave some food out or something?" Jake questioned.

Reggie shook her head. "Tom takes care of himself."

That was all she had to say on the subject. She turned and headed for the car. Shrugging to himself, Jake followed.

Five minutes later they were on the road. Two minutes after that, Reggie fell into a light slumber, her head against the window.

When she awoke, the light had already faded to dusk. She could just make out Jake, tapping one finger on the steering wheel while he whistled along with Billy Joel's "Allentown."

In the lull of half consciousness, she contemplated his hands and thought he would make a wonderful basketball player. Such long, lean fingers with wide palms. She could see him stroking the rough, orange skin of the ball or perhaps palming it for a particularly powerful pass.

When he'd kissed her, he'd tasted of coffee and experience, of hot nights and knowing touches.

It had been so long since she'd allowed herself to think of those things.

When Brian had called during her father's trial, she hadn't even spoken to him for more than a minute. She'd simply replaced the phone on the receiver, too afraid that if she stayed on the line, all the anger and confusion and fear would come rushing out like a giant wave. She couldn't do that. She couldn't give voice to all that. O'Douls didn't cry.

"You're awake." Jake's surprised voice cut through her thoughts. Slowly she tilted up her head to catch his gaze. "You should go back to sleep," he said. "It's only been half an hour, and you were up all night."

"I don't need much sleep," she said, though she did feel tired. She looked out the window. She didn't know what road they were now on, but the traffic was thicker, forcing Jake to slow down. He didn't seem that impatient at the wheel, however. Personally she found rush-hour traffic to be unbearably agonizing.

"You're from Boston, aren't you?" he asked.

Her head swiveled around, her eyes startled. Slowly, almost warily, she nodded.

"Your voice," he said in response to her unspoken question. "I kept thinking the accent was familiar. Finally I got it. Boston. It's not a thick accent though, just the way you say your *A*'s. How long did you live there?"

"My whole life," she finally replied. Her heart picked up in her chest, and if it had been light enough, he would have seen that all the color had drained from her face. She didn't like to talk about Cambridge. Not after the trial.

"No kidding?" Jake said beside her, his voice casual as his fingers continued tapping out the beat of the song on the wheel. "I lived in Cambridge for four years, but I suppose you know that. Where'd you live?"

She licked her lips, then looked back out at the fading light. Cambridge, that's where she'd lived. And that's where the FBI probing that had toppled her father had begun. "We moved around a lot," she said finally.

Jake's eyes shifted to her suddenly, his gaze made contemplative by her evasion. Mentally she cursed the man and his perceptiveness all over again. She really didn't want to talk about this.

"What about Madeline?" she said suddenly. She looked at him sharply, on the offensive now.

Jake's finger stopped in midtap, his brown eyes widening in unprecedented surprise.

"What about Madeline?" he asked back.

"You've been dating her," Reggie said shrewdly. "Won't she mind that you're returning home with another woman?"

Jake shook his head, his finger resuming his tapping while he whistled along to the chorus. "Nah. The thing with Madeline died when I was in Poland. It was never serious."

"It doesn't seem that any of them are." Buchanan had been right; Jake went through women as casually as wine.

Jake looked at her narrowly. "And what about you, hot stuff? How many young men have fallen prey to those kisses you deliver so passionately?"

Her cheeks flushed, but her chin came up a notch. "Oh, I stopped counting at fifty," she retorted airily, waving a hand in casual dismissal. "I would've notched 'em in the bedpost, but wrought iron's a bear to carve."

Jake laughed, but she could have sworn there was a glint of seriousness in his brown eyes. "Every good businessman considers the competition."

"Tom will be flattered then." Her gaze returned to the window, catching the gigantic house suddenly appearing in view. A couple more miles, and they would be at his place, she figured. She straightened in the seat, running a hand through her short, close-cropped hair. She still felt tired.

At the fourth huge, black iron gate, Jake slowed down the car. Rolling down the window, he punched in the gate access code. Silently, impressively, the gate swung inward.

"I have to warn you," he said as he pulled inside, "it's not all furnished yet. I'm not home much."

Reggie simply nodded, her attention caught by her first live view of the circular driveway before the house. In the middle of the oval, a large stone fountain crowned a smooth, green emerald of grass. She pulled her eyes away and forced them to register the three-story, brick structure rising before her. She'd seen the surveillance photos of Jake's home, but the grainy, black-and-white shots just didn't do it justice.

The house was built of classic red brick. White trim added an elegant touch, particularly the three white columns of the patio. The car came to a stop, but she continued to stare.

"What do you think?" Jake asked beside her, his voice devoid of teasing for a change. In fact, he sat forward with more tension than he liked.

"Very nice," she said at last, her gaze still sweeping down the curved tower that comprised the left side of the house. When she was little, she used to dream of living in a tower room. She must have read Rapunzel a hundred times. Unconsciously she fingered the shorn locks feathering her neck. "Tasteful."

Jake nodded and suddenly grinned. He scrambled out of the car, going around to her side as she opened her own door.

"I'm still working on the inside," he said as he took her arm and led her up the three steps to the double doors. "I tried the decorator route, but they kept mumbling about 'Trashed Palazzo.' For that kind of money, I didn't think I ought to be aiming for a garage sale look, even if it was King Henry's garage. Now, of course, my brother Garret is getting into the furniture business, so I think I'll have him finish it for me. If I can ever get it through his thick skull that it's not charity."

Reggie pulled her eyes off the structure enough to look at him. "The former SEAL?"

"That's Garret," Jake confirmed. He reached into his jeans pocket for his keys, then deftly unlocked the door. He grinned at her, then winked. "I'll carry you over the threshold for a small fee."

She arched a brow.

"Just a kiss," he swore.

"I can walk just fine."

"Yeah, but you kiss like dynamite."

Looking at him coolly—though a faint blush crept up her cheeks—she reached forward and opened the door herself. "After you, Mr. Guiness."

"How about a kiss on the cheek?" he tried one last time.

"How about walking into your house?"

"All right, all right. But you can't blame a guy for trying." He grinned at her as easily as a schoolboy, and she found herself wondering if he would always grin that much. God, he could make a woman's heart stop with that smile.

"After you," she said, and followed him into the house.

Chapter 4

The house didn't contain much furniture, Reggie agreed four hours later when she crept out of the guest bedroom for an impromptu tour. Since the FBI had the house under surveillance, she'd taken the opportunity to catch up on her sleep. Jake had also taken a nap, but now appeared hard at work in the study next to his bedroom.

She decided not to disturb him, exploring the rest of the house on her own. Creeping down the dark main stairs, she made it to the entryway and snapped on the light switch. A low-hanging chandelier of black wrought iron flared with electric candles, illuminating the round entryway with brilliant light. Looking around, Reggie could see the darkened archways of adjoining rooms scattered about like a waiting labyrinth. For a moment, she stood uncertain. Then she straightened her shoulders, selected one archway and proceeded.

This time, snapping on the lights nearly blinded her with stainless-steel brilliance as a huge kitchen burst into view. Hulking metal doors revealed a walk-in refrigerator, conspicuously unstocked, and an industrial-size freezer, which contained slightly more. A side wall dripped with stainless-steel and brass pans, nearly groaning with the weight. To sustain the onslaught of preparing sumptuous feasts, four ovens laid in wait, gaping mouths hollow with hunger.

Obviously the house was made for entertaining. If the kitchen hadn't confirmed that observation, then the forty-foot-long dining room did. At the head, a mammoth marble fireplace preened and simpered with red swirling Italian marble. Intricate woodwork framed it elegantly, arching up to the vaulted ceiling. Following the woodwork's ascent, Reggie found herself staring at an inlaid oil painting, Greek gods and goddesses frolicking above her head. She looked back down, shaking her head at such extravagance. The room was meant to be impressive, but mostly it seemed just empty and overdone, the brilliant, Austrian crystal chandelier drooling like a floozy over a single metal card table with four folding chairs.

Reggie crossed the empty expanse to the pitiful table, touching the marked-up vinyl and smiling for the first time. Her father had kept such a table for poker, but somehow, she just couldn't imagine millionaire Jake sitting in a folding chair. Then again, she could envision him tilting the chair recklessly back on the freshly waxed parquet floor, booted feet propped up on the tabletop while he dared fate to do its worst.

She shook her head again and kept walking, her stocking feet padding soundlessly on the oak floor. Tucked off the kitchen she discovered a small sunroom. A white wicker love seat with pastel pillows sat against one wall, accompanied by two glass end tables and a menagerie of plants. She tried out the love seat, staring at the inky blackness of night through the French windows. The wicker love seat wasn't Jake, either, she decided. Had a lover picked it out?

She crossed back into the entryway, this time choosing an archway to the left of the door. Here, she discovered the first room Jake clearly cared about: the billiards room.

Walnut paneling gave the room a dark, smoky feel, but it was countered somewhat by a left-hand bay of whitepaned windows. In the middle of the room, the pool table lorded as the clear centerpiece, complete with a hanging, stained-glass lamp. Reggie ran an expert hand across the green felt cover. Single slate table, of course. She smiled in appreciation. She inspected the collection of cue sticks lined like soldiers on the wall. The man had a distinguishing eye.

She took one down, then rolled it on the table experimentally. Straight, well balanced. She bet Jake Guiness was good, and her blood hummed in anticipation of a good challenge. Frank O'Doul had enjoyed a good pool game, and he'd taught his daughter a thing or two.

She put the cue stick away and investigated the bar. Four types of Scotch and a collection of liqueurs. She shook her head in reluctant admiration. Clearly Jake had his priorities established, and she suffered the uncomfortable sensation that her father just might have liked Jake Guiness.

Her lips twisted and she stood abruptly. Both were little boys who liked games. Did they share corruption, as well, the sickening need for money? Would Jake also betray anything for the power of the dollar?

She stalked out of the room, no longer so enamored with the damn table. Next door, she found a newly refurbished weight room, paneled with mirrors and boasting a state-of-the-art weight training system. She had no stomach left for admiration, she decided, and walked out before she could touch the weights with anything akin to longing.

She retreated to the upstairs. Of the seven bedrooms, only Jake's and a guest room where Reggie was now staying were furnished. Her room possessed a crimson-covered futon and low-built dresser. She would have dismissed it completely, but further investigation revealed the Chinese screen to be genuine and highlighted with 18-carat gold. Probably from his travels.

She moved into the tower room, her feet padding softly on the empty floor. Not a single piece of furniture marred the curved walls—just windows, which looked out over the brick fence to a wide street of discreet wealth. Gaslights glowed every twenty feet, throwing well-tended sidewalks into oily light. Dim shadows of trees obscured the other brick houses, leaving just a dark backdrop dotted by the occasional yellow window. The long, sleek shape of an imported car purred down the lit street, slowing at another huge gate before the heavy wrought iron granted entrance.

She leaned her forehead against the window and wondered what went on behind those other walls. When she'd been little, she'd wanted to be rich. Money could buy anything, she'd decided. Maybe even a new Mommy. Now, of course, she understood the fallacy of the dollar. Still, did people in million-dollar houses get to buy at least some happiness? A part of her still wanted to believe.

A light flickered down the street, catching her eye. After a minute, she made out the dim outline of a car parked in the shadows. The door had opened, revealing momentarily the shape of a head. Then the door closed, casting the auto back into darkness.

Her backup, she thought, giving the auto another critical glance. In the morning, she would claim to go jogging and update the agents waiting in the car. Simple enough.

She turned away and walked down the hall to stand before Jake's room. He didn't seem to be around. She decided that counted as an invitation and entered.

A bedside lamp revealed a huge room of startling simplicity. A raised area contained a solid oak four-poster bed covered by a blue-and-burgundy quilt. Near the foot of the bed, a huge fireplace oozed more red Italian marble. Logs were already carefully arranged inside, waiting for a single match to spark an aura of coziness and intimacy. She turned her gaze away, focusing on the night table instead. It looked sturdy and well built, holding a lamp, a clock radio and a pair of black-framed reading glasses resting on *The Pursuit of Excellence*.

"Not the same as murder notes," Jake commented behind her.

She turned abruptly, finding him leaning against the doorway, his arms crossed. Her cheeks flushed guiltily, but he simply grinned.

"Had your fill?" he asked. "I think it's rather boring after your place."

She brought her chin up, fighting back the rise of color to her cheeks. "Just looking around."

"Oh, dear," he declared mockingly. "I hope I hid the Vermeer well enough."

Her cheeks flushed even darker and she stepped back down into the main area. "I like the furniture," she said at last, seeking a neutral topic. It seemed to be the right thing to say, because he immediately smiled with genuine gratitude.

"Thanks. My father made it."

She arched a brow, running her hand along an oak armoire with new appreciation. "It's well made."

"Absolutely. Sturdy stuff, just like a good ole North Carolina boy." He pushed away from the doorframe to walk lazily toward her. He'd showered, and she could smell the fresh fragrance of soap and shampoo as he approached. The dark tendrils of his hair looked damp where they curled on his neck, thick and gleaming in the pale light. He stopped just a few feet away, looking at her with his warm, knowing eyes.

"Sleep well, darlin'?" he whispered.

"Yes," she said, then tried to clear her throat when the word came out slightly breathless. He wore a thickly knit, pine green sweater, the rounded collar wide enough to reveal the corded strength of his neck and the faint dusting of dark brown chest hair. She could see the pulse at the base of his throat, pounding and strong.

"Hungry?"

She dragged her eyes up to meet his winking gaze. Mutely she shook her head.

Stepping carefully back, she focused her eyes on the walls of the expansive room. They were empty, as most of the house was empty, giving the sense that he might stay here, but he didn't live here.

"How long have you owned the place?" she asked at last.

He shrugged, his eyes lingering on her face. He noticed she now wore a pair of slim-fitting jeans and a crew neck, ribbed shirt of navy blue. She looked trim and sporting and very, very attractive. He walked forward, grinning to himself when she took another unconscious step back toward the bed.

"Two years," he said and continued his advance.

She halted warily, and he froze, the careful hunter not wanting to spook his prey.

"That's a long time to not even put a picture up."

"I bought it originally as an investment." He made one casual, half step forward.

"And now?"

"Thought I might keep it, fix it up. Sooner or later, I need to cut back on my traveling. God knows I'm sick of eating airline peanuts for dinner."

"I would've thought you'd have gathered a lot of…things from your travels." She slid a bit closer to the wall as if suddenly realizing the bed area was behind her. He adjusted accordingly.

"I suppose I gathered a few 'things.'"

"I don't see any of them here."

He paused, grinning broadly and shaking his head. "Reggie, are you looking for the Vermeer again? Why, you know, I thought of hanging stolen artwork all over the walls, but my decorator just didn't agree. So I stuck it all in the freezer instead."

She frowned. "You don't have anything—" She caught herself, realizing what she'd just admitted.

Jake wagged his finger at her while arching a naughty brow. "The freezer, Reggie? You even looked in the freezer?"

"I was hungry," she muttered, her green eyes gazing at the floor.

Immediately he took the last four steps forward, catching her just as she brought her gaze back up. Suddenly he was there, soap scented and dangerous. Her breath caught in her throat, her eyes growing wider. She tried to take a step back, but her heel encountered wall.

"I'm hungry, too," he whispered, lowering his head.

She stiffened, steeling herself for his kiss, but his lips simply stopped, a mere two inches from her own. She felt the whisper of his breath as he looked into her eyes, waiting.

She licked her lips, her gaze falling to the full, strong outline of his mouth. Dark whiskers shadowed the softness, a late-day beard that would rasp against her cheeks. How long had it been since she'd felt the erotic tingle of a beard scoring her tender skin?

Her lips parted with longing.

She leaned slightly forward, narrowing the two inches to one.

"Kiss me," he whispered. "Please."

At the last minute, she caught herself, sanity flashing like a red siren through her overloaded senses. With a deft twirl, she ducked under his arm, scooting quickly to the relative safety of the open room. Fists clenched with her effort at control, she turned back to him with dangerously dark eyes.

"That's not appropriate," she said steadily.

He merely arched an eyebrow, walking languorously toward her as if he were a dark, jungle cat. "I'm not looking to write an etiquette book," he drawled.

Her cheeks flushed lightly, but she kept her chin up, her lips pressed tight.

"I did not come here for your entertainment, Mr. Guiness," she snapped. "You want a kiss, call Madeline. I have a job to do."

She pivoted back around, marching smartly to the door. She made it halfway down the hall before it became clear he wasn't going to follow her. Her shoulders relented some, her jaw relaxing a fraction. In almost half wonder, her fingers touched her lips, which had been so close to his. She caught herself with a shake of her head, and continued walking to her room with her hands at her sides.

* * *

She paced the confines of her room for half an hour trying to work it out in her mind. Buchanan had been right: Jake was nothing if not a womanizer. She'd told Buchanan not to worry about it, but had she been wrong? In her arrogance, had she underestimated Jake as Buchanan had claimed?

Because, God knows, a fraction of an inch more, and she would have kissed him.

She pivoted and paced in the other direction. The weakness galled her to the bone. That she should desire a man who so obviously liked the pursuit, a man who went through women like water, was demoralizing. When had she grown so weak?

The best she could do was rationalize it in her mind. For five years, she'd focused solely on her job. She was a healthy, young woman. Of course she was vulnerable to certain basic biological needs. But she had no intention of resolving those needs with Jake Guiness.

Women were more like an infatuation than a passion for Jake. He found them, he enjoyed them, he let them go.

The man really savored the conquest.

She pivoted again and marched the length of the room. Besides, she pointed out sharply to herself, she was an agent and a damn good one. She wasn't going to let him distract her that easily. He might be used to women who went weak in the knees, but she was made of sturdier stuff. Her hands balled at her sides and she took a deep breath.

She still remembered what it had been like to have Chelsey Harper grab the basketball out of her hands. The knowledge that she'd failed, that she'd let her guard down.

That look on her father's face . . .

Her restless footsteps finally stilled. She'd visited her father seven times in prison before his death. Each time, she'd expected him to be somehow different. Exposed, maybe, or vulnerable—the hero with his laurels toppled to the ground. But each time he'd still been Frank, sitting across from her with his red-flushed jowls and crinkled eyes, asking her about the job, yelling at her to be more aggressive.

"Don't let them damn OPR bastards get you down. I raised you better than that, young lady! Now you get that chin up, you hear me? Come on, I want that chin up now! That's better. That's my girl. Now go show 'em what your old man taught ya. Give 'em hell."

Frank O'Doul had never backed down a day in his life, not even when he'd been found guilty of accepting bribes to feed his gambling problem. But he'd never admitted to a problem, not to Reggie, not to his brothers, his partner, anyone. Frank O'Doul was never wrong.

The phone call telling her of his coronary attack was still the biggest shock Reggie had ever received. How could the man who could do anything suddenly be dead? How could her father, her big, red-faced father actually die?

How could he leave her when she still had so much to prove?

Reggie turned away from the wall, holding its blankness accountable for the unwanted memories that had crept through her guard. She didn't want to think of her father right now. For too many years, she'd done everything to be the son he'd always wanted. And for too many years, she'd carried the weight of his betrayal. Now, she lived her own life.

And she was good enough to catch the Highwayman.

Taking another fortifying breath, she stepped back into the hallway and headed for the light coming from the study. Jake looked up the minute she stepped into the room.

"Well," she started presumptuously, "are you hungry yet?"

He smiled, leaning closer to the computer screen. He glanced at his watch, then whistled. "Wow, nearly midnight. No wonder I'm starved."

Reggie nodded, approaching the desk. Was it her imagination, or did he tense a little? As she watched, his hand moved casually across the keyboard, saving the document. He leaned a little more, as if to get more comfortable, except that now he blocked the screen completely from her view.

Feigning some casualness of her own, she crossed to the left, picking up a paperweight filled with seashells.

"What do you suggest?" she asked, glancing over carefully. She could just make out line after line of text on the screen. His fingers moved again, the application abruptly closing out. Her brow furrowed deeply, her gaze quickly perusing his desk. It was bare of any documents.

"We could order out for pizza," Jake said. He reached up and flipped a switch. Not the power switch, she realized, but the screen switch. On cue, the screen went blank. He sat back easily now, grinning a bit, but she wasn't fooled.

"Sounds great," she muttered. Her gaze came up sharply. "Maybe we could phone it in, and you could go pick it up."

"I thought I wasn't allowed out of your sight?"

She shrugged. "I'm sure it's just a short drive." And she wanted the opportunity to search his office.

His hand moved negligently on the keyboard, hitting Escape. Closing out of the system, she thought. Her frown etched deeper. What had he been doing that he didn't want her to see?

Abruptly, he stood. "I'm sure there's something in the kitchen. Let's check it out."

She half-nodded, still glancing at his desk. Nothing. She found his gaze warily, not able to keep all the suspicion from her eyes.

"I forgot something in my room," she said slowly. "Why don't I just meet you downstairs?"

He smiled and shook his head. He took her arm. "We'll get it together," he declared as she gritted her teeth.

"I hate to take you away from your work." She tried one last time.

"No problem, I was already done."

"Taking care of correspondence?"

"Nope."

"Looking at some financials?"

He grimaced. "Definitely not."

"Following the stock market?"

"Market closed at four."

Her eyes narrowed dangerously. "So what kind of business do you take care of at eleven-thirty at night?"

He looked at her with a charmingly innocent smile she didn't believe for one single minute. "Nothing interesting, Reggie."

"But—"

"Let's eat. Nobody works well on an empty stomach."

With a last penetrating look, she followed the urgings of his arm. She would come back later, she promised herself, and list the files by date and time. That ought to reveal which item he'd been working on. She began to smile as he led her down the stairs.

"Oodles of Noodles or macaroni and cheese?"

Reggie looked at him incredulously, tilting her head high enough to peer over him into the opened cupboard. Sure enough, it was stocked to the hilt with boxes of macaroni and cheese and cellophane packages of Oodles of Noodles. And she felt guilty the nights she had microwave popcorn for dinner.

"You're serious?" she said at last, her green eyes still registering shock.

For one moment, Jake looked concerned. Then he seemed to shake the expression from his face, grinning familiarly once more. "Keeps well and cooks fast," he said cheerily. "Come on, what did you eat in college?"

"Oodles of Noodles," she confessed, though that had been nearly seven years ago.

"Oodles of Noodles it is," Jake declared. "Chicken, beef or mushroom?"

"Mushroom." He handed down the package of Ramen noodles, and she accepted it still shaking her head. There were certain things about Jake she had a feeling she would never understand.

Jake pulled a large pot off the wall, filled it with water and set it on the stove to boil. Then he rummaged through the huge, empty refrigerator and a few other cupboards.

"The good news is," he said at last, "I have ten bottles of wine, two jars of peanut butter, four kinds of jelly, three boxes of Nilla wafers and some butter. The bad news is, that's about it. Sorry, but I wasn't expecting to stay here much this week. Usually I just eat out, or, of course, make Oodles of Noodles. I'm telling you, college is worthwhile for its survival skills alone."

"And if you do stay a bit? What do you do then?" Reggie asked. The water reached boiling, so she ripped open both packages of the tightly meshed noodles and dropped them in. She pulled open drawers until she found flatware, and selected a fork for stirring.

Jake shrugged, hopping up on the counter to supervise. "There's a service that supplies temporary house staff. I generally hire someone for the time I'm around. When I entertain, I hire a catering company that takes care of everything. Hey, the noodles look done." He grinned. "Dinner in three minutes, you gotta love it."

In spite of herself, Reggie smiled back. In college, Oodles of Noodles had gotten her through hundreds of late nights. These days, she had a tendency to forget about meals altogether, sometimes going as long as two or three days before she found herself wondering when her last meal had been. There was always just so much to do, and eating seemed so mundane in comparison.

While she drained the excess water into the sink, Jake retrieved two bowls. He appeared back at her side carrying two thin, china bowls of a lovely bone color. He peered down at her work.

"Ah, draining out almost all the water. A true connoisseur."

Reggie looked up at him with an appraising smile. "Don't tell me you actually ate them as soup in college? Way too messy."

"Nope, I always drained them, too." He winked at her, his grin warm and intimate. "You struck me as a good noodle woman right from the start."

Reggie's cheeks colored, and for a minute, she felt a pang deep in her stomach. She looked away, her gaze falling onto the two bowls instead.

"Wedgwood china, Jake?" Her eyes softened on the fine bone color, the delicate gold trim. It was so lovely, like a butterfly you held in your hand and prayed not to crush. "We can't eat on this," she declared with an emphatic shake of her head.

He looked at her, genuinely puzzled. "Why not?"

"It's...it's..." She struggled for the words, but couldn't find any. Her mother had had china from her mother, and it was dragged out once a year for Easter. Even Reggie, who had given up on so many other things, observed that custom as the new keeper of the china.

Jake's face softened, his hand brushing her cheek. "It's okay, darlin'," he whispered gently. "We won't break anything. For you, I'll be on my best behavior." He smiled, slow and wicked, but somehow gentle as well.

Her hands began to tremble, that deep pang knifing through her belly again. She half wished he would go back to being an outrageous lout, and half wished he would look at her softly again, maybe lean a little bit closer.

She dumped the noodles into the two bowls, no longer able to meet his eyes. Beside her, Jake ripped open the two flavor packs, adding one to each bowl. He pulled down two wineglasses, and tucking a bottle of Chardonnay under his arm, he led them into the dining room.

Their footsteps echoed in the empty, vaulted room as they approached the tiny card table. Jake seemed unconcerned, just as he was unconcerned about the fine china, or no doubt the expensive wine he was about to serve with pre-packaged food. Reggie decided if he could be nonchalant, so could she.

But the room, for all its vastness, seemed somehow intimate, with just the two of them sitting catty-corner at a banged-up card table. The pop of the wine's cork bounced off the vaulted ceiling like the echo of a bon voyage party. The pouring wine tinkled in the silence, refreshing and promising with its crisp, tantalizing smell.

Jake picked up his glass, looking at her with lingering brown eyes. "A toast?" he proposed.

Her own hands nerveless, Reggie picked up the glass. "All right," she said quietly.

"To the start of a beautiful relationship?"

"To catching the Highwayman," she said. Jake raised a brow, but tapped her thin crystal glass with his own. They both drank, the wine dry and cool and soothing.

With a grin, Jake set down his glass and attacked his noodles. Reggie watched him for a while, her own fork aimlessly wrapping the noodles around its tines over and over again. Jake ate with smooth, fluid movements, twirling his noodles with careless, practiced ease. He seemed relaxed and happy and unconcerned with life. Should a man suspected of international art theft be so relaxed? she wondered. Should the leader of a one-hundred-fifty-million-dollar holding company seem so stress free?

She didn't know, but she envied him his nonchalance. She took a bite of her own noodles, registering the salty tang of mushroom flavoring. It evoked memories of other late nights in intimate dorm rooms with another man by her side. Brian had known how to make her laugh. And he'd known how to glance up and meet her eyes with just the right warm gaze. Until suddenly textbooks were forgotten, and his lips were on her own, and down onto the floor they would fall.

She laid down her fork and concentrated on the wine. Across from her, Jake frowned.

"Don't like the noodles?"

She shook her head. "They're fine." She looked around the vaulted ceilings, feeling restless again.

"The room then?" Jake said, following her glance. Suddenly he wiggled a devilish eyebrow, his voice teasing. "If the dining room's not to your liking, I know the perfect alternative—curling up on a blue-and-crimson quilt on a four-poster bed, lighting a fire in the fireplace for a bit of atmosphere..."

Her cheeks flushed at the description of the intimate scene. "I'm just not as hungry as I thought," she said, shrugging.

He frowned, his gaze serious. "You don't eat much, do you?" Somehow, it sounded like an accusation, and she immediately stiffened.

"I don't see how that's any concern of yours."

He leaned over, looking at her intensely. "Relax. Enjoy the noodles, enjoy the wine. No one ever goes to their grave thinking, 'I wish I had worked more.'"

She would. She was more than certain she would. "Strange advice coming from a millionaire," she retorted quietly.

Jake took a long sip of his own wine, watching her with startlingly perceptive eyes. Finally he set the glass down. "Work is good, but relaxation is an art, darlin'. Everybody needs a holiday."

Holiday? She hadn't even taken a weekend in the past six months. There was so much to do, so much to learn, so much to prove. And time flew by so fast, opportunities closed before you realized they were even open. She didn't want to lose any more opportunities.

She finished the glass of wine, feeling it course through her veins. For a minute, she felt light-headed but she dismissed it. She'd had her first sip of wine at age eight; she knew how to handle alcohol.

"Speaking of relaxing, are you going to work after dinner?" she prodded, her green eyes suddenly cool and watchful.

Jake sighed, leaning back and shaking his head at her impenetrability. "No," he said at last. "I know when I'm tired, and frankly, right now I'm looking forward to sliding between the sheets of my own bed and pulling my mother's quilt up to my chin."

Reggie took two more forkfuls of noodles, then set her fork down permanently. "I could use some sleep, too."

She rose, picking up her bowl, and with a reluctant sigh, Jake followed. "Still half a bottle of wine," he suggested as he followed her into the kitchen. "I'm telling you, that fireplace in my room is something else."

She rinsed out the cold, swollen noodles and placed the bowl gently in the sink. "Good night, Jake."

She walked out of the kitchen without looking back. Behind her, Jake poured himself another glass of Chardonnay, and stared at the empty archway with thoughtful eyes.

Reggie slid out of the futon a little after two in the morning. For a moment, she stilled, tuning her ears to the house. No sound penetrated the inky blackness, sleep settling thickly into the air. She crept over to her bag, pulling out the pair of gray sweatpants. Pulling them on, she padded out of her room on bare feet.

No lights illuminated the hall. She paused for one moment outside the closed door of Jake's room, but all remained still. She slipped into the study, shutting the door carefully behind her.

Nerves tight and adrenaline humming, she padded quickly to the desk, snapped on the desk light and reached for the computer's power switch. Simultaneously she saw the 3×5 index card sitting pleasantly on the keyboard.

Nothing interesting here, darlin'. Sweet dreams.

With a low oath, she picked up the card. No, she thought, he couldn't have known. She snapped on the computer anyway, but her heart was already sinking in her chest.

How could he second-guess her that way? He didn't even know her. And what the hell was he hiding?

She booted up the system, opening the file manager to view all file details. The dates and times of last activity appeared next to each file. Scanning down, she looked for the day's date and an approximate time of 11:30 p.m. But nothing registered the day's date, nothing at all.

Swearing, she sat down hard on the desk chair. Then it came to her. All he'd had to do to throw her off was change the date and time on the computer's clock, then resave the document. That simply, he'd covered his tracks.

She exited the program and shut off the machine. Then she picked up the index card and prepared to shred it into tiny, insignificant bits. At the last moment, she stopped herself.

Temper, Reggie, she reminded herself. She had to learn to control her temper. Eyes narrowing in contemplation, she very carefully returned the card to the keyboard.

He'd known she would come looking, and he obviously had something to hide. So what was Mr. I-Am-Being-Framed really up to? She stared at the blank computer screen for a minute longer, but it refused to relinquish any hints.

With a sigh, she stood, looking around the room for any final clues. When none magically appeared, she adjusted the chair and desk contents back to their original positions. When everything looked undisturbed, she snapped off the light with a final sigh.

Let him think she hadn't even thought to check the files. She'd underestimated him, now it was time for him to underestimate her. Sooner or later, he would let his guard down.

And she would be waiting.

Chapter 5

At six, Reggie was up once more, pulling on her gray sweats and shaking away the last remnants of sleep. Moving quietly, she found her thickest socks and laced up her running shoes. She paused briefly in front of the mirror, raking her fingers through her short-cropped hair. It looked slightly flatter than last night, but none too worse for the wear. She'd shorn off what was left of her hair when she'd entered the Academy in order to save time in the morning. When you were expected to be on the course running by 6:00 a.m., every minute counted.

She smoothed her bangs down, fingers pausing as she noted the dark shadows staining her unadorned eyes. When was the last time she'd slept more than six hours? When was the last night she'd managed to sleep without waking up every hour on the hour?

She turned away from the mirror, telling herself it didn't matter. At the Academy, they'd pushed everyone hard. Mind over body. Only the strong survived. Well, she'd been one of the survivors.

She cracked open her door and peered down the hall. Still no sounds of life, but she imagined it was much too early for Jake Guiness. She crept down the stairs and let herself out.

She did a few preliminary stretches, then began jogging. After only two blocks, a dark Lincoln Towncar came into sight, parked next to the curb where she'd seen it last night. Just as she was about to pause before it, she heard the sound of another approaching car. She veered back to the right-hand sidewalk, circling the block once more. This time when she came around, no one was in sight.

She jogged over, spotting two men sitting in the front seat. As she approached, the window glided down soundlessly.

"Regina O'Doul?" the man at the wheel said. He was wearing a dark gray suit, wrinkled from sitting in the car all night. She nodded, hesitating slightly until both men flashed their credentials. She came up to the window.

"Agent McGraw," the mustached driver said. He jerked his thumb to the younger, heavier man sitting next to him. "Agent Black. Hear you got the winning assignment."

Reggie shrugged. "A job's a job," she answered coolly.

Agent McGraw gestured to the brick-lined neighborhood, grunting sonorously. "You call this undercover work? Growing out your hair and getting a tattoo, that's undercover. Maybe getting roughed up a few times or being asked to kill a man to prove your loyalty. That's a job, rookie. Not chowing prime rib in a million-dollar suite."

Reggie's cheeks flushed from the sarcasm, her green eyes sparking a dark fire. With effort, she controlled her temper. She was young, and when it came to fieldwork, she was green. For some agents, that would always be an invitation for comment. "I don't think anyone cares how we catch the Highwayman," she replied, her voice measured, her eyes hard, "just so long as we catch him."

McGraw grunted what might have been agreement, but Reggie knew she still didn't have his respect.

She took a deep breath. "Look, I didn't jog over here for your compliments, sir. I came to report. The situation has not changed since yesterday. The current plan is to remain at this site until the day of the Charity Ball. Do you have any news?"

Both men shook their heads, McGraw's look still condescending, though Agent Black offered her a small nod.

"Report over," she said stiffly and stepped back. "I think I'll finish my morning jog."

She turned away and before either of them could comment she resumed jogging. Her pace remained light and even, until the car was nothing but an insignificant speck behind her. Then, and only then did she unleash the raw, burning anger inside her. She should have shown more composure. She should have been better, stronger, smarter.

She ran hard, listening to the beat of her feet against the pavement. She ran feeling the intensity in her knees, the punishing grind of bone on cartilage. She ran with lungs burning and her heart thundering, and then she ran some more.

And through it all, she could hear McGraw's condescension and see the bitter memory of her father turning away after that one last championship game. She even saw the lone index card lying on the keyboard. *Nothing interesting here, darlin'.*

She ran faster and let the wind sting her eyes.

When was she finally going to get everything right?

She completed a three-mile loop, caught the tinkling sound of church bells and ran the loop again.

When she finally returned to the house, she had a new idea.

She peeled off her sweatshirt with her chest still heaving. In the guest bathroom, she splashed water over her beet red face and blotted the sweat from her neck and chest. Her T-shirt clung to her lithe frame, soaked through from her exertions. Her foot sported a new blister, and her left knee ached.

She shut off the water, ignoring all the aches and pains, and listened to the house instead.

No sounds penetrated. She glanced at her watch. A little after 7:00 a.m.

After weeks of following Jake Guiness, she knew that he was a bona fide night owl, often working or partying until three or four in the morning, then rising at nine for work. However, he'd gone to bed by one last night, early for him.

Did that mean he would rise earlier as well?

She gripped the edge of the sink and contemplated her options. She looked at herself hard in the mirror, her face still red and dotted with perspiration, her bangs spiky around her eyes. It was now or never, she told her reflection.

She opened the bathroom door, listened one more time, then crept down the edge of the hall. Sliding into the study, she removed the index card, slid into the desk chair and flipped on the computer. It powered up with a loud *"bong,"* making her jump in the stillness. Nervously she glanced at the doorway, straining her ears for sound.

The house seemed quiet.

Biting her lower lip, she opened the file manager. Since she'd been watching Jake Guiness for a while now, she thought she might know a thing or two about him. Now if Jake with his easy grin, laughing eyes and notorious wit was going to redate a recent file, what would he use?

She ran down the list until she saw the date she'd been looking for: April 1, 1896. April Fools'.

Her hand trembling on the mouse, she opened the file, one eye on the empty doorway. Just a couple more minutes and she would be done. Just two minutes more...

The screen filled with text. Quickly her eyes scanned down, recognizing the file as a download from Nexus by its headings. Jake had been researching something using the on-line database of magazine and newspaper articles.

Maneuvering quickly down the document, she skimmed the lines. Slowly all the color drained from her cheeks, her stomach suddenly dropping until she was left with nothing but a hollow void. Her teeth bit into her lower lip, drawing blood. But even then, she couldn't stop reading.

By the end of the document, a deep resilience took hold of her. With amazingly steady hands, she closed out the document and exited the program. Turning off the computer, she diligently replaced the index card and covered up all signs of her visit. She walked into the hallway with legs that felt at once weak and amazingly strong. She looked at his door, but it was still closed.

She returned to her room and sat down on the futon in her sweat-stained T-shirt. She sat there for a long time, her arms wrapped around her knees. Slowly she rocked back and forth, the wheels in her mind turning, the sense of violation warring with the need to understand.

Jake Guiness had indeed been researching. He'd downloaded all the information on her father's trial.

Reggie did her best to avoid him during the day. With his permission, she set up a second phone line and spent most of the day in her room, talking to other agents on the case and brainstorming out loud. Jake came by once to ask her about lunch, but she was on the phone with Buchanan, so she'd waved him away. She didn't think about eating again until four.

She didn't feel quite up to facing Jake just yet. She felt far too exposed and vulnerable to handle his teasing comments and persistent advances.

Except she couldn't hide in the room forever. She was supposed to be watching him, after all.

She finished reading the notes she'd drafted during her conversations. Already, the Technical Services Division had installed wiretaps and three bugs in the Kendall estate where the Children's Charity Ball would be held in just ten days' time. Security checks were continuing on the catering company, and three other agents were in charge of monitoring probable leads, Kirk Richardson, Emelia Emmons and Drake DeSioux. Each had been present at all four thefts and each were renowned art connoisseurs.

Richardson, a tall thin man with a carefully trimmed beard, represented the fourth generation of English wealth.

Raised in Africa, he'd recently come to America two years ago and bought up a lot of property in Newport and Virginia. Viewed as cold and snobbish, he was now going through his third divorce, and his finances were no longer stable. Reggie had contemplated him quite seriously at first, except at fifty years of age and a chain-smoker, he didn't have the physical strength or technical acumen for the thefts. On the other hand, he could very well be directing the operations.

Emelia Emmons was middle-aged, busty and known for her string of affairs with twenty-year-old tennis pros. She preferred to wear minks and diamonds, and drank most men under the table. Filthy rich, she was the daughter of a Texan who made his fortune in oil and married her off to a solid Southern family for title. Emelia's husband had died in an unfortunate horsing accident, though she didn't seem to mourn his passing for too long, having being discovered in bed with a groom the next day. For the most part, she was considered uncouth and overly brash, except she had the most amazing eye for art and the wealth to fulfill that passion. She was also known to be competitive, ruthless and vindictive.

While Emelia did not possess the physical strength to be the thief, she'd recently taken up with a mysterious young man who looked quite capable. They only had surveillance photos of the tall, leanly built stranger. He seemed to only meet Emelia at hotels, not at public events. Interesting, considering that Emelia was not shy about bringing her young playmates to even the loftiest social events.

Drake DeSioux, however, was the suspect Reggie worried about the most. For starters, she didn't believe De-Sioux was his real name, and in fact, background information on the man was suspiciously lacking. He claimed he was the last of a defunct royal East European lineage, appearing in New York ten years ago. He spent money lavishly, without appearing to have any source of income. He relished art, the opera and fine wine. He also tipped the scales at over two hundred and fifty pounds and was known for his biting sarcasm. From what she'd heard, there was little about the man Reggie trusted. He seemed incredibly bright, ingenious and ruthless, the perfect Dr. No. But then who would be the thief? Business associates of the man were also hard to find.

In the final analysis, Jake Guiness remained the closest match to her profile, putting her at square one. Jake, who seemed intent on playing his own game.

In response to her thoughts, there was a firm knock at her door.

"Come on, Reggie, you have to eat sometime," Jake called through the door.

Reggie gathered her notes together and slid them beneath the mattress of the futon. She brushed her hands over her crimson jersey, then raked them through her short-cropped hair. She took a deep breath, composed her face and opened the door just as his fist was descending once more.

His hand froze in midair. "There you are, darlin'. I was beginning to think I was going to have to call the cavalry. Busy day?"

"Busy enough," she said simply. Her green eyes met his face openly, hard and composed. Slowly she searched his gaze for some sign of what he knew—any lingering bit of malice or laughter or pity. But Jake Guiness just grinned that damn grin, looking once more casual and careless.

"Can I buy you dinner?" he suggested with a wiggling brow. "I'll let you provide dessert."

"Macaroni and cheese will be fine," she said, her voice purposely distant and cool.

His flirtatious expression slipped a bit, and he looked at her more closely. "You all right?"

"Why? Any reason I shouldn't be?"

He shrugged, his gaze slightly wary. "You just don't seem yourself."

"How should I seem?"

He leaned forward, his deep eyes penetrating. She simply smiled tightly. He definitely looked uncomfortable now.

"I'll take you out for real food," he tried again, his voice more somber this time. "Restaurant of your choice."

She shook her head. "It isn't necessary. Mac and cheese is fine. Dinner in eight minutes."

"You're sure?"

"Yes."

"Absolutely sure?"

"Yes."

He nodded, but his brown eyes remained sharp. Finally he pushed away from the doorframe and led the way downstairs. She followed, not saying a word.

"So did you learn anything interesting today?" he asked when they finally reached the kitchen. Reggie simply shook her head and opened the cupboard.

"I had a boring day as well," he continued dryly, "thanks for asking."

"One box or two?" Reggie asked.

He frowned at her once more. "I eat a whole box, so you'd better make two. I saw you jogging this morning."

Her hand froze in the cupboard. "I had a nice run," she said carefully.

"You keep a good pace." He patted his flat stomach suggestively. "I don't think I could keep up."

She kept her eyes off his hard belly and on the boxes of macaroni. She pulled down two. "I've been running for a bit."

"Yeah? Does it usually involve talking to two guys in a car?"

"They needed directions."

"For five minutes, Reggie?"

She turned on him, her green eyes blazing, her brow fierce. "They were complicated directions, Jake."

He held up two hands immediately, taking a step back. "Just making conversation," he said slowly, but his eyes lingered thoughtfully on her face.

He looked so damn sincere, she felt her jaw tighten with anger. How dare he tease her, how dare he pretend to be attracted to her, when all along he was reading about her corrupt, gambling-addicted father who'd blown an entire career at the tracks! Just how gullible did he think she was!

"Stop making conversation," she ordered tightly, ripping a pan off the wall. "I'm not here to make conversation, Jake. I'm not here to be your friend. I'm an agent on assignment. And I don't give a damn if you counted your toes all day long, just as long as you didn't run out and steal a van Gogh. Got it?"

He looked at her for a minute, a series of unreadable emotions flickering across his face. Abruptly he grabbed the pan and yanked it from her grasp with surprising strength. No muscle in his face gave him away, but suddenly, she could see the anger slowly burning in his brown eyes.

"You can make up all the rules you want, Reggie," he said quietly. "I'll play by the ones I want to." He turned to the sink, abruptly twisting on the faucets and sticking the pan under the pouring spout. "You know, when I was little, my mom would send us to our rooms to clean up our acts before dinner."

She stiffened behind him, and even as she fought to control her temper, it spiraled beyond her grasp. "Damn you," she swore to his back. Tears burned her eyes, the emotion choking her throat so tight she could barely speak. "Don't you talk to me about family and rules and all that crap. I read your computer, Mr. I-Am-So-Clever. I saw your file on my father!"

He stilled at the sink, then abruptly nodded his head. "Ah, so that's what this is all about." He turned off the water, and as if they were merely discussing the weather, he carried the pot to the stove and set it to boil. "I had a feeling April Fools' might be a little too obvious."

She took a deep breath, struggling for control but encountering little success. "How dare you spy on me like that," she whispered fiercely. "What were you hoping for, Jake? Did you want to know if like father, like daughter? You had no right!"

He nailed her with serious brown eyes. "You're in my house, investigating me for art theft. I had every right. Didn't you spend time investigating me?"

"You're a suspect!"

"And you're the agent I'm now working with! For God's sake Reggie, you have an incriminating photograph of me as well as circumstantial evidence that ties me to these crimes. Did you really think I would just sit back and wait to see what happened next? Would *you?*"

Her chin came up stubbornly, her eyes still burning, though she resented the emotion. O'Douls didn't cry because O'Douls didn't hurt.

"That still doesn't give you the right to investigate *me,*" she repeated, her chin up, her gaze unrelenting. "He was my father."

"It must have been tough," Jake said abruptly. His eyes took on a new gleam, which might have been pity. She stood even straighter.

"We got through it."

"Did you, Reggie?" he asked softly. "Mitch said you started on the admin side of the Bureau...."

Unconsciously she winced, validating his words more strongly than any other reply could have done. Without thinking, he reached out.

Instantly she stepped back, her green eyes wary and burning. "My father was a good man, Jake. When I graduated from the Academy, he stood in the front row cheering at the top of his lungs. He was a decent man who let his gambling problem get out of control because he was too stubborn and too proud. He was wrong to accept those bribes, and he admitted it and served his time. End of story."

"If you say so."

"I say so!"

"Okay," he said simply and turned back to the sink as if it really was that easy. Behind him, her eyes narrowed as she shook her head. That he could blunder through her life that way and then say it was his right!

"Be careful, Jake," she finally said to his back. "Because I'm watching you."

She sat across from him, quiet and picking at her macaroni for most of dinner. He concentrated on the wine, letting her be. To a certain extent, he could understand her anger. If he'd found out that someone had suddenly dug up information on his past and his family, he would be upset, too. Then again, he had discovered exactly that, and he was learning to deal with it.

He hadn't consciously started out with the idea that he would expose Regina O'Doul. He'd simply wanted to know more about the woman who would be responsible for either arresting him or clearing all suspicion. He considered knowing the competition to be solid business strategy, and he'd been as surprised as anyone when the O'Doul name suddenly evoked newspaper article after newspaper article on Nexus.

Frank O'Doul had been caught in an overall sweep of the Cambridge city police department by the FBI, which had been investigating complaints of corruption and misconduct. O'Doul had pleaded guilty to one count of falsifying loan documents and three counts of bank fraud. He and several other officers routinely took out mortgages against a city councilman's condos, except that the "mortgages" were really undeclared second mortgages, illegal bribes from the councilman. Apparently O'Doul needed the $25,000 he'd collected to pay off some gambling debts.

Jake wondered what it would be like to watch your own father on trial, to hear him declare guilt and receive sentencing. He couldn't stomach the idea, and he couldn't see Reggie taking it well, either.

She seemed fierce to him, passionate and driven and determined. But she certainly didn't seem corrupt. At least, he had no reason to believe that at this point. Actually he was secretly pleased that she'd deduced which file he'd been reading. Beautiful, intelligent and passionate. He hadn't encountered such a worthwhile opponent in years.

He leaned over a bit, finally capturing her gaze. Her huge green eyes still looked wary, and he unconsciously frowned.

"I thought we might go to Middleburg tomorrow," he said quietly.

Her fork froze on the china plate. "Middleburg? As in Middleburg, Virginia?"

He nodded patiently. "There's a big hunt tomorrow, one of the last of the fall. Almost everyone will be in attendance, including the Richardsons, the Kendalls, the Grand-prés, the Westons, everyone. Might be a good chance to do a little research."

Reggie nodded, chewing on her lower lip as she turned the idea around in her mind. "What kind of hunting?"

"Fox hunting, of course."

Her eyes grew slightly wider. "As in run down a defense-less little animal with a pack of hounds?"

He grinned at her. "I see you've heard of it."

"I can't ride," she said immediately.

He arched a fine brow. "Reggie, this is research we're talking about."

She straightened immediately, almost embarrassed by her previous admission. "Of course. I'll fake it. How hard can that be?"

"Hard enough," he assured her. "I'll tell you what. We'll divide and conquer. I'll take on the people who are riding, while you sit at the Tuscany Inn, savoring the pasta and quizzing everyone else who drops by."

She looked at him suspiciously, and he felt a start of rare impatience. First anger, now impatience. So far, she was succeeding wonderfully in making him feel all the things he generally avoided. How jolly for him.

"Reggie, not everyone rides at once. People get hungry, people get thirsty. There'll be plenty of nosing around to do."

"Then, we can both sit at the Inn," she said.

"I've ridden at Middleburg several times, Reggie. If I don't participate, people will get suspicious."

"You can always tell them you have a demanding new girlfriend." She smiled sweetly.

"And give up a perfect opportunity to quiz more people? If I ride with the hunt and you wander through Middleburg, we can cover twice the ground. Just think of it. You'll be Nancy Drew and I'll be Frank Hardy."

"Or I'll be Nancy Drew and you'll be the Highwayman," she muttered.

He sighed, setting down his fork. "Reggie, this is my neck we're talking about here. I'm the one being framed by those photos. Can't you cut me a little slack? We'll be in the same area, and if this neighborhood's 'lost cars' are anything to go by, I'm sure there'll be plenty of other blue suits to watch my every move."

He actually had a point there, she granted him that much. Given who would be at the hunt, she could justify requesting several additional agents to cover the scene. Since she couldn't ride, it made sense for him to talk to those people. Except . . . except she just didn't know how far to trust the clever, quick-witted Jake Guiness. Perhaps he'd engineered this whole scenario precisely because she couldn't ride. "I'll have to give it some thought," she said at last. "Certainly it would be more effective than sitting around here."

"I tried to make it more entertaining," Jake said pointedly, picking up his fork. "But alas, you spurned my advances."

He tilted his head sideways, planting a forlorn expression on his wicked face. For one moment, he looked so ridiculous she almost smiled. Almost. He caught the faint twitching and grinned broadly.

"Truce, darlin'? I promise to behave, or at least as much as I behave for anyone."

"Truce," she agreed reluctantly. Regardless of his motivation, his suggestion to go to Middleburg was an excellent one, a chance to get to know all the players before the true Saturday night performance. Besides, she was getting antsy holed up in this empty house, alone with Jake.

"All right, then," Jake declared. "It's time for pool."

She looked confused, but he was already rising and gathering up the china with enough careless clattering to make her wince.

"Now?"

"Of course. Come on, Boston girl. I'm sure you've been to Jillian's."

She nodded, having spent more than her share of nights at the pool hall. With its hardwood floors and brass railings, the hall had seen some of the best pool games. Her father had loved it.

"Can you play?" Jake called from the kitchen.

"A bit," she said and bit back a smug smile. The evening was looking up.

She tried to appear casual as she selected her cue stick. From her earlier investigations, she figured Jake was no slouch at the game, and she hated to give away too much too soon. He poured them both glasses of whiskey, giving her time for her selection.

By the time he handed the glass of rich, amber alcohol to her, she was ready.

"Eight ball?" he asked, racking up the balls.

"Sounds good."

She let him break, taking a deep sip of the fine whiskey. It burned her throat with a familiar fire, sparking color in her cheeks and a gleam in her eye. Jake sunk two on the break, and hit in two more before missing. She wasn't worried, though.

She took her time with the first shot, picking the right ball, exploring the different angles. She leaned down low, relishing the feel of the smooth cue between her fingers. It felt solid, slick, straight. She hit the ball hard, sending it ricocheting off the left embankment to bury itself in the far, right corner pocket.

Behind her, she felt Jake's eyes brighten with interest.

"Not bad," he said, grinning at her. "But somehow, I never doubted your abilities."

She just smiled at him and selected her next target. Jake began to laugh, and the laughter mixed with the whiskey in her blood to warm her from the inside out.

She sunk five more balls before scratching.

Jake walked over to retrieve the cue ball on his own, stopping much closer to her than necessary. His gaze caressed her flushed cheeks and smiling eyes.

"Let me guess," he whispered devilishly. "You hustled pool to pay your way through college."

"Nah." She corrected him. "Tuition was too high for that. I just used it for clothes money."

He smiled broader, his eyes fueling a warm, low-spreading fire in her belly. He leaned closer, until she could smell the single malt whiskey on his breath. "That's good, 'cause you haven't seen nothin' yet."

He motioned her back, and she moved with a challenging swagger. He didn't disappoint, sinking all but the eight ball. Leaning against the bar, Reggie nodded at him thoughtfully.

"Guess you're not a stranger to Jillian's, either."

"Guess not."

"Think you're going to win?"

"Darlin', I hate to lose."

She smiled even larger. "So do I, Jake. So do I."

She sauntered forward, cocky and arrogant, the cue stick in her hand. He simply grinned, liking the bounce in her step and loving the way she leaned down low over the table, revealing the graceful outline of her long legs and curved hips. He'd left her a tough shot, the cue ball tight against the embankment, far from her own solid-colored targets.

She took her time setting up, and he sipped his whiskey while enjoying the view. She picked her strategy, bending over once more, and his whole body went hard. God, she was something else. She aimed the cue straight and true, going for finesse when he would have thought she'd go for strength.

She struck the cue hard on the left, spinning it right, away from the embankment. It arched around beautifully, picking off a solid already hovering at the lip of the pocket. She didn't look up again until she was down to the eight ball.

"Ready to like losing, Jake?"

"It's not over yet."

She arched a brow. "I'll let you call the pocket."

He grinned. "Cocky. I like it. Care to match that arrogance with a little wager?"

Immediately she stiffened, her emerald eyes hard. "I don't bet," she said sharply.

"A kiss, Reggie. A simple kiss. That's all."

Her gaze narrowed. "So if I win?"

"You kiss me."

She arched another skeptical eyebrow. "And if you win?"

"I kiss you, of course."

She smiled, relaxing once more as she shook her head in amusement. "Nice try, Guiness. I suppose you also have a bridge to sell me?"

"Stairway to heaven."

She waved the cue stick impatiently. "All right, here's the deal. If I win, you can't make a pass at me again."

He managed to look horrified. "But then what would I do with myself?"

"You'll learn. And if you win," she appeared to contemplate the idea, then dismiss it completely, "I suppose you can have a small kiss."

He nodded, satisfied. "Do I still get to call the pocket?"

"Do you need to call the pocket?" she challenged.

"Reggie, I've seen you play and I want my kiss. I'd be more than delighted to call the pocket."

He examined the position of the eight ball, thought about picking the most difficult shot, then decided to be slightly sporting and selected the second most difficult. "Left middle pocket," he declared.

She nodded, her brow already crinkled as her eyes alighted upon the goal. Chewing on her lower lip, she circled the table once, then bent down over the ball. The shot was hard, but it could be done. It just required exact angle and velocity.

She bent down and felt the first beads of sweat on her forehead. Taking a deep breath, she pulled the cue stick straight back and fired.

The eight ball careened off the first embankment, slammed into the second and nailed the third. But Reggie could already see that the angle was slightly off as the ball raced toward the homestretch. It hit the lip of the pocket, wobbled back and forth, then stilled on the green cloth.

She stared at it for a long moment, feeling the disappointment strong and hot in her gut.

"My turn," Jake said.

He walked almost negligently to the cue ball, bent down easily and tapped the eight ball in. He straightened and grinned. "I seem to recall a certain forfeit."

"You didn't call the pocket," she said immediately, frustration stabbing through her.

His grin stilled, his brow crinkling. "The pocket was self-evident."

"You didn't call it," she said again, her voice tight, her chin stubborn. She knew she shouldn't be saying these things. She knew she was at the age when she was supposed to be gracious. But the disappointment churned like a monster in her gut. *You weren't good enough, Reggie. Should've done better, Reggie. Winning is all that counts, Reggie.*

Jake set down his cue and looked at her from across the table, his brow furrowed. Abruptly he nodded, crossing his arms in front of himself and adopting a blatantly challenging stance. He knew at least one way of getting through to her. "Afraid to pay up a little kiss, Reggie?" he said boldly. He looked himself up and down. "Didn't realize I was so intimidating."

Immediately her chin popped up, her eyes taking on an unholy gleam. "I didn't say that," she said tautly.

"The way I see it," he continued slowly, not giving an inch, "you lost the game, and now you're crying sour grapes because you're afraid of a little kiss."

She looked at him darkly, then abruptly walked around the table. "You want your kiss, fine!" She came to a rigid halt in front of him, her hands balled at her sides. She stuck her lips out. "Take it."

He laughed, that low, smooth sound like warm whiskey and lush velvet. It rolled across her, seeping into her veins and for a moment, her stance weakened. He seized the opportunity, swooping down on her with stunning swiftness.

He'd tried and failed with finesse before, and he was a man who learned quickly. This time, he did not ask but took. His large hands seized her shoulders, dragging her body against his. One large palm smoothed down her back, flattening her breasts against his chest, cupping her buttocks. Just as she opened her mouth in outrage, he ducked his head and possessed her lips.

His tongue drove in with deep, knowing strokes. He delved the moist recesses of her mouth, tangling with her tongue and sucking slowly on her lower lip. He plundered deep, drawing her out, raking his tongue across her teeth.

Suddenly her arms were no longer down by her sides, but wrapped around his shoulders. She pressed closer, slanting back her neck, granting him deeper access. He pressed the advantage surely, nipping on the corner of her mouth, sucking on her lips. He trailed hot kisses across her cheekbone, burying his face in the crook of her neck, finding the sensitive curve of her throat.

He bit tenderly, harshly, and felt her gasp and quiver against him. Her hands tangled in his hair, pressing his mouth against her neck, urging him on with her hands. He scored her neck with his teeth, moving up to suck voraciously on her earlobe. She shuddered in his arms.

Slowly he backed her up, step by step, until her buttocks were pressed against the pool table. With his knee, he urged her legs apart and almost wantonly she complied. Her short nails raked down his back, her lips now greedily seeking his. He tangled with her tongue once more, tasting whiskey and heat.

She was urgent against him, warm and needy. Her trim body was well toned, arms and hips curving seductively. He hoisted her onto the pool table, wrapping her legs around his waist and pressing against her intimately.

She gasped, her legs grasping tightly and her neck falling back. He could see the pounding force of her passion in her pulse. She was beautiful and ethereal in her desire, pure and wanton. He rotated his hips and felt himself already teetering on the brink.

He ducked his head low, dragging down the collar of her shirt to kiss between her breasts.

"My room," he whispered hoarsely, forcing his glazed eyes back up. "Reggie, let's go to my room."

She shook her head as if in a daze, pulling his head back up until she could kiss him deeply, tracing the corner of his mouth, rasping her palm along his beard. It was rough, just as she'd known it would be. Rough and delicious and wonderful against her skin. She wanted whisker burn against her neck, her breasts, her thighs. She wanted the pleasure, the pain, all of it.

He rocked against her, drawing the breath in tight gasps from her throat. She'd given this up five years ago. All this passion, this feeling, this intimacy. She'd had to focus. Still needed to focus...

Her heavy-lidded eyes dragged open, the emerald depths filled with need, with pain. For one moment, she looked into his eyes and he could have sworn he lost his soul.

Just as abruptly, her eyes closed, heavy and damp-lashed. She pushed vehemently against his shoulders.

"No," she whispered. "No, no, no. I don't want this. I don't need this."

She pushed harder, and he stumbled back feeling drunk. Immediately she was off the table, wiping her mouth with the back of her hand.

"That was more than a kiss," she accused thickly.

He drew in a ragged breath and tried to count to ten through the tight need in his groin. "Darlin', you weren't complainin'," he muttered roughly. Oh God, he hurt. Not since he was fourteen had he hurt this bad. He paced the room, drawing in deep lungfuls of air. But he just had to turn around and see her kiss-swollen lips to feel the desire stab through him like a knife all over again.

"Leave," he ordered hoarsely. She stood there, head ducked and eyes wary. "Damn it," he growled, "get out of this room before I forget my upbringing entirely. I'm only a man, Reggie, and so help me God, I want you."

Her eyes opened wide, startled and shocked. Then she pressed her hand against her mouth and fled.

Jake stalked over to the bar and poured himself another good stiff drink. He downed the burning whiskey in one swallow, his face contorting into a grimace. He slammed the shot glass down.

She was going to be the death of him yet.

Chapter 6

"Rise and shine, sleeping beauty." Jake popped his head through the door, his gaze finding her sitting up on the futon. "Already dressed? How disappointing."

She just looked at him and finished stretching out her leg. It had taken her a long time to fall asleep after last night's episode. Then, she'd merely dreamed heady visions of his lips and his hands, over and over again. Her own lack of self-control was appalling.

Jake leaned against the doorway looking sporty in white riding pants, high black boots, a crisp white shirt and tie and a long, nicely tailored scarlet jacket with gold buttons. He crossed his arms, tapped the riding crop against his left boot and grinned knowingly. "Jogging again?"

From the futon, Reggie tore her gaze away from his lean, discreetly outlined figure. How was it that at six-thirty in the morning he could look so polished and debonair, while she just looked like a tired FBI agent about to go running? "Of course," she muttered finally, fingering the collar of her loose cotton jersey.

Jake pushed himself away from the doorframe and entered the room. Immediately Reggie stiffened, but he ignored her, strolling to the window instead. He cracked open the blind and peered down the street. "I see another car in need of directions, Reggie."

She glared at him as much as she could from her seated position on the floor. "Then I'd better go help them. How much time do I have to run?"

He pivoted sharply and sighed. "I imagine you could go around the block a couple times—if you had to."

"I have to." She stood, frowning at him pointedly when his gaze lingered on her bare legs with unabashed appreciation. The memory of his lips on hers was still too familiar, as was the feel of his hard body pressed against her own, his hands on her back, his hips rotating against her.

She drew in a deep breath and headed for the door without looking back. She had to get a grip on herself. She still did not trust Jake Guiness, and she refused to turn into some blithering idiot just because he grinned at her.

When she reached the sidewalk, she started running with more force than necessary.

"Reggie, they don't kill the fox anymore."

She sat in his early model Porsche, gripping the door with such force her knuckles had gone white. Jake didn't seem to notice the tight look on her face, swinging them around another sharp curve at breakneck pace. He wore black leather gloves and the most unholy grin on his face.

"The hounds generally run the fox into a tunnel or hole, and that's the end of it. The fox lives to run another day. The hounds get a good workout. It's not *that* inhumane."

"Tell that to the fox," she muttered through clenched teeth. Another hairpin curve came up and Jake actually accelerated. She closed her eyes and contemplated rediscovering religion. She liked driving fast, but only when she was at the wheel. And even she drove with more sense than this madman.

Jake began to speak again from the driver's seat, and Reggie wished he would shut up and concentrate on the winding road. "Look, there are generally thirty-five, forty riders. I'll go with them. Generally some people follow along in cars to watch. Maybe you can find someone in that group. Or, as I said, simply hang out at one of the inns. Everyone ends up eating sooner or later. Middleburg isn't that big. Hell, it only has one traffic light. You'll meet everyone you ever wanted to talk to."

"Fine," she said tightly, having already made the arrangements this morning for several agents to cover the hunt. Jake's proposal was a practical way of handling things, and the day showed a great deal of promise.

Once more, she tried to picture a fox hunt in her head, and once more she failed miserably. Maybe Buchanan had been right—she didn't have the background for this kind of thing. She'd never ridden a horse; she knew nothing about hunting and, frankly, mixing with the rich and famous just sounded stressful.

As if reading her mind, Jake reached across the tiny car and patted her clenched hand. "Relax, Reggie, it won't be so bad. A lot of things have changed in the countryside of the elite. Nowadays, a bit of everyone is present at these things. CEOs and account executives ride alongside fourth-generation wealth, state senators, even movie stars. You'll see families from D.C. and locals enjoying the event. You'll be fine."

"Do you do this often?" she demanded, refusing to relinquish her death grip on the door. She would feel a lot better if he kept both hands on the wheel.

He shrugged, withdrawing his hand as if he'd read her mind. "When I'm around," he replied casually. "Anymore, with the number of Fortune 500 execs and politicians running around, it's hard to ignore the networking opportunities. Plus, the countryside is just plain beautiful and Middleburg is as great as it gets. You'll see."

She nodded, hoping he was right and that the tight ball of tension would suddenly dissolve in her stomach. What if she was too inexperienced for this? What if she didn't know how to act?

The thick hedge of trees suddenly gave way, and she lost her train of thought as she sucked in a low breath of wonder. Suddenly they were in the country. Huge, rolling fields opened up, thoroughbreds prancing around giant loaves of hay. Low black-railed fences crisscrossed the gentle greenery, complemented by thin lines of crimson-leaved trees. Here and there, small stone farmhouses came into view. Farther back, Georgian-style mansions sat elegantly on gently sloping hillsides. Country homes of the rich and famous peeked out over huge stables and dome-topped granaries. A bright fall sun illuminated it all with rich colors of green, rust, gold and blue.

"Wow," she breathed. Beside her, Jake smiled, inordinately pleased by her response. That was what he'd thought the first time one of his Harvard buddies had brought him here. Back then, his knees had shook with nervousness, too, as he'd entered a world unlike any he'd ever known. Each time he arrived, he still felt that bone-deep thrill, adrenaline combining with nerves and excitement and sheer exhilaration.

Middleburg represented a slice of colonial times, untouched, undisturbed and uncompromising.

"Wait till you see the rest," he laughed from the driver's seat, his eyes bright, his smile broad with enthusiasm. "You'll love it, Reggie. You'll positively love it."

They pulled over on the outskirts of the town to a milling madhouse. Gleaming thoroughbreds pawed the ground next to panting hounds and racing children. Already some riders were up in their saddles, making last-minute adjustments as they led their mounts to the fringe of the mayhem. One man walked around with a gleaming horn in his hand, two hounds already trotting at his heels.

Jake parked next to a Blazer, and they both climbed out into the din. For one minute, Reggie simply breathed in the rich, milling scents of drying leaves, cut hay, oiled saddles and horses. It was at once fall and colonial and rich and natural, and she didn't think she'd ever smelled anything like it. It consumed the senses, teasing and coaxing and mysterious.

She felt her pulse quicken.

Beside her, Jake watched her with a knowing smile, understanding completely. He gestured to the crowd. "Go ahead and mingle if you'd like. I need to find McGregor to make sure he brought the extra horse for me. I'll catch up in a minute or two."

Reggie nodded, half dismissing him as her eyes searched the crowd. She spotted a voluptuous woman in a short black riding jacket mounting her horse with the help of a fine young man. Farther back, she got the fleeting glimpse of a tall, thin man standing ramrod straight. So Emelia and Kirk were already here, she noted. That just left Drake for her to find. Reggie forgot all about her nerves and doubts, as she began walking through the crowd.

Jake found McGregor quickly and claimed the extra mount. Rubbing the rich, brown neck of the thoroughbred, Jake began searching the crowd once more for Reggie. He saw her homing in on a portly gentleman still sitting in a car, and began to smile.

Drake DeSioux. He should have known.

Jake simply watched Reggie for a bit, admiring the way she wove through the chaos with sure steps and athletic grace. She wore a thick knit green sweater that highlighted her eyes, while soft denim caressed her legs. She blended in with the fall crowd, yet the sun sparked her dark red hair like a halo, forming a beacon for his eyes to follow.

He'd brought plenty of women here over the years. He'd brought ones who'd complained about the treatment of the fox; he'd brought ones who'd complained about the crowds. He'd brought others who'd gushed over the Mellon mansion, and some who'd preened at the sight of a movie star. None of them had ever seen the place the way he did, had ever understood it the way he did.

The day wasn't about the mansions or movie stars, not even about the rolling hills and falling leaves. Middleburg to him was the scent in the air, the electric current of pent-up tension, the pawing of horse's hooves, the tight, anticipated yelps of the hounds. It was the rush of adrenaline, the feeling all-around that something new and unexpected and fundamentally interesting was about to happen. Deep in each brush, high in each branch, or tucked behind each rock, adventure just waited to explode.

He felt it each time he came, a tightening of the groin that was nearly sexual. The thrill of the challenge.

His eyes fell on Reggie, who now paused at the car, talking to DeSioux. He'd known she would feel it, too. Of all the women he'd met, she would be the one to understand.

She was a hunter like him.

He forced his attentions back to the horse, frowning at the force of the desire clenching his gut. In general, he left passion and intensity for his brothers. He much preferred his more cerebral and casual approach to life.

And right now, he had plenty of riddles to solve.

"It's a beautiful day for riding."

Thin, narrow-faced Kirk Richardson stopped pulling on his fine leather gloves long enough to peer down at Reggie with watery blue eyes. "Too bloody beautiful," he said, snapping on the first glove. "The heat will carry the scent right over the hounds' heads. We'll never track anything."

"What do you do then?" Reggie asked politely. She leaned casually against the low black fence where he was mounting up, hoping she appeared friendly but nonthreatening. Her conversation with DeSioux had been a disappointing commentary on man's concept of progress being little more than dressing up the same primal acts.

"Ride," Kirk said curtly, snapping on the second glove and flexing his fingers experimentally. "Perhaps we'll flush one out and then the chase will begin." He stopped looking at his gloves long enough to rake her up and down with insipid eyes. "Not a rider, heh?"

Mutely Reggie shook her head. She didn't like his eyes.

"Visiting from Washington, then?" The words carried a fine edge of disdain. Already he was turning away from her.

"Not from Washington," she said immediately. "I came with Jake Guiness. I'm Regina."

Richardson stilled, his gaunt features tightening just a fraction. "I heard he was back," the older man said slowly. He turned around, his watery eyes speculative and perhaps a touch wary. Kirk looked at her more intensely, then seemed to nod to himself.

"Redhead," he muttered. "I should have known." Then louder, he added, "So you're the new flavor of the month?"

Reggie flushed, not needing his reminder of Jake's habits. But she kept her chin up, looking at Kirk squarely. "Maybe I'm the flavor of the year," she suggested coyly, giving him a sideways glance. She picked up a piece of straw on the fence and began to absently twirl it. "He's taking me to the Children's Charity Ball next weekend. I'm quite excited. I understand the Kendalls have one of the finest collections of Flemish tapestries, let alone their collection of Renaissance art."

Kirk's pale eyes narrowed. "Are you a collector?"

She shrugged, her mind turning over the best answer to that question. "An interested enthusiast," she said at last. "And yourself?"

"Gathered indigenous sculptures for years, but I'm beginning to branch out some. Now I hear Guiness is the one who's acquiring the more interesting pieces."

Unconsciously Reggie frowned, uncertain about what Richardson was alluding to. She looked through the crowd, trying to spot Jake by the horses where she'd last seen him. But while his friend was still grooming a horse, Jake was nowhere to be seen. Her frown deepened. On instinct, she looked for Emelia, only to confirm that she was missing as well. Her jaw tightened, the wheels of speculation unflattering in her mind. So much for Jake catching up with her in a minute or two.

"Jake hasn't mentioned much about his collection," she said at last, turning back to Kirk. "He must not keep it in his Virginia home."

"Oh, no," Kirk assured her coldly. "I believe it's all in Rhode Island. You should ask him sometime, my dear."

She most certainly would. And she would be drilling the original investigating agents about it as well. Information like that should have been in Jake's file, and she wanted to know why it wasn't. "And yourself? Will you be at the Kendall estate?"

"Of course."

"Perhaps we can take in the tapestries together?"

He looked at her for a long time, no expression on his narrow face. She could see him trying to subtly scan the crowd over her head. She didn't need a mind reader to know he was searching for signs of Jake. At last, his pale eyes came back to her face, lingering like a watery caress.

She forced herself not to flinch.

"Maybe we can," he said softly. "Maybe we can."

She never could find Jake. She walked through the milling throngs several times, even stopping and introducing herself to his friend McGregor. Everyone she talked to had seen him going this direction or that, but he never did turn up. Nor, for that matter, could she find a trace of Emelia.

By the time the horn blew and the riders and hounds set out, she was quietly fuming. Jake certainly hadn't wasted any time hightailing it as far away from her as possible. And given the fact that she was the one primarily responsible for him, she couldn't believe she'd let him slip away that easily. Sure, they'd agreed he would go with the riding party. Sure, there were other agents around to monitor his every move. But he could have at least told her what he had planned for the afternoon!

When she got her hands on him . . .

She made her way through Middleburg, lingering at the hunting-art galleries, classic clothiers and tack shops. She found kid gloves and jackets of leather so soft it could make

you weep. She even tried on the full hunting outfit for effect. She ran into plenty of people, introduced herself often
and collected names.

Many of the names she recognized from the guest list to
the Charity Ball, and these she followed more closely. Drake
DeSioux drove back into town around noon, reporting that
the hounds had yet to flush a fox. She invited him to lunch,
but he turned her down, saying he'd had enough of the
charades and was returning home.

She promised to see him again at the Kendall estate and
tried not to shudder when he kissed the back of her hands
with smacking, devouring lips.

She washed her hands three times before sitting down at
the Tuscany Inn to eat. She drank two glasses of red wine
and ate too much bread soaked in spice-laden olive oil.
Around two, Jake still hadn't reappeared, and she devised
all sorts of new ways to slowly torture Jake Guiness.

At two-thirty, he walked through the doors of the Inn as
if it was the most natural thing in the world. His warm
brown gaze fell on her at the tiny table and he smiled
broadly.

"Honey, I'm home," he declared for the whole restaurant to hear. The other diners laughed good-naturedly,
watching with genuine smiles as he swooped down upon
Reggie and caught her shocked form in a passionate embrace. Just as abruptly, he let her go and plopped down in
the seat across from her. "So, little woman, what's for dinner?"

She simply stared at him, suddenly so real and larger than
life before her. He smelled of horses, warm leather and cool
fall days. Absently, he picked a bit of straw from his thick,
dark brown hair and smiled at her wickedly. "Remember,
darlin'," he purred low under his breath, "we're lovers
now."

He continued smiling to the others, reaching out and
clasping her hand. He turned it over, and began to rub his
callused thumb over the center of her palm. The goose
bumps raced all the way up her arm, and his sharp eyes

caught those as well. "Did you miss me?" he whispered.
"Please say yes."

"Where have you been?" she asked at last, her voice
sharp. She leaned across the table, yanking her hand out of
his, then came to her senses long enough to realize other
people were still watching. She set her hand back by his.
"And don't tell me you've been riding," she whispered
fiercely under her breath, "because I watched the group
leave, and you weren't with them."

"But of course I was," he told her easily. "You must have
just missed seeing me. In black hats and scarlet jackets, you
know we all look alike."

"Don't even try it," she warned in a low voice. "I trust
my own eyesight a hell of a lot more than I trust your little
stories. And I just happened to notice that Emelia Emmons
was missing as well. Funny, I thought she would've been a
bit old for your tastes."

For a minute, his easy grin seemed strained, but then his
lips recovered. He picked up her hand, never taking his gaze
from hers.

"Jealous?" he whispered.

"Don't insult my intelligence. I know perfectly well your
interest in her is professional."

"And what kind of professional relationship would that
be, Reggie? Do you think she's my partner, or the one trying to frame me?"

Reggie's green eyes hardened dangerously. "Why don't
you tell me?"

He shrugged, looking nonchalant, yet somehow sharp.
"Why I don't know," he mocked her softly. "Why should
I be interested in her at all? Is there something about her I
should know?"

For a moment, Reggie frowned, suddenly wary. Jake
could be so deceptively dangerous at times. "No," she said
slowly. "I suppose you shouldn't be interested in her at all."

"Of course," he said easily. "Just like there's nothing
about Kirk Richardson or Drake DeSioux that I should
know."

Her cheeks colored delicately, her eyes at once chagrined and rebellious as they met his gaze. The smile was still on his face for all casual observers to note, but his brown eyes were deathly serious as they bore into her own. "What a tangled web we weave," he quoted softly.

"You forget your role in all this," she snapped back, shaking her head. "You don't have to know everything. You're simply supposed to cooperate with me." She leaned closer, her eyes penetrating. "And what about the Rhode Island art collection, Jake? When were you going to mention that?"

"I like beautiful things," he said simply. Then abruptly she saw his jaw harden. "Besides, Reggie, you're the agent."

The words were cold and they stung. She winced unconsciously, but even then his gaze didn't soften. It didn't help matters to know he had a valid point.

She drew herself up as straight as she could in her chair. "The truth of the matter, Jake," she said levelly, "is this isn't your game. It's mine. And I can make all the rules I want, because I wasn't the one caught breaking into someone's house and waving at security cameras. We agreed you'd go with the riders, not that you'd disappear altogether. You violated the arrangement."

His brown eyes remained hard and assessing. "You're in over your head," he stated softly.

She snapped, her cheeks flushing so dark, her eyes growing so bright that for a moment it looked as if she might inflict bodily harm. Her hand tightened in his with enough force to make his jaw clench. "I will solve this case," she swore in a low voice. "And if you are the Highwayman, Jake, I'll think nothing of dragging you down."

"So that's it then?" he said quietly. "Should I be shaking in my boots?"

She shook her head, amazed at how deep his words stung. "I suppose that's it then," she said, "since obviously you trust me so much."

"I trust you as much as you trust me."

She laughed sardonically and fought against the deeper hurt his words invoked. "Order some food, Jake. After all this sleuthing, you should be famished."

He nodded, and she wondered if she saw a flash of disappointment in his eyes. She decided she didn't care and picked up her wine instead. But now it tasted sour on her tongue, and when the fresh pasta finally arrived, she'd lost her appetite completely.

Jake ate his smoked cheese ravioli slowly, savoring each piece while he turned over the day's events in his mind. Across from him, he could see Reggie poking uselessly at her angel hair pasta with sun-dried tomatoes. He frowned and ate another ravioli.

He disliked attacking her as he'd done, but he hadn't seen a choice. Whether it wounded her ego or not, he fully intended on conducting his own research. For crying out loud, someone was trying to frame him. He took that quite personally and had no intention of lounging back and letting some novice field agent save the day. Besides, she could have a little more faith in his innocence, he concluded darkly.

Worse, as much as he wanted to like Reggie, the case was beginning to worry him. After spending his afternoon talking to Emelia, he'd determined that she didn't have enough brains in her head to pull off the kind of stunts the Highwayman had. Even if she was merely bankrolling a more enterprising young man, he couldn't see her concocting an elaborate charade to frame a man. Her cunning was more overt than covert. She didn't appreciate dry humor or understated intelligence. She liked the obvious, and her ego demanded recognition.

And Drake DeSioux? Maybe. He was the wild card in the group, always had been. No one understood the man, and Jake didn't like him. The same went for Kirk Richardson, who just maybe had the cunning to frame someone else for the crimes.

The only missing link was that Jake didn't care for any of the three possible players; whereas, he had a great deal of respect for the Highwayman. He was a true master of his craft. The question became: Where could one learn such a trade backward and forward, inside and out, until you knew you were the best? Jake had a few ideas in that area, and none of them were reassuring. Plus, the more he thought about it, the more he was convinced there were at least two people involved—the Highwayman and a mastermind. If he was being framed as the Highwayman, who would wind up being the mastermind?

This case wasn't simple, and Reggie was new at this sort of thing. Even if it hurt her ego, she ought to consider that. Besides, she was the kind of person who rose to a challenge. The harder he pushed her, the better she would respond. Or so he told himself.

But he did hate to see her picking at her food that way, so tense she could no longer eat. He'd never encountered anyone as driven as she was, and for a moment, he felt a rare flash of anger at this unknown father who'd burdened her so.

He found his hand drifting across the table and lightly tapping her own. Her green eyes looked up, so wary that he winced.

"Gino's angel hair isn't good enough for you?" he teased lightly.

She looked dully at the twirls of pasta she'd made on her plate. "I ate too much bread beforehand."

"How about trying a bite of the ravioli," he coaxed, picking one up with his fork and offering it to her. "The smoked cheese is excellent."

She looked at him for a tense minute, but the hardness had melted out of his eyes. Now they were the soft, teasing depths she'd come to expect. Very slowly, she took the ravioli off his fork, chewing almost absently. With a start, she realized it was quite good.

"I have a surprise for you," he said.

She looked at him sideways. "Surprise?"

He grinned. "It'll make you very happy."

She simply waited, not saying anything.

"I talked to Kendall," he said casually, "and convinced him to invite us a few days early to the estate."

She picked up immediately, her shoulders straightening, her eyes brightening. "Really? How perfect! We can scope out the place, keep watch and check on all the arriving guests." Her mind raced with the possibilities.

Jake laughed, pleased by her enthusiastic response. "Told you I could make you happy, darlin'." He squeezed her hand warmly, wiggling a wicked brow. "And that was with the lights still on."

She flushed warmly, too caught up in the anticipation to mind his flirting. Already, her mind brimmed with things to do. She picked up her fork and began to twirl the fine pasta once more. "When do we get to go?" she asked.

"Tomorrow?" he suggested. He moved his thumb warmly over the top of her hand, enjoying the feel of her soft skin. If he turned her hand over, he knew he would find small calluses at the base of her fingers from weights and racquets and perhaps sharpshooting. He could picture her in a thin tank top, biceps curving as she curled a ten-pound free weight.

"Perfect," she said, waving her fork in the air. "That allows plenty of time for legwork before the party. Just perfect."

She smiled at him, and for one rare moment, she squeezed his hand in gratitude. "Thank you."

He nodded, feeling slightly dazed by the force of her genuine smile and decided it was better that she hadn't smiled at him that way earlier; he most certainly would have fallen to his knees and pledged eternal devotion.

She took another bite of her pasta, and he could see the wheels in her mind rushing ahead. His gaze fell to her lips, which glistened now with a fallen drop of olive oil, and his body hardened instantly. He shifted slightly in his chair and decided he'd lost his appetite for food.

He was hungrier for richer things.

He waved for the single waiter to come over, discreetly requesting the check and inquiring if one of the Inn's six rooms might be available. By pure luck, a family had just canceled, freeing a room. Jake took that as an omen of things to come and promptly reserved the room upstairs.

He waited until Reggie had finished her pasta before mentioning the news.

"I thought we might spend the night here," he said casually, his thumb lingering on her hand. "It's getting late and I'd like to clean up before heading back."

"Late?" Reggie frowned. "It's only four."

He smiled easily. "But we'll want to walk around and see Middleburg. The art galleries are amazing."

"Yes," she agreed. "I saw them earlier. In fact, we can leave now."

His smile tightened a fraction. All those years of women swooning over his invitations. He ought to have known he would pay for it sooner or later. He leaned over and looked deeply into her eyes. "Reggie, we're supposed to be madly in love. Now wouldn't it look strange if we simply left such a quaint, romantic location?"

She frowned, worrying her lower lip as she contemplated this new argument. For a moment, she looked at him suspiciously, but he simply returned her gaze guilelessly. Not that it meant anything. Jake seemed to follow the "all's fair in love and war" premise.

Then again, for the first time in a while, she was beginning to feel relaxed. Maybe it had been the wine or the food or the heady day spent exploring and talking outdoors.

"We don't have bags," she said at last, a final feeble argument.

Jake grinned wickedly. "How wonderfully decadent. Do you think the maids will talk?"

She blushed becomingly, and the desire in his groin became near pain. "I suppose it would only strengthen our cover," she said.

"Absolutely," he agreed. Success was so close he could practically taste her lips upon his own. He shifted again in his chair.

"All right," she said with a shrug. "Just make sure you get two beds."

"I'll work something out."

Fifteen minutes later, he was leading her upstairs, the anticipation so fierce in his blood he practically bounced with each step. Beside him, Reggie was lost in her own thoughts, no doubt catching the Highwayman twenty different ways at the Kendall estate. More power to her, he thought, and unlocked the door with relish.

He stepped inside, not surprised by a quaint room with antique furniture and a single, Colonial-style bed. "I'm afraid it was all they had left," he said honestly.

Reggie stopped in the middle of the room, her green eyes warier. "We can work it out," he said instantly, not wanting the mood to end so soon. "Just let me shower first, then we'll figure out the arrangements."

She sighed, but nodded, her eyes already falling to the queen-size bed with its feather pillows and thick quilt. The exhaustion flowed like lead through her veins. She sat down on the edge to test the mattress. Soft. She liked soft mattresses.

"Go shower," she said, running her hands across the blue-and-mauve quilt. Beautiful. Her eyes already felt heavy. There were several agents posted outside the Inn, so if Jake tried to leave town, he wouldn't get far. As long as there was backup available, maybe she could catch a small nap.

Jake nodded, finding the towels and heading for the shower while whistling under his breath. He showered quickly, rinsing away the last remnants of horses and hay and sweat. He stepped out with a grin, briskly drying off. This was going to be wonderful, he told himself. Positively divine.

He whistled as he came back into the room, the sound abruptly dying on his lips. Curled up on the edge of the bed, Reggie now slept with the quiet serenity of a child.

Jake approached, looking at her curled figure with longing. The frustration stabbed through him sharply, and for one moment all sorts of lovely ways to wake her up flashed through his mind. He bent down, his lips just inches from her own.

But this close, he could see the dark shadows under her eyes. He, of all people, ought to know just how badly she needed the rest.

With a soft sigh, he settled for touching her cheek lightly. Then with a small, muttered oath, he sat down in the wing chair and contemplated his options.

And alternative plans for seducing the incredibly captivating Regina O'Doul.

Chapter 7

She awoke once to the feel of the bed sagging beside her. From somewhere deep within the woolly haze of sleep, she tried to rouse herself. A deep, whiskied voice whispered in her ear, "Go back to sleep, ma chéri." A heavy, capable hand curled comfortably around her waist, drawing her into a firm, lazy embrace.

She faded back into slumber, thinking somewhere far off that it was nice to be in his arms once more.

When she woke up fully, the room was pitch-black. For a moment, she simply lay there, eyes open, orienting herself. She felt hot, her thick-cabled sweater sticking to her skin. Gradually she registered the solid wall of heat against her back, the heavy weight of the arm around her middle and the thick barrier of the comforter pulled up to her shoulders.

She forced herself to exhale, her green eyes alert in the darkness. Jake still hadn't moved, and she determined the heavy rhythm of his sleeping breaths. Moving carefully, she freed herself from his embrace, setting his arm down over his stomach. He shifted, rolling over to the left, and muttered softly under his breath. He returned to sleep, and still watching him, she backed her way out of the bed.

From the dim glow of the moon, she could see his nude torso, pale, sculpted and pure. She promptly pulled the quilt up to his shoulders, fairly sure she didn't want to know what other pieces of clothing he was missing.

Moving to the relative safety of the center of the room, she glanced at her watch: 11:00 p.m. She shook her head, running her hand through her hair.

The nap had been much needed, but it had also been disorienting. Now, her internal clock didn't know what to do. Should she curl up in a chair and sleep until morning, or do some work and then go to sleep much later?

She remained torn, finally peeling down to her black tank top so she could at least cool down. She tossed her sweater carelessly onto an old wing chair.

She paced the room a bit, running her hand over the old, nicked furniture while her mind wondered. News of Jake's art collection in Rhode Island disturbed her greatly. He'd been right. As an agent, she should have known about it. When you were investigating a man for art theft, you certainly didn't overlook those kinds of details.

Her brow furrowed in the darkness. So why hadn't the surveillance team picked that up? There were fourteen agents involved in this case, two of whom had done the preliminary legwork on Jake Guiness. His recent art acquisitions didn't appear to be secret, at least Kirk had known about them. So why did Kirk, another suspect, have information the FBI didn't?

Her frown deepened, creasing her forehead as the possibilities tossed around in her mind. She didn't like the series of loose ends beginning to appear, and as the agent managing the case, it was up to her to make sure this kind of investigative sloppiness didn't continue.

Unconsciously she began to rub the knotted muscles in her shoulder. Her jaw tightened to the point her teeth began to ache. With a small, frustrated sigh, she loosened her stance, shaking out her arms. Then, moving on instinct, she assumed an opening position from T'ai Chi, relaxing her muscles, blanking her mind. She flowed smoothly through the warm-up exercise, the fluid, graceful movements loosening her body and allowing her to focus.

The Highwayman had stolen four times. The Highwayman would most likely strike again at the Kendall estate. The Highwayman—and others involved?—wanted to retire. The Kendall estate would be the last job. The last job and then . . . ?

The light next to the bed suddenly snapped on. She froze, her right hand still stretched before her while her left hand curled upward at her side, her left leg thrust back.

"Little late for gymnastics, isn't it?" Jake said groggily from the bed. She turned her head as he sat up, the quilt falling to his waist, revealing his bare, contoured chest. Under the harsh glow of the lamp, his skin glowed faintly bronze, his shoulders broad, his collarbone strong, his sculpted pectorals covered by a light dusting of curling brown hair. She forced her gaze up to note cheeks shadowed with an eighteen-hour beard and a forehead covered by thick, rumpled brown hair.

"Just stretching," she said tersely and shifted into the next position, forcing her gaze to focus on the far wall. "You can go back to sleep."

Instead she heard the bed creak ominously as he threw his legs over the side. She heard him stand, but didn't dare shift her eyes. Instead she squinted them forcefully, stepped forward and rotated back smoothly into the next stance.

"Karate?" His voice was gravelly, roughened by sleep.

"T'ai Chi." She shifted again, refusing to look at him even as she became uncomfortably aware of his gaze lingering on her bare arms. She wasn't wearing a bra beneath her tank top, her athlete's build not requiring that kind of support. When his gaze skimmed over her, however, she was much too aware of just how thin the material was.

"Studied T'ai Chi for long?" he asked casually, his gaze finally resting on her face.

"Long enough."

"Long enough for what?"

Her green eyes came up levelly, pinning him for the first time. "Long enough to know what I'm doing," she said, her voice tinged with steel.

He merely arched a brow, crossing his arms in front of himself while standing nonchalantly in nothing but a pair of green plaid boxers.

"You look good," he said softly.

She stiffened, losing focus and teetering for a moment. Instantly, brutally, she brought her gaze back to the wall. "It isn't about looking," she said through gritted teeth. "It's about concentration, focus, harnessing the energies of your body."

He raised a sardonic brow. "Sounds serious. Does this mean you have to register your hands as lethal weapons?"

She pivoted sharply, giving him her back. She wasn't even going to dignify that comment with a reply. But he remained unperturbed, merely walking around until he stood in front of her, the small confines of the room dictating that he stand very close. She felt the heat of his presence, caught the faint odor of fresh soap and shampoo. Couldn't he at least put on a shirt?

Jake leaned over until he caught her eye. "Want to give a demonstration?"

"No."

He grinned at her. "Come on. As we've already established, my fate is in your hands. The least you could do is demonstrate just what you can do."

Her green eyes narrowed thoughtfully, his challenging words evoking the response he no doubt desired. Abruptly she relaxed the position, standing straight instead.

"All right," she said at last. "I guess a brief trial wouldn't hurt."

His grin broadened exuberantly. He stepped forward until his lips were just inches from her own. Unconsciously she held her breath, but he didn't try anything. He just leaned over slightly and whispered into her ear, "To the victor, go the spoils."

She stepped back, no longer sure what he had in mind and needing the distance. "Is everything for you a game?" she asked sharply.

He merely raked his gaze leisurely up and down her thinly clad frame. "Guilty as charged, darlin'. But I think you can handle the challenge."

She moved back another step, shaking out her arms and feeling the power of his warm brown eyes in the quickening of her pulse. Ruthlessly she forced herself to focus. "You can start at anytime," she said levelly. She motioned him forward with her hands. "Just try to attack me. Anyway you want."

He nodded, not moving immediately forward as she expected, but leaning back instead. He walked back and forth a couple of times, his brown eyes narrowing with the concentration. Abruptly he smiled at her and rushed.

At the last minute, she stepped deftly to the side. With a quick sideways thrust, she caught him square in the stomach and he folded over immediately. She danced out behind him, listening to his attempts to catch his breath.

"Nice," he sputtered at last.

"You weren't even trying," she accused.

"I'll have to remember that," he gasped. At last, he straightened, gripping the corner post with one hand. "Take two?"

"All right."

He didn't try to rush her this time. Instead, after a few minutes of studying the room, he abruptly scrambled over the bed, grabbing her from behind.

Immediately she sagged in his grip, using her body weight to throw him off balance. Jerking back both elbows, she delivered two sharp jabs to his kidneys. His arms fell away, his breath rushing out in a tight gasp.

But just as she pivoted clear, his hand whipped out and caught her wrist. She immediately turned into him, slamming a straight hand toward his sternum. He turned instinctively, taking the blow in the shoulder and using her momentum to catch her closer to him. He caught her second wrist, enclosing both in his strong grip.

She relaxed momentarily, knowing the futility of fighting his greater strength. Rather than relaxing himself, he merely smiled at her grimly.

"I'm trying this time, darlin'," he whispered. "So you're gonna have to do better than that."

Her eyes narrowed fiercely, her chin jutting up. Looking him straight in the eye, she jabbed her knee up. As he twisted his hips to block the blow, she brought her foot back down to catch him sharply on his insole. His face blanched with pain, and she used the opportunity to wrench one wrist free. Catching his own wrist, she pivoted to face forward and flipped him neatly over her back.

He hit the floor with a solid thunk, sprawling out ungracefully and blinking his startled eyes.

She smiled down at him, but her eyes were fierce. "Was that good enough, Jake? Or do you still think I'm in over my head?"

He moved stiffly on the floor, wincing from the motion. He gazed up at her, contemplating his next move in this elaborate dance. She looked angry, but more than that, she looked capable. She had that flush in her cheeks, that glint in her eye. If he tried to get up, he had the feeling she would toss him back to the floor. He liked that about her—she gave nothing less than one hundred and fifty percent.

"I seemed to have overlooked some talents," he said at last. He reached up a hand. "Truce? I'm getting old, you know. I don't think my poor body can take much more."

For a moment, she allowed herself to examine that "poor body." Sprawled half-naked on the floor, it looked lean and firm. Jake obviously used those weights in his house and used them regularly. He'd honed a strong, capable body to complement his sharp, quick-witted mind. A potent package. And didn't he know it.

"What now?" he asked from the floor. "I thought we agreed the victor got the spoils." His lips curved devilishly, making him look dashing and roguish even splayed on the floor. He wiggled a dark brow. "So what kind of spoils do you want, darlin'? Your wish is my command."

"Get up," she said, tersely.

He immediately looked injured. "Get up? What kind of boring victory wish is that? Reggie, Reggie, Reggie. We gotta get you out of the office more."

She scowled. "What do you mean by that?"

"Well, here you have a strong, young, red-blooded man at your mercy, and the best you can do is ask me to stand? Surely a devious, brilliant mind like your own can do better than that. Why, if I'd won, I'd certainly have come up with some interesting forfeits by now. Say, that tank top."

"You would've taken my shirt?"

"It's a very nice shirt," he assured her. "And frankly, I'm going to have to become more creative in my seduction techniques. You're quite a challenge."

"Gee thanks," she commented dryly, though her heart was beginning to beat faster in her chest.

"Do you mind, Reggie? Does it bother you to know that I want you?"

Her mouth went dry. Her mind scrambled to find some kind of stinging retort, but in the end she couldn't get beyond the simple exhilaration invoked by his words. He wanted her. Her gaze fell to his half-naked body once more, taking in his long, tapered legs, his smooth, cleanly defined chest. "All right," she said abruptly, licking her lips nervously.

"All right what?" Jake asked. "Hardwood floors aren't that comfortable you know."

"I've determined my prize," she acknowledged, slowly sinking onto her knees, leaning over his shoulders. He didn't appear surprised. He'd been slowly goading her along this path, but somehow she couldn't muster any outrage. He might think he was still in control of things, but she would prove him wrong.

His face stilled, his brown eyes looking at her carefully. "You did win," he concurred. "And fair is fair." He found himself holding his breath and lying quite still, lest the slightest movement startle her back into sanity.

She leaned forward slowly, each move careful and pensive. Her eyes skimmed his face, taking in the thick lashes that framed his eyes, the shadowy growth of his whiskers, the full outline of his lips.

Very softly, she brushed his lips with her own, hearing his sudden sharp breath. She returned to his lips, settling her mouth more firmly this time, gently exploring the full softness of his lips. She parted them slowly, easing her tongue inside to taste him as if he were a sweet, sinful delicacy.

She stroked her tongue deeper, finding his tongue and twining hers around it. He tasted rich and masculine, a heady flavor she'd sampled before but never truly savored.

She leaned closer now, brushing her breasts over his bare chest, reveling in the soft intake of his breath. She straddled his body, settling her pelvis low on his hips, and kissed him deeply.

Immediately he groaned, his hands reaching for her waist. Just as quickly, she caught his wrists with her hands, snapping his arms flat above his head.

"My kiss," she whispered fiercely. "Mine."

He nodded mutely, his brown eyes too molten to argue. She leaned back over, her breasts settling against his chest once more, and he sighed blissfully.

Her kiss grew bolder, her tongue stroking him deeply, reveling in the richness of his mouth. She nibbled on his lower lip, toying with the fullness, then traced featherlight kisses along his jaw, his whiskers tickling her lips. Her stomach grew heavy, her breasts full and swollen.

The more she kissed him, the more she ached. She pressed against him harder, as if she could melt her lithe frame into his and achieve a completion never known. The passion was dizzying, the desire intoxicating.

What would it be like to let his hands go? To feel his strong fingers gripping her waist, guiding her hips against his. To have his palm cupping her breast, his fingers teasing the sensitive nipple like a master.

She wanted so much, needed so much, the intensity scared her. It would be easy to give herself to him, to quench the hunger that roared like a famine in her blood. In the past few years, she'd forgotten just how lonely being lonely could be.

And then what, Reggie? And then what?

With a low moan, she rolled off him, reaching for the bedpost and pulling herself away before she could lose her will.

His hand wrapped tightly around her ankle, stilling her as she squeezed her eyes shut.

"Don't go." His voice was hoarse and ragged, tearing at her control. If he'd been teasing, it would have been easy. If he'd sounded suave, she wouldn't have thought twice. But instead, the raw ache of his voice cut her to the bone until she sagged against the bed and wished for a strength she no longer had. His hand crept up her calf muscle, stroking her curved leg.

"Reggie . . ."

She vaulted up onto the bed, cursing them both.

"One kiss," she cried, her hands clenched against her stomach. "One kiss was all I wanted."

She heard a sharp thud from the floor, and knew he'd just slammed his fist against the hardwood. A part of her wished she could do the same. Instead she grabbed the quilt in huge fistfuls and squeezed with all the power she could muster.

"You don't fight fair," Jake muttered from the floor. He pulled himself up at last, looking at her with eyes that were supremely frustrated.

"I learned from a master," she snarled right back.

"You're going to kill us both, Reggie."

"Frustration builds character."

"I don't want any more character," he snapped. "I'm eccentric enough as it is."

Abruptly she looked at him and quite weakly began to laugh.

"Hey," he protested from the floor, looking injured. But she only laughed harder, collapsing on the mattress until tears streamed down her cheeks.

"It's not funny," he insisted, pulling himself onto the bed. "I've got a reputation to uphold."

She laughed harder.

"Lady, you're killing my ego." But a smile began to tickle the corners of his own mouth. "Does this mean you find me eccentric?"

Reggie nodded her head, struggling to pull herself together. With one hand, she wiped the tears from her cheek. He leaned forward and swiped one hand across the other cheek.

She looked up warily, but his composure had returned and he simply grinned charmingly.

He leaned forward, his brown eyes warm on her face. "You're missing out, Regina O'Doul," he whispered. "Laughter might be fun, but I know better ways to bring tears to your eyes."

She shook her head, carefully pulling away from his magnetic grin. "Maybe you do need more exercises in character building."

He waggled a dark eyebrow at her, his gaze hot as it slid down her body. "Someday, Reggie," he promised softly. "Someday."

She pulled back to the far corner of the bed and decided she didn't want to think about it. Wordlessly she pointed to the small chair next to the door. With one last challenging look, he slid off the bed and pattered obediently to the chair.

"The least you can do is throw me a blanket," he called out, settling his overgrown body into the small, blue covered armchair. She obliged by tossing him the quilt and a pillow. Then she resolutely gave him her back, ignoring his muttered curses as he draped his lean body across the chair's fragile frame.

As she turned out the bedside light, she could still feel his gaze warm on her back in the darkness.

* * *

When the first rays of morning penetrated her sleep, she awoke groggily, blinking her bright green eyes like an owl just emerging from its hole. She went to stretch out, long and lazy, then abruptly became aware of the arm once more wrapped around her waist.

Turning carefully, she came face-to-face with Jake, curled like a puppy around her form. She shook her head and wondered if she should really be surprised that he'd crept back into bed the first chance he'd had.

He stirred slightly and she held her breath. But he simply murmured something soft and unintelligible. Then, in a strangely endearing gesture, he curled his arm tighter around her waist, rubbing his cheek against her hair, and fell once more into sleep.

She let out her breath slowly, blinking against the sudden tightening of her throat. He was just sleeping. No doubt he'd curled up with many women just like that.

Big, stupid brute.

She turned abruptly and sought the edge of the mattress. Immediately his arm tightened around her waist, pinning her in place.

Eyes darkening dangerously, she rolled over again, arching back her head to look at his closed eyes.

"You're supposed to be sleeping in the chair," she accused darkly.

"Chair hurt my back," he muttered, still not opening his eyes. He tried to snuggle closer, but she placed both of her hands on his bare chest to fend him off.

"So did being tossed on the hardwood floor," she said pointedly.

He cracked open one drowsy brown eye. "You wouldn't hurt a sleeping man, would you?"

"Just try me."

He sighed, a small forlorn sound that didn't fool her for a moment. Behind her, his hand began to slowly stroke her back, a movement that both comforted and sparked her nerves. "I'm just lying here," he said in his most innocent voice. "Just lying here, sleeping away, minding my own business. Surely two adults can share a bed."

"Two *adults*," she agreed emphatically.

He cracked open his other eye, peering down at her with a warm gaze that curled her stomach. "Hey," he said softly. "I'm as adult as the next man. At least adult enough to know that sleeping here with you is a helluva lot more fun than sleeping in the chair."

His hand slid forward and quite unexpectedly cupped her breast.

Her green eyes opened in shock, and even as the desire bolted down to her tightening stomach, she pushed vehemently at his chest. Immediately he sat up, releasing her so fast she fell back against the mattress. He looked down at his right hand with a narrow gaze, then as she watched in stunned silence, he promptly slapped his own hand.

"Bad hand," he said to it. "Bad, bad hand." He slapped it again, then looked up at her with his most apologetic gaze. "I don't know what to say. You try to raise 'em right and look what happens."

His hand snaked out again and wrapped around her waist. Immediately he ducked down, nuzzling her neck and nipping at her earlobe. Then just as quickly he released her and slapped his hand once more.

"Stop that, I say! Cease! Desist!" His hand seemed to tremble in front of him even as she watched in bemused fascination. Then like a wild beast, his hand broke for it, finding her ribs and dancing along the sensitive flesh.

"No, no!" Jake cried with mock protest, then tickled her harder. She squirmed and batted at the wayward hand, but it found each sensitive spot with ease until the laughter escaped from her throat in breathless gasps.

Jake leaned over, tickling her other side and rasping his beard across her sensitive neck.

"Stop, stop," she cried breathlessly, searching for his wrist and finally latching on to it. She pulled back his hand desperately, tears swarming in her eyes from the laughter. Her bones felt like jelly and her cheeks were flushed. "Stop that," she tried to say fiercely. But when she glanced up, she saw him smiling warmly down at her and the force faded from her words.

"I like your laughter," he said softly. He brushed her short hair back, then curved his thumb down her soft cheek. "You're beautiful in the morning, darlin'."

Immediately she shook her head, struggling for her composure but finding none. Her stomach still ached from the laughter and now tightened with something far deeper. Her eyes grew luminous on his face and one half of her wished he would let her go even as the other half wished he would draw closer.

She was an agent on duty, a small voice whispered in the back of her mind. She couldn't afford to lose her edge.

But Jake simply kept smiling, and she felt her resistance melt like a frozen stream that had gone far too long without any warmth. At her side, her hand began to tremble. Very slowly, her lips parted.

Jake watched the faint emotions flicker across her face, recognizing the first instant she drifted from apprehension to submission. His brown eyes darkened and shifted to her parting lips, full and ripe for the taking.

He leaned forward automatically, catching himself just inches away, her soft breath fluttering against his cheek. With the steely will of a man who knew what he wanted, he bent down and simply brushed his lips against her own. Then, his hands fisted from the effort, he pushed himself away and rolled off the bed.

If he pushed, she would have an excuse to pull away. No, last night he'd determined that the best way to seduce Reggie was to get her to want to seduce him. Unfortunately his overwound body already protested the new strategy. He was going to have to take the coldest shower this side of the Arctic to survive implementation of Plan B.

"Breakfast?" he said with his back still to her. He hoped to sound casual, but his voice came out half strangled.

Behind him, he heard the rustle of the blankets as she sat up. He didn't dare look, knowing that if he had to see her bare arms, slender and curved, he would snap in half.

There was another long moment, then finally she uttered a soft yes. He nodded back, taking three more deep lungfuls of air before he trusted himself to stand.

He moved around to the phone and rang the front desk. Moments later, a bellhop appeared with multiple shopping bags.

"What's that?" Reggie asked sharply from the edge of the bed.

"New clothes. I can't very well wear my riding pants again." He pulled out a soft pair of khakis from one box, then opened a second box containing a shirt and sweater.

"When did you go shopping?" There was a dangerous edge to her voice, but he was too busy unfolding the deep crimson sweater to notice.

"Yesterday," he replied casually. Apparently the reference to his truant afternoon wasn't a good idea because she jerked the sweater from his grasp, her green eyes flashing fire.

"You did all this yesterday afternoon when you were supposed to return to my side?"

He arched a sardonic brow. "For God's sake, Reggie. I just went to buy clothes. That's all."

She shook her head at him. "The deal was you were not allowed out of my sight until we heard back from Ivansson. Well, we haven't heard back, meaning you had no business going anywhere without me."

His lips thinned, he stood and impatiently yanked his sweater from her hands. "I just went shopping," he insisted. "Besides, this town's crawling with so many agents I couldn't sneeze without being photographed by one of them. Give us both a break, why don't you."

She was more than aware of the number of agents in the vicinity. Still, she brought her chin up stubbornly, her green eyes hard. "Maybe you just pointed out why you had to come back."

Jake stared at her, then shook his head in disgust. He raked his hand through his hair, feeling himself getting angry when he *really* did not want to start his day with anger. "Sooner or later," he said in a low voice, "you're going to have to trust me."

"Why, Jake? You're the one bending the rules—sneaking off to meet with Emelia, going off by yourself, conducting your own investigation. Why give you more credit than you're giving me?"

"I believe we had this conversation last night," he snapped. He yanked on his sweater with more force than necessary, realizing he'd forgotten his shirt. With a muttered oath, he ripped the sweater off and practically tore the box in two getting out the shirt.

Watching him darkly, Reggie suddenly stomped over to the bed. When she knew she had his attention, she very calmly reached beneath the mattress and pulled out the 9-mm she'd stashed there last night before falling asleep. She made a great show of pointing it toward the window and examining the lean, slick lines of the black, medium-size weapon. It didn't have the power of the Smith & Wesson .357 Magnum, but with fifteen rounds in the magazine, it got the job done.

She clipped the leather holster to the back of her jeans, and looking straight at Jake, tucked the safetied gun back into the small of her back.

"Don't take my cover too seriously," she warned him softly, her green eyes hard. "I'm a federal agent on a case, Jake. Leave my sight again, and I'll arrest you."

"You're bluffing," he retaliated evenly. "You need me to get into Kendall's party."

She merely arched a slender brow. "Not really, Jake. I had quite a nice conversation with Kirk Richardson yesterday. I think he'd be delighted to escort me."

At his incredulous stare, she smiled grimly and picked up her sweater. "You're not the only one who did some research yesterday, Jake. Did you really think I'd eaten pasta all day long?"

He didn't say anything, but the set of his jaw was hard. "Kirk Richardson is a pig," he said at last, his voice so low he barely recognized it. His hands were actually knotted at his sides, and he had the most unholy urge to punch Kirk Richardson's aquiline face. What was wrong with him? He *never* got mad.

"Maybe," she concurred, "but I'm not looking for a saint, just an opportunity."

He stepped forward and was finally rewarded by a tinge of wariness in her eyes. He brushed his thumb across her cheek, noting that she no longer flinched, but remained staring at him with steel in her spine.

"But I don't think you'd like kissing Richardson, darlin'," he whispered softly, his own eyes hard. "I don't think he'd be nearly as much fun as I am."

"Don't leave my sight again," she said simply. "You agreed to a deal, and I expect you to follow it."

"Reggie, I'm not the Highwayman."

"Jake, you agreed to the deal. Now follow it, or I will arrest you. It's that simple."

He shook his head. "So far," he drawled, "I don't think there's anything simple about it."

"Then let's just hope for your sake that we catch the Highwayman quickly." She smiled at him sweetly. "Or maybe you want to confess now, so I can save us both time and energy by arresting you this minute."

His brown eyes remained clear and frustrated. "You are a hard woman, Reggie O'Doul."

"Just so long as you understand."

"Oh, I understand all right. You wanna make the rules. Fine. Just fine. But I insist, rules were made to be broken."

"This isn't a game, Jake."

He smiled wryly and finally stepped away from her, picking up the empty boxes scattered across the floor. "Actually, darlin', I'm beginning to think we're caught in the biggest game of all."

"What does that mean?" she demanded.

He just smiled and shrugged again. "If only I knew..."

Chapter 8

They backtracked to Jake's house before beginning the long drive to the Kendall estate in Connecticut. Once back in her room, Reggie quickly showered, changed and called Buchanan.

"Who was in charge of checking into Jake's Newport home?" she said without preamble.

"Reggie?" came Buchanan's dry voice. "Hello to you, too."

"I don't have much time, Buchanan," she said curtly. "We're about to leave for the Kendall estate."

"Already?"

"Jake arranged it. This way I can scope out the place."

"Yeah, but so can Jake," Buchanan said pointedly.

Reggie's hand tightened on the receiver. She wanted to discount his words, a part of her thinking that despite what she said to Jake, she was becoming more convinced that he wasn't a thief. He was a rogue, but he had integrity. Then again, she wasn't exactly unbiased anymore. "Have you heard from Ivansson?" she asked sharply.

"On safari. Won't be available for at least another week."

"Damn." Reggie chewed on her lower lip while she digested the news. She really would like to have cleared up some things one way or the other by now. Hopefully, her secretary was having better luck reaching Mrs. Ivansson in Paris. "And Jake's Newport home?" she repeated. "Who originally looked into that?"

Buchanan sighed, and she heard the crinkle of papers as he sifted through the piles that permanently occupied his desk. "Evans, maybe. Or it might have been Dewitt. I'd have to look it up. What's up, Reggie?"

"I talked to Richardson. He mentioned that Jake was collecting the 'more interesting' of art pieces for his Rhode Island home. I asked Jake about it, and he didn't deny it. Now, how is it we're investigating a man for possible art theft, and everyone knows about this but us?"

Buchanan sighed harder. "There's been a lot going on, Reggie, and it took a while to weed the suspects down and fully staff the case team. I imagine a piece or two fell through the cracks, or maybe Evans or Dewitt do know but haven't had time to write it up yet. You know how it goes. Listen, I'll check up with them and get them on it. They'll report all findings to you. In the meantime, I assume all this means you're making progress?"

Reggie had to fight back the urge to laugh cynically. "I'm getting more opportunities," she said at last. "The next few days should be interesting."

"We'll have people posted around the estate," Buchanan assured her. "If things get too hot, don't be afraid to call in the cavalry. I'm not expecting you to be the Lone Ranger."

Reggie nodded, asked if there was anything else she ought to know, then hung up when Buchanan said no. She called back her secretary and learned that he had located Mrs. Ivansson's hotel and had left an urgent message. Perhaps they would get lucky and have an answer by day's end.

Completing her phone calls, Reggie chewed on her lower lip and wondered why everything felt wrong. Her shoulders were tense, her nerves on edge. Maybe Buchanan had been

right, and it was simply the toll of pretending to be someone she wasn't. God knows, Jake wasn't making her life a
piece of cake.

With a sigh, she rolled her neck, massaged her shoulders
a few times and packed her bag. Time for act two, the Kendall estate.

When she walked down the stairs fifteen minutes later,
Jake was already standing in the foyer. He looked up once,
bag in hand, then did a quick double take. Slowly enough
to make her cheeks color, his eyes skimmed down her figure. She'd changed into a pair of burgundy silk pants, the
thin material cut wide at the ankles to skim and flow as she
walked. A matching silk top had long, billowy sleeves that
ended in French cuffs. Over the whole outfit, she wore a
straight-cut, off-white silk sleeveless vest, fastened by a single string at her waist.

"Very nice," Jake said. "Casual, yet elegant, and not at
all what I would picture you wearing."

She arched a fine brow, but he merely shrugged. "Does
this mean you're now officially posing as the lover of the
rich and famous?" he asked.

"My gray sweat suit hardly seemed appropriate," she replied dryly.

He grinned. "I don't know. I always thought sweats were
sexy. And in that tank top—"

"Are you ready to go?" she interrupted.

He held up his garment bag and computer case, but his
eyes were still skimming up and down her long, lithe body.
She'd added the barest tinge of eye makeup, and now her
green eyes seemed to blaze out of her pale, delicate face. He
offered her his arm.

"Let me guess," he remarked casually as he led her back
out to his Porsche and popped the hood, "the loose vest
helps disguise the 9-mm still tucked into your waist."

She offered him an appraising look, setting her small bag
in the nose of the car. "Very good, Guiness."

He smiled and shook his head as he laid his garment bag
over two shopping bags, added his compact computer case,

then closed the hood. "Chic, elegant, and armed to the teeth. How very nineties of you, darlin'."

"A girl can't be too careful," she told him.

He grimaced ruefully, unconsciously rubbing his back. "And around you, sweetheart, neither can a guy."

She had to admit, there was something about riding in a Porsche. Through the winding back roads and up Interstate 95, they seemed to glide more than drive. Then there were the looks of the other drivers, sneaking furtive glances as the Porsche zoomed by. Jake was in good spirits, chortling with the radio and tapping out the beat on the steering wheel.

She found herself relaxing, smiling and humming a bit under her breath. The six-and-a-half-hour drive—completed in five hours and forty-five minutes with Jake at the wheel—passed in easy complacency.

Then they turned off I-95 at the Stamford exit in Connecticut and homed in on their destination.

Reggie had seen some snapshots of the Kendall estate before, but grainy black and whites didn't prepare her for the full effect. Winding down River Road, they passed regal house after regal house perched along the Stamford Harbor. They passed tennis courts, the yacht club and the circular driveways of beautiful stone homes. Jake kept driving, until at last they came to the point. Crowning the tip, the Kendall estate sat by itself, a tall, elegant mansion surrounded by blue, blue water.

Jake slowed down, shifting into low, and Reggie held her breath as they pulled up to the house. Overall, the Kendall estate wasn't huge, containing twelve bedrooms including the renovated servants' rooms. From the outside, it was a striking construction of beige stucco walls with dark brown, Tudor trim. Twin towers and a gabled roof gave it an elegant presence.

It wasn't as overwhelming as Reggie had feared, and she relaxed as they walked up the broad stairs to the massive, dark oak doors. While Jake pressed the bell, she looked around for evidence of security.

A flag in the corner of the lawn proclaimed a state-of-the-art security system, but Reggie couldn't make out any evidence of video cameras. And certainly the lawn was exposed for all eyes as any hedges, fences or trees would have spoiled the 270-degree view of the water. On the one hand, the bare lawn left a burglar no place to hide. On the other hand, the house appeared to be protected by only a wire system, and there were innumerable ways to bypass them. Surely the Highwayman wouldn't find much of a challenge here.

The door opened. Jake immediately beamed and shook the hand of an older gentleman with striking gray hair.

"John! So nice to see you again. It's so great of you to have us! Allow me to introduce my friend Regina O'Doul."

Reggie smiled, shaking John's hand and gritting her teeth at the older man's bemused look. Obviously Jake had brought many "friends" before. Coupled with Richardson's past "flavor-of-the-month" comment, Reggie was beginning to believe her status as Jake's friend put her in the same social category as a small, fluffy dog—well mannered, well-groomed, and completely inconsequential.

"It's a pleasure," she said politely. "Jake's told me so much about your beautiful home." She smiled pleasantly, if not a little vacuously. Then on an impulse she could only attribute to the devil, she found herself linking her arm through Jake's, resting her head on his shoulder and declaring, "Why, when we're married, sweetheart, I think we'll build a home just like this one."

Jake stiffened immediately, and Kendall's face registered shock. The older man recovered first, slapping Jake on his other shoulder.

"Guiness! Congratulations, you sneaky devil. We'd all but given up on you."

Jake turned and looked at Reggie, but she simply smiled serenely. She figured she would live to regret her impulsiveness, but it served Jake right after all the "flavor-of-the-month" comments.

"It's a bit of a shock to us all," Jake murmured at last. "You know what they say. When love strikes, it strikes hard—kinda like being tossed on your back on the floor."

Reggie smiled even larger, though her eyes were a bit hard. "How romantic of you, dear. I just hope for your sake love doesn't *strike* too often."

Kendall cleared his throat, clearly not understanding all nuances of the exchange. His gaze fell automatically to Reggie's exposed—and ringless—left hand. Immediately, Jake covered her hand with his own.

"We're keeping the engagement quiet for now," he said by way of explanation.

Kendall looked more confused than ever. A good host, he steered the conversation to neutral ground by giving them a tour of the house.

The entryway was the most striking. From the doorway people could look straight through the vaulted foyer to a solid wall of glass revealing a striking view of Long Island across the water. The unencumbered entryway rose two stories to a ceiling painted as a cloud-swept sky, and the green marble floor could fit one hundred people. On the left, a sweeping staircase carried people up to the second floor, which contained the bedrooms. Gilded railings allowed people on the second floor to look down at the beautiful foyer or out to the view. In the back of the house, an exposed patio boasted beautiful frescoes in pale blue, deep burgundy and indigo. Huge porcelain pots overflowed with pansies, geraniums and fuchsias.

For the Children's Charity Ball, Kendall explained, the foyer would be set up like a casino. The dining room would offer a dazzling buffet, and people could dance out on the patio.

"Will access to the rest of the house be restricted?" Reggie asked, then mentally berated herself when Kendall gave her a startled look at the direct question.

"Ah, no," he said at last. "I don't believe so. After all, some of the guests, yourselves included, are staying here."

Jake made a show of patting Reggie's hand and gave her a rather patronizing smile. "Reggie's been reading too many newspapers again," he said in his most condescending voice. "Thoughts of the Highwayman simply terrify her."

Reggie batted her lashes at him and smiled so brightly her cheeks hurt. Her grip on his arm, however, tightened enough to make him wince.

"Ah, yes, the Highwayman," Kendall said with a quick nod of his head. "Definitely we've taken extra precautions along those lines. You needn't worry, Miss O'Doul. During the actual ball, there will be security guards posted in the library and the dining room, where the main pieces are. Also, we recently upgraded the security system of the library, since it has the Waterhouse paintings. The new door locks don't have an access code, but require my thumbprint to open. Rather amazing what technology can do these days, isn't it?"

Reggie nodded, though she absently worried her bottom lip. During the actual event, the collection sounded very vulnerable. Of course, the Highwayman did generally strike after the event. She glanced at Jake and could tell by the distant look in his eyes that he was turning over the matter in his mind, as well.

After finishing the tour of the downstairs, Kendall showed them to their room and regretfully excused himself to attend to business.

"What do you think?" Reggie asked, the minute Kendall had closed the door behind himself.

Jake merely arched a sardonic brow. "About what, my dear fiancée?"

She flushed a little, pacing the room as the wheels in her mind turned. "The Highwayman will strike," she said after a brief pause. "He has to. The Waterhouse paintings are too tempting, the security system too lax."

"You don't think a print-activated system is secure enough?"

She snorted indelicately. "You could remove Kendall's thumbprint from his drinking glass using simple makeup powder and tape. Voilà, legitimate access to the security system without half the hassle the Highwayman's accustomed to."

"Very good, my dear. I believe you missed your true calling."

She leveled a hard stare at him. "The assumption is, of course, that the Highwayman will be at the party to snatch one of Kendall's glasses."

Jake nodded. "A fair assumption, but one that hardly limits the suspects. Unless, of course, you plan on following Kendall around all night wiping clean everything he touches."

Reggie frowned and nodded. She pivoted and paced in the other direction. "If the Highwayman isn't an overnight guest, however, he still has to access the house."

"That wire system's not too difficult."

She looked at him pointedly. "You would know."

He shrugged nonchalantly. "You're the one who just described how to trick a personalized system. Maybe I should be watching you."

She glared at him, swiveling and pacing once more.

"Reggie, you're making me dizzy." He walked toward her, placing his hands squarely on her shoulders. Immediately she stiffened, and he shook his head at her. He leaned down and whispered in her ear, "Now that we're engaged, don't you think you should relax a little?" He smoothed his hands slowly down her arms, feeling her tremble. "I think I should get an engagement kiss."

She tried to pull away, but his hands merely tightened on her arms. Her green eyes darkened dangerously. He pulled back enough to arch a brow at her. "Darlin'," he drawled, "you're the one that announced our engagement, not me. I'm just doing my best to maintain our cover."

"It was a mistake," she snapped back. "I simply reacted without thinking."

He smiled at her. "Perhaps, Reggie. But we can't just 'recant' our engagement. People will do nothing but talk, and then how will we get any work done? Nope. You made your bed, and now I think you have to lie in it. Lucky for you, I know all sorts of fun things to do in bed."

Her cheeks flushed even darker, her eyes snapping with frustrated fire.

"I think we should check out the library and dining room for ourselves," she said, keeping her chin up.

"In a minute," he murmured. He lowered his head, then paused. "I'm waiting," he whispered against her lips.

"You'll be waiting a long time!"

"Come on, Reggie. One simple kiss. It's the least you can do after ending my bachelor reputation."

"I'm sure your reputation will recover."

He leaned even closer, his lips a fraction of an inch from hers. In spite of her best intentions, she trembled. "Come on, Reggie," he cajoled. "What are you afraid of?"

They were the right words to say, and they both knew it. Immediately her arms wrapped forcefully around his neck. "All right," she growled. "One kiss."

She dragged his head down, slanting her mouth across his. She pressed her body against his generously, reveling in the feel of his hands spreading across her back. Arching her neck, she opened her mouth and drew him in.

She kissed him slow and languorously, as if she intimately understood just how to touch his mouth, how to caress his lips, how to romance his tongue. Her hands played with the dark fringe of his hair, sending goose bumps up and down his spine while her hips rubbed seductively against his own.

He felt himself pressing her even closer, kissing her even deeper, when he knew he would pay the price. His body was already hard and aching, his hands demanding and wanting as they cupped her buttocks.

She groaned against his lips, a whisper of a sound that fired his blood. The room spun away, until all he could think of was the thin barrier of silk that kept him from her skin.

His hands drifted up, seeking the edges of her shirt and finding the gun instead.

She tore out of his arms, her hands automatically checking the semiautomatic weapon in the small of her back. Her breath was still labored, her cheeks flushed, but her chin was set stubbornly.

He groaned to himself, his body protesting vehemently. Damn it, seducing FBI agents should come with its own guidebook. He wasn't used to feeling up a woman and finding a 9-mm gun instead. He would have to remember to keep his hands off her waist, or at least wait until he had her so thoroughly enthralled she wouldn't notice.

"Can we proceed now?" she asked crisply.

He wanted to laugh, but didn't think he could manage the sound.

"Sure," he managed hoarsely after a minute. He needed a cold shower. Hell, he needed a fifteen-mile jog, three hours of lifting and then a bath in solid ice to recuperate from her.

"I say we start in the dining room," she said levelly, already turning around and marching for the door.

"Sure," he said again. He began to follow, and after the first few steps, even managed to stop wincing.

He felt better by the time they were downstairs. He had his usual grin back on his face, and he was whistling tunelessly as they walked into the dining room. Reggie came to an abrupt stop, her green eyes unconsciously growing round.

The room was impressively ornate and Gothic. The walls were paneled in dark, Circassian walnut, the ceiling inlaid with a richly colored oil painting that had probably been lifted from a European castle. Beneath their feet, a faded gold-and-burgundy Isfahan rug remained plush and tightly woven despite three hundred years of wear. A black walnut table squatted in the middle of the room, its curved legs thickly scrolled like a gargoyle with too many tattoos. Its well-polished top gleamed like a midnight lake, drowning the Isfahan rug and sucking the light from the windows. A lone flower arrangement sprouted from the middle, blue, crimson and cream silk flowers fighting the dark. Behind the creamy silk rose petals, two Renaissance oil paintings hung in thick gilded frames.

"Wow," Reggie said after a minute. She walked to one of the two windows, unconsciously seeking sunlight.

"It's something else," Jake agreed.

"Can you imagine—" She broke off abruptly. "Then again, I imagine you can."

"I can what, Reggie?"

"It's just so much," she said at last. "Such an overwhelming display of money, art and age. For God's sake, this rug alone is worth more than what I will make my entire life." She glanced at him. "Does it ever get less overwhelming?"

He shrugged, bending down closer to examine the weave of the carpet. "Yeah, I suppose. But how much less overwhelming can a room like this get? It's designed to strike awe in everyone's heart. John probably offers his estate for this ball just so people can come and be awestruck."

"Is this what you'll do to your dining room in Virginia?" she asked, walking over to stare at the first oil.

"Who me?" He shook his head with a frown. "Come on, Reggie, I'm just a good ole Southern boy. Why would I do this to my house? Money doesn't come with an inherent style, you know. It is what you make it."

"You drive a Porsche," she said, pointing this out rather stiffly.

"Lord have mercy on my soul," he drawled back. When she glanced back over at him, he smiled. "Come on, Reggie, you know me better than that. Besides, I can't even drive my Porsche home without my brothers stealing it. And let me tell you, you'd never believe what Cagney can do to that car. Sure, he looks quiet and composed all the time. But you put him behind the wheel of a sports car, and he's even worse than Garret."

She smiled, feeling relieved when she'd never understood her uneasiness to begin with. She just knew she didn't feel comfortable in this room, and she wasn't sure she could ever feel comfortable in such a house. It seemed too foreign, too exotic for a girl who grew up in a two-bedroom apartment in Cambridge.

"Did you always want to be rich?" she found herself asking. "Is that why you went to Harvard?"

He stood again, looking at her from across the room. "I wanted the challenge," he told her honestly. "However, I have to say I really like the money."

"Why? So you can overwhelm people?"

He shrugged, glancing around the dark, rich room. "Not overwhelm, but maybe stand out. Everyone wants to feel special, Reggie. Come on, we're practically drowning in a sea of humanity. Money lets you buy special things, makes you feel elite. Business is a game, and I suppose the suits and cars and houses are all the trophies." He looked at her, his eyes skimming critically down her fashionably garbed figure. "Isn't that why you buy such nice clothes, Reggie? I bet on the really tough nights, you go straight from work to the malls. Buy yourself a real nice suit, so you can go to work the next day feeling successful, competent, on top. Am I so far from the truth, Reggie?"

Her flushing cheeks told him he wasn't.

There had been days, especially right after the trial, when it seemed all she'd done was buy nice clothes. Trips home to visit her father often meant hours of scouring her closet, trying to find the one suit that stated successful, competent agent.

"It's hardly a sin," Jake said softly, walking toward her. "I bet your father liked seeing you in those sharp, blue suits."

She looked away, not liking the way he followed her thoughts or the intensity suddenly choking her throat. Yeah, she tried wearing all the trappings for her father. She'd wanted to show him just how successful she'd become. Wanted for him to say the words he never said, but that she knew as an adult he must have felt.

Jake brushed her cheek with his thumb, but she walked away from him to examine the window for wires.

"Tell me a happy memory," he said abruptly.

"I don't know what you're talking about," she said from the window.

"Sure you do. Tell me a good memory, of you and your father. Then you'll feel better again. It was just the two of you most of the time when you were growing up. I imagine you did a lot together."

She nodded slowly. "We went to basketball games," she said at last. "He always had tickets for the Celtics. We'd go to the Garden and sit in really bad seats, eating stale pretzels covered in mustard and cheering until we were hoarse."

"Favorite game?" he pushed.

She paused for a minute, though the game came to her immediately. "Fifth or sixth game of the play-off series. Detroit trying to inbound the ball with just seconds left on the clock. Larry Bird stole the inbound pass and tossed it to Dennis Johnson for an easy lay in to win the game." It had been one of the last games she'd seen with her father. She could still remember them both jumping up and down on their seats with the excitement and adrenaline. The ball had gone in and they'd screamed at the top of their lungs, beating their feet against the bleachers. Frank had hugged her so tight, her ribs had ached and they'd both cheered, laughed and cried. At that moment, she'd never loved him more.

"Nineteen eighty-seven," Jake supplied. "Celtics beat Detroit in the play-offs, but lost to L.A. in the finals."

She turned and looked at him with genuine surprise. "Very good, Guiness."

He smiled, closing the distance between them. "I like basketball."

She tried to turn away again, but Jake merely came up behind her, his body so close she could feel the heat.

He brushed the back of her neck with his lips, and the tremor ran down her spine to her toes.

"I think I like being a fiancé," he whispered in her ear. He nuzzled her neck until her lips curved uncontrollably from all the goose bumps running up and down her arms.

"Stop that," she whispered, trying to push him away.

He merely grinned at her, his eyes so warm they melted her from the inside out. Resolutely she stiffened her spine, but her lips kept smiling. He leaned a little closer and she held her breath.

He brushed her hair with his fingertips, his eyes on the glowing strands with rapt fascination. Sparked by the setting sun, the dark strands burned red and fiery. He liked the way the blaze framed her pale face, highlighting her green eyes, crowning her delicate features.

"Now that we're engaged, will you kiss me every evening?" he asked huskily.

Her eyes widened a fraction. "Do you think you could handle being kissed every evening?"

"Interesting point," he concurred.

She nodded and took a step back. Immediately he reached for her arm.

"Don't," he said. She stopped, startled, her heart in her throat.

"I think we should go check out the library," she whispered, but her round eyes remained on his, waiting.

He shook his head, his brown eyes suddenly soft, nearly tender. "I want to watch the sun in your hair for a minute longer," he murmured. "You know, that's one of the first things I noticed about you. Your hair. From a distance, it looks dark. But then the light hits it and catches it on fire. You have beautiful hair, Reggie."

She opened her mouth to protest, but no words came out. She had to swallow twice before she could recover her composure. "I think you have too much time on your hands if you noticed all that about someone's hair," she said at last.

He smiled softly. "It's a worthy way of passing the time."

"Do these lines work on all your women?" Her voice was barely a whisper.

He shrugged. "I don't know. I never really tried before. You, on the other hand, require a great deal of effort."

She forced her chin up. "So happy to know you're finally meeting your match."

"I want you, Reggie," he said abruptly. "Tonight. I really think we should make love." While her eyes were still rounding with the shock, he used the opportunity to catch her hand, turning it palm up and brushing his thumb across the sensitive surface. "I mean, I'm as big a fan of foreplay as the next guy, but it's been days, Reggie. If we keep going on like this, I could seriously hurt myself."

Her jaw worked once, twice, then she forced out the blustery words. "I think the only thing that's been hurt is your common sense," she muttered. "You're taking this undercover business entirely too seriously."

"Shh," he whispered, lifting a single finger to silence her lips. "Someone might hear you, darlin'. Besides, I think the lady doth protest too much. You are attracted to me, Reggie, and you know I'm attracted to you. Why fight the inevitable?"

"Nothing is inevitable," she growled. Her heart was thundering so hard in her chest she thought it might leap out. She'd known he was capable of almost anything, but to bring up the subject of sex as casually as if they were discussing where to eat for dinner? Worse, he had a way of saying the words so that they almost made sense. There wasn't a man in the world as dangerous as this one.

With a tug, she freed her arm and walked posthaste toward the library. "You can stick around, or you can go to the room," she said over her shoulder. "But I plan on working."

With a sigh, he fell into step beside her. "I don't give up that easily, Reggie."

"Neither do I, Jake."

Chapter 9

"What do you think?" she asked at last.

Jake looked up from his examination of the first painting. "Frame's wired."

She shrugged. "The frame's too heavy to steal anyway. He'll cut the canvas out."

Jake nodded, moving to the second, smaller oil. The library contained six original paintings, two Flemish tapestries and three shelves of rare books. A virtual thief paradise. Jake was looking forward to spending the next couple of days perusing the library himself.

"I don't know," Reggie said at last. "Once he enters the house, I don't think it will be much of a challenge."

"And entering the house isn't much of a challenge at that," Jake agreed.

"He can slip through a second-story window," she added.

Jake shook his head. "Not even that hard." She looked over at him sharply, but he merely shrugged. "You heard what Kendall said. Half the party's on the patio. If I was the Highwayman—" She raised a fine brow but he ignored her. "If I was the Highwayman I would simply rent a masked costume and wait until about 1:00 a.m. By then, most of the guests would be drunk on champagne and nobody would be paying much attention. He could simply walk onto the grounds, join the dancing on the patio and slip inside. When the crowd thinned out, he could find a closet to hide in, and *bamm,* he would be all set for when the last light turned out."

"There'll be attendants watching the grounds," she said pointedly. "At two thousand dollars a head, you don't want anyone crashing the ball."

"Sure," Jake agreed. "And I'm certain from nine till eleven, bouncers will keep a good eye. But who's looking for an uninvited guest at 1:00 a.m.? Things are dying down at that point. I'd say if anything, this is the easiest job the Highwayman's had yet. If I was him, I'd be insulted."

Reggie turned and raised a quizzical brow. "What do you mean by that?"

"The other jobs required skill, finesse, style. I admire that in a person. And leaving behind the single red rose and a small poetic verse, what a beautiful finishing touch."

"For God's sake, Jake, we're talking about a thief. Aren't you romancing this just a little?"

He shrugged. "Sure, but so are half the women in the country. Come on, everyone wants to know who the Highwayman is. Once he gets out of jail, he'll be the hottest stop on the social circuit."

"The world is sick," she declared.

"Why, Reggie? The thief has style and flare. You don't see much of that anymore. He operates outside of the rules. Everyone loves a rebel."

"For one thing, maybe *he* is a *she,* ever think of that? And secondly, a thief is a thief is a thief. Case closed."

He looked at her speculatively from across the room. "I take it you consider Robin Hood to simply be a thief as well."

She looked at him in exasperation. "The Highwayman is not Robin Hood, Jake."

"Just answer the question."

She met his gaze squarely, her chin coming up. "All right. As a matter of fact, Robin Hood was a thief. If Robin Hood lived today, I'd arrest him. It's my job. If the man really wanted to fight poverty, he should've worked at a soup kitchen."

"How charitable of you," Jake remarked dryly. "Haven't you ever done a single rebellious thing, Reggie? Surely your life isn't that black-and-white."

She appeared warier now, her hand unconsciously gripping the curved marble ivy that decorated the fireplace. "I've had my moments."

"One thing, Reggie. Name one rebellious act."

Her chin came up again, her eyes stubborn. "I dated Brian," she declared.

He raised his eyebrows. "Dated Brian? I stand corrected. You're a virtual wild woman, O'Doul."

Her chin trembled slightly, her knuckles whitening on the red marble leaf. "My father hated him," she said levelly. "He said I shouldn't get serious about anyone, I would get sidetracked, forget what I wanted. But I dated Brian for two years anyway."

"And then?" Jake persisted.

She tore her hand away from the marble trim and walked as nonchalantly as possible to the far bookcase. "Then I broke up with him to enter the Academy."

"Bet your father was proud." His voice was hard, harder than he'd intended it to be. She whirled on him coldly.

"I *always* wanted to be an agent, Jake. My father liked the idea, but it was my dream, too. My father was right, you know. Giving up Brian was a small price to pay for becoming who I wanted to be."

"And I'm sure that thought keeps you warm on all those lonely nights, Reggie."

She winced, turning away sharply. "You can be very cruel, Jake."

"No," he said, and for the first time he sounded troubled. "Generally I'm not cruel at all."

He turned away as well, walking toward the window, and peered out at the blue water. If he was smart at all, he would leave her alone. He would stop teasing her and seducing her and simply help her catch the Highwayman so this thing would end. Then they could both go on their merry way. No harm, no foul.

Except he just couldn't quite bring himself to let it go at that. Maybe all his teasing wasn't quite teasing anymore. Maybe Mitch had a point about women who disliked you on sight.

Reggie cleared her throat and finally broke the silence. "Maybe." She cleared her throat again and her voice came out steadier. "Maybe, I should ask Buchanan to contact Kendall about beefing up security. A couple of dogs might be a good addition, plus an all-night watchman in the room."

"I think," Jake drawled slowly from the window, "that *we* should do it."

She hesitated, and immediately he turned toward her. Forgetting his own internal advice, he bore down on her. "What's the matter, Reggie?" he found himself asking intensely. "Don't you trust me?" In the back of his mind, a warning voice told him this wasn't a smart thing to do, but then he'd done a lot of stupid things since meeting the infamous Reggie. He wanted to know. He really wanted to know.

"That's a loaded question, and you know it!" Reggie exclaimed as if she'd just read his mind.

"What's so loaded about it, Reggie? Actually I think it's quite simple. Sooner or later, you have to decide whether I'm the Highwayman or not. You can't have me both help you catch the thief and be the thief. It makes no sense."

"We haven't heard back from Ivansson yet," she hedged.

His eyes darkened. "To hell with Ivansson," he said succinctly. "This is about you and me now. Do you, or don't you, trust me?"

"How can you of all people ask that?" she asked grittily. "Look at all the times you've sidestepped me. And how am I supposed to trust my own judgment when you spend the other half of your time trying to get me into bed? No sane person would answer that question."

"Then be a little crazy, Reggie."

"I thought we just established that I'm never crazy."

"Do you or don't you trust me?"

"Stop asking me that!"

"Then answer the question! All you have to do is answer the question."

"And if I say no?"

"Is that your answer?"

"Go away, Jake."

"I can't, darlin'. I'm not allowed out of your sight, remember?"

"I won't answer that question."

"Yes or no?" He stood so close she could see his jaw clench.

Her eyes squeezed shut and abruptly she could see her father sitting at the defense table. "The defendant pleads guilty, your honor." *Guilty, guilty, guilty.*

Her eyes popped open. She looked him straight in the eye. "No," she said tightly. "I do *not* trust you."

He stilled for a minute, then pushed himself away, a vein suddenly throbbing in his temple.

"Liar," he said and walked out of the room.

When Reggie returned to the bedroom, Jake was lying down on the bed, his feet crossed and his eyes closed. As quietly as possible, she unpacked her bag, hanging up her clothes in the closet and placing her sparse makeup kit in the adjoining bathroom.

Jake still didn't say anything, though she could tell from the tension in the room that he was awake.

For the first time, she missed his easy banter. He always had a way of making her smile, of making her relax even in spite of herself. She hadn't met anyone who could do that since Brian, lovely Brian who she'd left because she just had to be an agent.

What if Jake was right, after all? What if she had walked away from the only joy she'd ever known, simply because she understood the critical demands of her father much better than she understood happiness?

She knew how to hunger, and she knew how to stay up nights and torture herself with all the things she needed to accomplish.

She certainly didn't know how to simply be.

And suddenly, standing in the center of the room, Jake silent on the bed, she felt so unbearably lonely. She didn't know how to tell him how it had felt to sit in that courtroom and hear her father—her big strong father—plead guilty. She didn't know how to tell him what it was like to wake up each morning, realizing her whole life had been a lie, and she'd pushed herself to meet the demands of a man who'd turned out to be a corrupt gambler, a greedy, insatiable, unhappy man.

She didn't know how to tell Jake that even in the end, Frank had still been her dad, red-faced, blustery and yelling at her to demand more responsibility at the Bureau. Even when he was in jail, even after pleading guilty, he was still somehow the unconquered hero, the father she wanted so desperately to be proud of her. The father, who'd even then, never said that he loved her.

And now there were so many late nights when she came home to her two-bedroom condo, looked around at the endless stacks of paper and wondered when she'd become so lonely. If she'd made all the right choices, why was there no one to understand, no one to cheer for her in the front row, no one to hold her close and stroke her cheeks on the bad days when maybe, just maybe, O'Doul felt like crying?

Wasn't there anyone out there who could look at her and see how hard she tried and how much she hurt with each failure? How much she wanted and how afraid she was of never achieving any of those things?

How much she wanted to love, and how absolutely terrified she was that no one would ever really love her? That in the end, she would be simply the same driven, insatiable, unhappy person her father had been.

"I didn't mean to hurt you," she said into the silence.

For the first time since they'd argued, Jake faced her, his brown eyes piercing. "What do you mean?"

"I didn't mean to hurt you," she repeated, her fists balled at her sides. "But you're the one who asked if I trusted you, and well—" Her chin came up a stubborn notch. "Don't ask questions if you can't stand the answers, Jake. You know I have to suspect you. You know I have to remain focused."

"Gotta remain the sharp agent, huh, Reggie?"

She clenched her jaw fiercely. "Yes," she stated levelly.

He sighed and sat up, his gaze still on her face. "Damn, you're stubborn."

"Runs in the family."

"So that's it, Reggie? We're back to being partners, but with you still contemplating my guilt?"

She looked uncomfortable, and then she wrapped her arms around her waist, a curiously vulnerable gesture. "Yes," she said again. She looked down at the floor. "So are we square now?"

He got off the bed and walked across the room until he could tip up her chin. For a long time, he simply searched her eyes, taking in the green depths that were defiant, yet carried a sheen he hadn't seen before.

"Does it matter to you, Reggie?" he asked softly. "Do you care if I'm angry or not?"

Her pale chin trembled in his grip, her green eyes luminescent. "I don't want you to be angry," she said at last, her voice unusually quiet.

If he hadn't known any better, he would have thought his hard-as-nails agent was actually sad. He frowned, then brushed his thumb absently over her smooth, soft cheek. Her lips parted a little, and he saw the longing bloom suddenly in her eyes.

Not passion, not desire, but *longing*.

His gaze stilled on her face, then grew suddenly intent. He bent down a fraction of an inch and sure enough, she trembled before him.

Very slowly, he moved his hands to cup her shoulders. She didn't try to pull away, but leaned forward almost imperceptibly. And once more, he saw the sheen in her eyes.

"Say it," he whispered.

She shook her head.

"Say that you want me."

"I don't." But her hands came up to his chest anyway, flattening over the thick softness of his deep crimson sweater. "Jake..."

He relented with a sigh, closing the last few inches and finding her lips with his own.

He touched her lips softly, gently, not wanting to push and giving her ample opportunity to pull away. But her strong, curved arms wrapped around his neck, her trim, lithe body settling against him. His tongue traced the full outline of her lips, dipping a little at the corner, waiting to dip farther and truly taste her.

She sighed again, a soft whisper that tugged at him, until his large, square hands smoothed down her graceful back, molding her against him, willing her to allow him even closer.

Open up, my tough little agent. Let me inside.

Her lips parted with another feathery sigh. He didn't immediately advance, but angled his head to the side, finding and catching her lower lip, then her upper lip. Tasting the corner of her mouth, then sipping from her lips like a man discovering the sweetest nectar.

Her body pressed against him more tightly, her arms becoming more insistent around his neck.

He kissed her fully, his tongue finding her mouth, tracing the satiny warmth of her inner lip, dipping deep into the moist recess and thrusting fully. She welcomed him with a low moan, her hands suddenly tangled fiercely in his hair, her beautiful eyes squeezed shut. And in the rich flavor of her mouth, he thought he could taste her tears.

What had finally affected the incredibly driven Agent O'Doul? He doubted he would ever know.

His hands flattened on her back, exploring her lean, graceful shoulder blades, her delicate, finely boned rib cage, then the narrow, feminine curve of her waist. He palmed her hips, his fingers strong and kneading on her buttocks, shifting her closer until she could feel what she'd done to him, how much he'd been wanting her, how much he needed her now.

Still he hesitated, advancing but not pushing, always waiting for that moment of her retreat. He smoothed his hands up her body, his thumbs finding the upward curve of her breasts. Then, because he simply had to, he curved his hands inward and rubbed his thumbs over her nipples.

She gasped, then shuddered, and he knew he was lost.

Suddenly patience was gone, and the man who had seduced innumerable women forgot about seduction. His hands trembled, his body shook with the need. His kiss deepened abruptly, harshly, until he no longer romanced her mouth but consumed it. In reply she angled her head back, accepting him, pulling him, demanding even more. Their tongues met and dueled, tasting and discovering and tangling together as each sought to become closer and closer.

His large hands wrapped around her head, burying themselves in her short, silky hair so he could ravage her lips. In response she rubbed her hips against him, her flat, lean belly rotating insistently over his hard, burning length.

"Jake," she whispered again.

He groaned and dragged her down to the floor. Together they ripped off her shirt, and in a flurry of feverishly choreographed moves, they rolled together in a luxurious pile of hastily discarded clothes, hot, satiny skin pressed against lush, moist desire.

She straddled him shamelessly, her back arched, her eyes heavy-lidded. His hands swallowed her breasts, his thumbs rubbing her nipples until she squirmed on top of him, her warm femininity rubbing along his turgid length. He drew her down, finding her nipple with his mouth, and she cried out as his lips fastened on the hard pebble and sucked deeply.

Sweat blossomed over her lithe, curved body, the moisture beading her upper lip and trickling down her cheek as he found her other breast and laved it generously.

Her hips wouldn't remain still, already rotating with incessant, urgent desire. He found them with his hands, settling her once more on his burning length. As she slid back on him, his teeth gritted and his neck corded with fierce need.

His hand reached out, blindly seeking his wallet in his pants while she continued to rotate suggestively. His hands were now moist with sweat, trembling with passion, but at last they latched onto the prize, and he fumbled to get the condom out.

In a last moment of lucidity, she took the foil from him. She looked at him with clear, luminous eyes, then wrapped her hand around his hard, burning length. He arched against her touch, his brown eyes nearly black, his tan skin glistening with sweat.

She held him carefully in her strong, capable hands, and while still looking at him, she rolled the condom onto his shaft.

For one moment, they simply stared at each other, their chests rising and falling with the tension, their gazes thick with desire. He reached out, and tenderly, he cupped her cheek.

Her eyes closed, her lips turning into his palm, and he saw the tremor race down her graceful spine.

Rising, he pressed her down onto the pile of clothes and covered her body with his own. She parted her legs wordlessly, opening herself to him and giving him her body since she didn't know how to give him anything more.

And with teeth-clenching control, he slowly sank into her waiting warmth.

It had been a while for her. He could tell by her nearly virginlike tightness, and by the sudden clenching of her jaw.

Her gaze did not waver, but her hands suddenly balled into fists at his shoulders. He knew it hurt her a little, muscles long unused having to stretch once more.

His body screamed for him to push deeper, to thrust, to take, to possess, but he remained poised over her, his neck corded, his arms sculpted with the strain. Very carefully, she rotated her hips, her eyes taking on that determined look he knew so well as she tested her own readiness and adapted to his penetrating size.

Her hands opened on his shoulders, her breath accelerating, her eyes darkening.

"Now," she whispered.

He groaned, her single word robbing the last of his control. He arched back his hips and thrust deeply. She met him fiercely, her legs wrapping tightly around his waist.

Suddenly there was no finesse or skill. It was simply urgent demand meeting urgent demand, primal need against primal need. He plundered her body, and her nails raked fiercely down his back. He plunged deeper, and she pressed herself against him tightly.

The tempo grew fierce and savage, their bodies slippery with sweat, the air heavy with the sound of their labored breaths. Then abruptly, she bowed beneath him, her fine white neck arching back, her mouth parting with a soundless scream of exhilaration.

He poured himself into her, taking her body, giving his soul, collapsing onto her slick, alabaster form.

She wrapped her arms around him tightly, burying her face against his neck, her body still shaking with the aftermath.

He rolled onto his back, dragging her on top of him and positioning her comfortably. They simply lay together, his hands caressing her back.

And for the first time in his life, Jake couldn't think of a single thing to say.

* * *

Sometime later, Jake moved them both to the bed, where they curled up spoonlike, her head pillowed on his arm, and in wordless silence they fell asleep.

They didn't wake up until nearly ten, well after dinner. Reggie couldn't quite meet his eyes and couldn't quite look at his bare chest without remembering the feel of him moving inside her. She caught his sideways glance and knew that he was remembering the feel of her body as well.

She thought they would make love again, her body already quivering with the anticipation. But instead he simply took her hand, and like two wayward teenagers, they slipped on robes and crept downstairs to ravage the kitchen.

Jake pulled out sandwich makings from the huge, stainless-steel refrigerator while she watched, still feeling curiously raw and vulnerable. She waited for his witty comments, waited for any word to break the tension. But instead, he fed her silently, his dark eyes filled with a new intensity that kept her hands shaking.

They ate turkey from each other's fingers, followed by tomatoes, then bread, then lettuce. Jake assured her it still counted as a sandwich.

Then he found vanilla ice cream. They ate it straight from the carton, sharing a spoon, while they sat on the cool tiles of the kitchen floor.

She still couldn't think of anything to say.

Later, they retreated upstairs, and since she didn't know where to look, or what to say, she simply slipped the robe from his fine, muscular body and led him back to the bed.

This time, when he slid into her body, she shut her eyes and bit her lower lip so he wouldn't learn of the emotions that bubbled so dangerously close to the surface.

Long after he fell asleep, curled tenderly around her form, she remained wide-eyed and awake.

You've got to keep focused, Reggie. You've got to keep focused.

She wondered if maybe Jake and Buchanan had been right after all: She was in over her head.

* * *

In the morning, Reggie called her secretary.

"We got a message from Mrs. Ivansson," her secretary reported. "I tried to clarify, but she has a very thick accent, which made things difficult."

"What did she say?"

"She said—and I quote—'There has been much confusion about Mr. Guiness. He is a fine man and a close friend. Of course, Mr. Ivansson gave him permission.'"

"Oh," Reggie said dumbly, grabbing paper and pen. "Give me her number."

Her secretary complied, and after confirming that there wasn't any other news, Reggie dialed the number in Paris.

She was in luck; Mrs. Ivansson was available to speak.

After confirming her identity, Reggie drilled the woman further on Jake's break-in of the Ivansson home. Mrs. Ivansson insisted again and again that Donnar and Jake had had an arrangement; Jake certainly wasn't a real thief. Furthermore, why were the FBI harassing such a dear family friend. Donnar would be most upset.

Ten minutes later, Reggie hung up, satisfied that Mrs. Ivansson was telling the truth and that Jake's story was confirmed. He was not a thief.

He was in the clear.

Reggie promptly dialed Buchanan.

"I heard from Mrs. Ivansson," she said immediately.

"Jesus, Reggie. Are you ever going to learn to say hello?"

"Hello. I heard from Mrs. Ivansson."

Buchanan laughed, and she could almost see him shaking his head. "All right, O'Doul. Did you say *Mrs.* Ivansson?"

"Yeah, I had my secretary track her down. She cleared Jake."

"Oh? You contacted her?"

"Yeah, since we couldn't reach Donnar. Is something wrong?" she asked sharply. For some reason, Buchanan sounded disturbed.

"Oh, no," he said hastily, "just pleasantly surprised. It's good to have Jake's activities clarified. I imagine that makes your position easier."

"Yes," she concurred, then hesitated for a moment. "Did you ask about Jake's Newport home?"

"I passed it along to Dewitt. Now that we can safely eliminate Jake as a suspect, though, it will probably fall to the wayside. We've got much more urgent matters that need our attention before the night of the ball."

"Security here is pretty bad," Reggie reported. "Jake offered an interesting scenario of the Highwayman trying to sneak onto the grounds as a guest. There are no fences and it's a costume ball."

"God, how easy. What's the security like inside the house?"

"Not much. The library has the real treasures, and it's protected by a print-activated lock. Still, lifting Kendall's fingerprint isn't that hard."

"No, so far it sounds almost too easy."

"During the actual party, a security officer will be in the room. Since the Highwayman doesn't usually strike until *after* the festivities, one security guard should do the trick. After lights out, though, I'll take up watch inside the library. This time, we're going to catch him."

There was a long pause. "Are you sure that's such a good idea, Reggie? Stolen art can be recovered. Dead agents remain dead."

Reggie frowned. "I'm trained for this," she said sharply, taken aback by his comment. The Highwayman had no history of violence, having simply bound and gagged the only security guard who'd stumbled upon him. Besides, she was a professional; this was her job, for God's sake! Couldn't someone believe in her abilities for just once?

"All right, all right." The older man immediately backed off, sensing his blunder. "Just keep your eye out. We haven't had any casualties yet, and I want to keep it that way."

"I'll be careful," she promised, her tone begrudging.

"Keep me posted."

"Of course."

They both hung up, but Reggie remained by the phone in the bedroom for a moment longer. It would appear that Jake wasn't the Highwayman, just someone being framed for the crimes. She felt a sharp pang of relief at his innocence, but it was quickly followed by confusion. She still didn't know what it all meant, professionally or personally.

She hadn't meant to sleep with him, hadn't meant to succumb to him as so many other women had succumbed. But already, she desired him once more.

It didn't help that each time she moved, she felt the telltale soreness between her legs.

She stood and squared her shoulders. She was strong, she reminded herself. She was independent and capable. She *could* sleep with the man and remain professional.

There was physical desire and there were emotions. If a sophisticated man like Jake could keep the two apart, well then, so could the cool Agent O'Doul.

She journeyed downstairs to the library to find him.

Jake was reading in front of the window, a first edition of *Catch-22* held delicately in his hand. She wondered if that wasn't somehow apropos.

"Hi." She halted in the middle of the cozy library, her hands tangling behind her.

"Hi, yourself," he said casually. He set down the book on his lap, his face easy and relaxed. "Looking for something to read?"

"Sure," she agreed, latching onto a convenient subject. "What do you recommend?"

"What are you looking for?"

She hesitated once more, then jumped right in. "How about tips on how to apologize."

He stilled in the dark blue wing chair. "How to apologize? As in a real, solemnly stated, sincerely meant apology?" He suddenly grinned at her and leaned back smugly. "I think I'm going to like this. By all means proceed. And make it good, darlin'. I have a feeling it could be decades before you'll apologize again."

She flushed furiously. "You're not making this easy."

"Give me one good reason why I should." The hard edge emerged in his tone, though his face remained grinning.

"You aren't exactly blameless," she said sharply.

"Reggie, are you apologizing or attacking?"

She looked down at the Turkish rug. "Sorry," she muttered. "In my family, we have a tendency to confuse the two."

"Point taken."

She took another deep breath. "We heard from Mrs. Ivansson today," she said at last, wanting to keep it simple. "She verified that you broke into Donnar's house with his permission. I imagine I could have trusted you a bit more. Though there were extenuating circumstances and as an agent, I had the right to remain skeptical!"

He winced. "I don't think you're going to be able to make a living off reparations anytime soon. But knowing how this must grate against your very nature and curdle your tongue, I accept your apology."

"And how graciously you did so," she remarked caustically. She'd really only apologized because she knew her lack of trust had wounded him yesterday. Given last night, she didn't want him to think she still didn't trust him. It seemed she could offer him that much consolation.

He grinned at her, that old spark back in his eyes. "So we're 'all squared away'?"

"I believe so."

He winked at her. "Then we can plan our midnight rendezvous in the library. You bring the strawberries, I'll provide the whipped cream. Did you know—"

"That won't be necessary," she hastily interrupted. "I think your plan has a lot of merit," she continued slowly. "In fact, I believe I will wait up in the library the night of the ball. But you're a civilian, Jake. Your role was to get me into the party without raising suspicion. You've accomplished that. You don't need to do anything more."

He frowned, his eyes darkening a fraction. "Am I under arrest?" he asked carefully.

"Of course not!"

"Then I'm free to do what I want, correct?"

"Jake, I can still nail you for interfering with a criminal investigation," she said quickly, seeing where his thoughts were headed. Then she frowned at him furiously. "Look, Jake. I just came down here to apologize to you. Now, can't you show a little faith in me by letting me handle this?"

"It's not a matter of faith," he told her levelly. "I think you're very competent, and I have the bruises on my back to prove it. But I'm still the one being framed in all this, Reggie. That gives me a very personal stake in what goes on Friday night. As they say, two heads are better than one."

"I can't do my job and worry about you!" she said fiercely.

He smiled at her. "Then forget I'm there. I'm an adult. I'm willing to take full responsibility for my actions."

"I'll handcuff you to the bed if I have to, Jake."

"How delightfully inventive. Maybe I should bring whipped cream, after all."

She groaned, a low, frustrated sound. "You are not coming Friday night, if I have to break every bone in your body!"

"I believe that's police brutality."

"More like justifiable homicide. Look, we're not talking about this anymore. You're not coming, that's final. So why don't we just—"

Jake grabbed her wrist and abruptly pulled her onto his lap. She was just beginning to sputter and pull away when Kendall appeared in the doorway.

"There you two are," the older man said. He smiled at them both, and Reggie could have sworn he slipped a quick wink at Jake. "Enjoying the afternoon together, I see."

"Absolutely," Jake said. "You have a fine library. Your collection of books is impressive."

Rather dumbly, Reggie nodded her agreement. She could feel Jake's hand sneaking up her back, and had to forcefully suppress her goose bumps. But then he tickled her ribs and she gave a little yelp.

Kendall arched an elegant brow. "Sorry to interrupt. I forget sometimes what it's like to have just fallen in love." He smiled kindly at them, already pulling away from the door. "I thought you might be interested in going to play golf, but I can see that you're busy."

"Oh, no," Jake said. "We'd be happy to join you. Have you ever played golf, darlin'?"

Mutely Reggie shook her head. Jake's hand was sneaking around her ribs again, waiting for an opportunity to strike. "Sounds delightful," she managed to say.

"Shall we say in an hour?"

"Agreed," Jake said. He nuzzled Reggie's neck, and she had no choice but to laugh and smile indulgently. With a final wave, Kendall ducked out.

She immediately hopped off Jake's lap and hit him in the shoulder. "Show some self-control," she hissed.

He merely smiled. "Darlin', we're newly engaged. People expect us to be gushy."

"I don't do 'gushy,'" she told him levelly. "We get to be civilized engaged people."

He managed a forlorn smile, giving her his best puppy-dog eyes. "No one lets me have any fun anymore," he said mournfully. "Wanna sneak up stairs and remedy that?" He was already nibbling on her fingertips.

She managed to shake her head in spite of the goose bumps rippling up and down her spine.

"I have something for you," he said abruptly. She looked down at him with startled eyes. Not saying anything more, he dug into his pants pocket and pulled out a blue velvet box. He stood, offering her the box.

She took a wary step back. He caught the movement and raised a sardonic brow. "Interesting response, Reggie."

She raised her chin. "Where did you get that? Did you go shopping again?"

He looked at her for a moment. "You know, Reggie, you're a hard woman to please," he said softly. She didn't reply, but remained staring at him. Finally he sighed and relented. "It was delivered this morning, Reggie. Satisfied? You'd be amazed what a phone and credit card can accomplish these days. Welcome to the nineties." He held out the box. "Don't jump for joy or anything."

She took the ring box rather tentatively, surprised to see her hands trembling. "I don't understand," she whispered finally, still not opening it.

"Well, we're supposed to be engaged now. Certainly Kendall will announce it to everyone he meets. After all, you just caught one of the most eligible bachelors around, if I do say so myself." He glanced down at her ringless left hand, gently capturing it and lifting it up. "Now is there anything wrong with this picture, Miss Undercover?"

Miss Undercover. So it was part of the game again, part of the job. Professional. Remember to be professional, Reggie.

She took a deep breath and slowly tilted up the lid of the box. Inside, sat a gleaming gold Irish wedding band with a single diamond nestled in the center of the heart formed by the two hands.

"Oh," she breathed quietly, looking up at him with startled eyes. "A *claddagh*."

"Do you like it?" His voice came out gruff, and he immediately cleared his throat.

"You didn't have to do this," she said, her gaze back on the band. It was truly beautiful. In her jewelry box at home, she had the *claddagh* her father had given her mother, but not even it was as beautiful as this one.

"Well, I did do it," Jake said. He took the box from her, surprised to find his hands unsteady. For crying out loud, Guiness, this was just to maintain pretenses. He cleared his throat yet again and took the delicate band out of the box. "Your hand?"

She held up her left hand, and he took it, suddenly hyperaware of the feel of her long, slender fingers resting on his palm. His throat grew tight.

"Now when the heart faces out, it means you're available, right?" he muttered. Wordlessly she nodded. "And when the heart's turned in, it means you're taken?" Again she nodded.

Very slowly, he turned the band so the heart faced inward and slid it onto her left ring finger.

"But we're not married yet," she whispered.

He smiled at her, but his look was fierce. "I don't share," he said. He bent down and brushed his lips across the sensitive spot by her ear. "That ought to take care of any talk," he said at last.

She nodded, her hand still resting in his. "It was very smart of you to think of it."

"You know how clever we Harvard boys are."

"Can...can you take it back when everything's done?"

"I could."

She nodded, turning her hand lightly to watch the gold reflect. She'd never seen a ring on her left hand before. She liked how it looked.

"Thank you, Jake," she whispered abruptly.

He raised a finely arched brow. "Wow. An apology and a thank-you all in one day. Be careful, O'Doul, you might win Miss Congeniality after all."

She immediately brought her chin up in fierce contradiction, but then he winked at her and grinned. "Gotcha!" he whispered and bent down to nip her neck.

She pushed him away with both hands. "Rutting goat," she told him.

He simply wrapped an arm around her waist and dragged her back down into the chair. "Yep," he agreed quite cheerfully and found her ear.

"Jake," she whispered weakly, her eyes already drifting shut, "we're supposed to be golfing."

"That's in forty-five minutes," he assured her, his teeth closing gently on her earlobe. "And I'm very talented."

"Yeah," she agreed and placed his hand on her breast.

Chapter 10

Jake had said that he'd taken care of the costumes for the ball, so Reggie had removed the matter from her mind. Unzipping the newly arrived garment bag the night of the ball, however, she wondered why she was surprised at its contents: one black Zorro's costume for Jake, one Spanish doña's outfit for her. She eyed the low-scooped neckline of the white peasant's blouse with open suspicion.

"I don't think any self-respecting matron would wear that blouse," she announced.

Jake looked at the ruffled collar, estimating revealed cleavage, and smiled. "I will have to personally deliver my gratitude to the costume company," he murmured. "You'll look divine."

She scowled. "That blouse is cut a little below 'divine.'"

He grinned and pulled out the fake rapier blade. With a couple of practice moves, he brandished the elegant saber in front of her. "Don't worry, I'll protect your virtue," he declared grandly.

Reggie merely shook her head. "Great, now the one person in the room I need protection from is armed. I'm going to sew an inset into that blouse."

"And ruin all my fun? Come on, darlin', it's a costume ball. It's supposed to be interesting. Think about the advantage you'll have at the Black Jack tables. If you ever get to losing, you can just bend over real low, and I'm sure the dealer will deal you twenty-one in no time. Hmm. Maybe I should wear the blouse."

She shook her head, half-exasperated, half-curious to know how she would look in such a daring costume. Being around Jake seemed detrimental to her sanity. With a wary look on her face, she handed him his black clothes and mask.

"Change, Zorro. We've got work to do."

With one last devastating grin, Jake took his costume and laid it out on the bed. In the past week, they'd grown accustomed to sharing the room. Nights found them as eager and greedy as newlyweds, tangling among the sheets. Afterward, they slipped into sleep tucked together like spoons.

It was at once intimate and easy, and Reggie had sworn not to think about it. Perhaps Jake knew how to maintain the bounds between physical and emotional. She was rapidly learning that she could not.

Her thoughts on the present, she clutched her costume to her chest and ducked into the master bathroom to prepare.

She pulled on the ruffled underskirt, then covered it with the scarlet overskirt. The white cotton peasant blouse slid on easily, cut wide enough to easily fall over her shoulders. She tucked it in while shaking her head, then tied a black satin sash around her waist. The costume included a tall, glossy black comb and black lace veil for her hair. A large, crimson-and-black fan provided the finishing touch.

She adjusted the black lace down around her shoulders, pulling on the blouse. She bent over, revealing a clear view of her navel. Yeah, it was cut low. If she were smart, she would wear a tank top beneath it. But as she adjusted the ruffled collar once more, she knew she wouldn't.

It was a costume ball, and she really did look, well, sexy. She even added makeup, darkening her eyelids with a smoky brown, then slashing rich crimson color across her lips. When she stepped out of the bathroom, her hands were shaking.

Jake was prancing around the room in shiny black riding boots, skin-tight black pants, a scarlet sash and an open black silk shirt. His cape was tossed over one shoulder, the mask obscuring his eyes beneath the low brim of his black hat. He parried the fake blade in front of the mirror, slashing Z's in the air.

His gaze found hers, and the blade stopped midmotion. She stood there, twisting her hands and waiting.

Slowly he straightened, the blade coming down to his side as he stood at attention. With dramatic flourish, he abruptly bowed, low and formal. He didn't straighten back up, but merely lifted his head to look at her with burning eyes.

"Breathtaking," he whispered. He closed the distance between them, long, lean strides bringing his body within a hairbreadth of hers.

"Grant me a kiss, my bonny sweetheart," he pleaded eloquently. "One kiss, and my heart is surely yours."

She knew he was just being melodramatic and grand, playing a game as he liked to play games. But the breath left her anyway, her heart melting slow and sweet in her chest.

He looked dashing and handsome, better than the real Highwayman, she wagered. And this was it, their final evening. If their ruse worked and they caught the Highwayman tonight, by morning she would leave Jake, returning to live as Reggie the full-time agent once more.

All cases came to an end.

"We should go down," she whispered, her gaze falling to the floor so he could not see the sorrow in her eyes.

"We should," he agreed. Very gently, he reached out a gloved hand and caught her chin. He tilted her head up, his eyes searching her luminescent gaze. Slowly he brushed her lips with his. "What do you want, Reggie?" he whispered.

He knew what she wanted. They both knew what she wanted. But she couldn't say the words. She beseeched him with her eyes, wanting him to simply act. He merely brushed her lips once more, a featherlight caress that tormented.

"Say it," he commanded. "Just once, I want to hear you say it."

"I can't."

"Can't what, Reggie? Can't stand to admit that you want someone?"

"I don't—"

He caught her lips once more, no longer light, but suddenly bruising. His leather-sheathed hands caught her bare shoulders, his mouth slanting across hers fiercely. Immediately her arms wrapped around his neck, her mouth opening, welcoming him. He delved his tongue in deep, and she pressed against him, urgently.

Just as abruptly he jerked his head up, his brown eyes burning. "Tell me you want me, Reggie. Tell me this is exactly what you want. Or are you too afraid of the words?"

Immediately she stiffened, her green eyes growing dark. "I'm not afraid," she whispered fiercely. Her mouth opened again, but somehow the words stuck in her throat.

He smiled, suddenly sad and cynical. "You can't, can you? I've been patient and honest about my desire. But you can't admit you want anyone. Not even me."

"Damn you," she whispered. Abruptly she pulled back her hand and hit his shoulder. When he simply smiled at her, she hit him again. "I don't want to want you," she cried. "I don't."

In the next instant her arms pulled his head down and she kissed him passionately. Her hands smoothed over his chest, finding the buttons and urgently unfastening. His hands were suddenly in her hair, just as demanding.

The hair comb fell, the veil, the sash, the skirts.

"I want you," she whispered fiercely against his lips, ripping off his shirt, his cape, his hat. "I want you, I want you, I want you." She tore off his pants.

He answered by pulling her blouse over her head.

They came together quickly, naked flesh pressing against naked flesh. His hands roamed down her back, finding smooth skin and gentle curves. She rubbed her long, supple leg against his, shivering from the crinkling feel of his crisp leg hairs against her denuded calves.

She buried her hands in the thick, silky forest of his hair, kissing him deeply as he settled her hips against his. With her height, she fit against him perfectly, their bodies clicking together as if they were two pieces of a puzzle, now made whole.

He pressed her down to the floor, rasping his two-days worth of beard against her cheeks, listening to her soft sighs. Then he dipped his head, kissing the base of her throat and burning a trail to the swell of her breast. He paused for just a moment, admiring the perfect curve of her high, firm breasts. Then his tongue found a nipple and he suckled gently.

She cried out, arching against the burning pull of his mouth. Her hands pressed him closer, wanting more, needing more. He sucked hard, and she felt the desire shoot down to her belly and burst into flame. Urgently she parted her thighs and wrapped her legs around his waist.

"Please," she whispered, her hands tugging on his shoulders. He merely turned his attention to her other nipple, leaving her insane with desire. She raked her short nails down his back, then found him with her hand. She would not burn alone.

The minute her fingers wrapped around him, she felt the tremor rack his frame. He moaned against her breast, and she caressed him intimately, reveling in the length and feel of him. His body was so well made, hard and sculpted and beautiful in its masculinity.

She shifted her hips and heard his sharply in-drawn breath of anticipation. Very slowly, she drew him closer, rubbing against him intimately.

"Condom," he said grittily, his voice so thick he hardly recognized it. Heaving himself away, he strode quickly to the bedside table and removed a foil wrapper from the drawer.

Rolling on the condom with trembling hands, he returned to her side, covering her body while her eyes still looked at him with mute need.

Very slowly she reached for him, parting her legs wide and drawing him in.

He gritted his teeth with the initial penetration. Her body was moist and hot and wonderfully tight. He sunk into her like a ship coming to port, knowing he wanted her.

Her eyes darkened exquisitely, her lips parting in breathless wonder. He rotated his hips seductively, and she sighed, a soft, voluptuous sound that nearly rent his self-control. She arched against him, locking her legs behind his back, taking him deeper.

He pulled back slowly, then thrust in mightily. Her hands tightened on his shoulders, her nails digging in as the desire clawed in her belly, desperately seeking escape.

She arched her head all the way back, closing her eyes and giving herself over to the sensations. He thrust in again and again, harder and faster as she moaned her ascent. Then abruptly she bowed, the desire spiking long and hot, the world suspending and lengthening, shattering like crystal through her mind.

She cried out his name and his control snapped. He took her savagely and they climaxed together.

Afterward, he rolled her onto his chest, wanting the feel of her spent body lax against his own. The sweat ran down their cheeks and neither could speak.

Very softly he caressed her short hair with his hand. Lying on his damp chest, tasting the salt, feeling the moisture, Reggie closed her eyes and fought the urge to weep. He touched her shoulder, smoothing a hand down her back in gentle comfort, and she squeezed her eyes tighter.

If she closed her eyes long enough, maybe the moment would last. Maybe she could lie with this man forever, his callused hand stroking her neck.

She wished her moments with him had never been this good, and understood that they could never have been anything less.

"Maybe we should shower," Jake murmured at last. He sifted his fingers through the short strands of her gleaming hair, marveling at the texture, the color.

"We should," she whispered. The words were so thick, his hand stilled in her hair. Had he touched her that deeply? Did he dare dream that much? He wished he could see her eyes, but knew instinctively that the minute he moved she would bolt. He let her hair slip through his fingers once more.

One thing about his Reggie, she could probably stand up to a small army with just her gun, but a mere whispered sentiment would send her running. He often wondered what she was thinking, those moments when her eyes glistened and her body shuddered with unnamed emotions. Sometimes he worried that she never would tell him.

What did a man have to do for her anyway?

There was a discreet knock at the door.

"Coming down?" Kendall called through the thick wood.

"In a minute," Jake called back. Reggie was already rolling off his chest and reaching for cover. He tried not to wince at the loss, and tried even harder not to notice how she refused to meet his eyes.

He pushed himself up on his elbows and summoned a grin.

"Race you for the shower," he said.

"You go ahead." She was still examining the floor.

"Darlin'," he chided, "that takes all the fun out of it. Come on, I bet I can give you a two-foot head start and still win."

Her chin came up, her eyes narrowing speculatively. "We can start even," she said, already rising for the occasion. "But I get to do the counting. One, two, three, go." She was already bolting across the room while he scrambled to his feet.

"Hey," he protested, but from the bathroom he could hear the sound of her laughter.

"You're old, Jake," she called out from the tub. He stopped in the doorway, arriving in time to watch her naked form lean over and turn on the water.

He managed to smile through the tightness in his chest.

"So did you have a nice chat with Richardson?" Jake murmured in her ear three hours later. She ignored him long enough to say "Hit me," and the dealer dealt her a ten, giving her twenty-one. She smiled triumphantly.

Jake whistled with admiration. "Are you cleaning out the house?"

"Doing my part," she crowed fiercely, looking at her healthy stack of vouchers. At the door, each guest received two thousand dollars of the play money in return for their two-thousand-dollar check to the Children's Fund. The fake money could be used at the various casino tables. At the end of the night, people would sign each of their collected pink bills and enter them in a drawing for a few token prizes. Since it wasn't real money, Reggie decided it wasn't gambling and had indulged to the point of doubling her supply of pink hundred-dollar bills.

Certainly her Black Jack game was going better than her attempts to understand Richardson.

"And Emelia?" she now asked Jake under her breath.

"Emelia hasn't had an original thought since '82," he replied dryly. "I'm willing to count her out. Now tell me about Richardson."

"Total bust," she confessed. "The man is tighter than a clam."

Jake raised a mocking brow from beneath his mask. "I thought you and he were developing quite a relationship."

Reggie frowned unconsciously, absently indicating that she wanted another card while the wheels turned round in her mind. She had thought she'd made at least small headway with Richardson at Middleburg. But tonight, he'd acted as if he'd never even seen her before. She didn't like it.

"Have you seen Drake?" she muttered back. Richardson had been easy enough to identify dressed as a British nobleman. Emelia had been overwhelming as Marie Antoinette, but Drake had been conspicuously absent.

"Maybe he's coming late," Jake whispered back, his masked eyes once more perusing the crowd. It was nearly eleven and most of the guests had arrived. "Want to dance?"

She looked at him crossly, and he immediately corrected himself. "Want to check out the patio?"

She promptly agreed, gathering up her handfuls of pink money with a look of sublime satisfaction. He liked that look on her face. He wanted to take her upstairs and put lots of looks like that on her face. But he settled for leading her to the patio where he promptly swept her into his arms and out onto the dance floor. Reggie didn't seem to mind, relaxing against him.

He smiled at her, she smiled back, then promptly looked over his shoulder to check out who stood at the edges of the patio. He shook his head, chuckling at her predictability. At least he had a great view of her charms.

By midnight, however, Reggie was becoming more tense. They still needed Kendall's thumbprint, but he kept drinking champagne, the condensation on the delicate flutes ruining any possible prints. Her only consolation was that the Highwayman must be encountering the same difficulty.

A little after midnight, Richardson approached Kendall, and Reggie held her breath. Richardson poured two glasses of cognac, handing one to Kendall. Consumed at room temperature, cognac did not cause perspiration on the glass as did chilled champagne. Was Richardson trying to get a thumbprint as well? Was that why he'd chosen to offer the host cognac?

She waited surreptitiously until both men finished sipping their drinks. They set the large, crystal globes on one of the disposal trays and walked away together. Still Reggie waited, half convinced Richardson would double back after some thin excuse and grab the glass. Minute dragged into minute without anyone approaching the glass.

Finally a waiter paused to pick up the whole tray of discarded dishes. Frowning with consternation, Reggie swept forward and plucked up the glass by its stem, not offering a single excuse to the bewildered waiter.

She didn't know what was going on anymore. She hated that feeling.

She found Jake.

"I'm going back up to the room now," she whispered in his ear. "I want to change and get in position."

He nodded, automatically cupping her elbow to guide her to the stairs. She stiffened immediately. "You're not coming with me," she stated firmly.

He smiled at her, devastatingly handsome in his black silk costume. "Of course I am."

"We had this discussion already," she said pointedly, struggling to keep her voice down and her smile in place.

"And we agreed we'd both be in the library," he concluded somewhat generously.

"We agreed I'd break your bones and handcuff you to the bed," Reggie corrected tightly.

He smiled at her charmingly and held up his slender blade. "Ah, but I'm armed now. Mess with me, madame, and I'll carve a *Z* in your hair."

"Stop it! This isn't some joke!"

He arched a fine brow, his brown eyes suddenly sharp. "Exactly why I plan on accompanying you. Now shall we go together, or shall I throw you over my shoulder and create a scene for all these nice people to witness? You know I would."

Her green eyes threatened exotic forms of death, but his expression never wavered. If he tried to move against her, she would no doubt toss him on the floor, creating a scene, and right now, she didn't want to be the center of attention.

Mumbling something low and uncomplimentary under her breath, she grabbed his hand and jerked him upstairs. He tried not to gloat too much.

* * *

They had to wait two hours for the last guest to leave. Jake had fallen asleep on the bed, his ankles crossed casually. Reggie, on the other hand, had paced the room enough times to wear a small tread into the wood. When she heard the foyer light finally turn off, her stomach immediately clenched. She took a deep breath, smoothing a hand over her black turtleneck and black jeans.

She double-checked the thumbprint she'd lifted from the glass, then pulled her gun from the waistband of her jeans. Softly she opened the door.

The minute the handle turned, Jake's eyes popped open and he rose. Reggie swore inwardly, but didn't say a word. She didn't have time to fight with him anymore.

She had a job to do.

She crept out into the blackened hall, sparing a quick glance at her watch. It was 2:33 a.m. She slithered down the stairs, Jake right behind her.

On the main floor she checked out all the nooks and crannies using standard procedure. When her probing indicated the foyer was clear, she took the impression of Kendall's thumbprint out of her pocket and held it up to the scanner. The red laser whizzed across, then a green light blinked twice in silent acceptance.

She cracked the door open slowly, leading with her 9-mm. She stepped solidly into the room, making a quick sweep. Just like Hogan's Alley, she told herself. Her palms grew slick with sweat.

Nothing moved, nothing stirred. Jake crept into the room behind her. It took them both a minute to stop looking for intruders and look at the walls instead. When they did, they both uttered the same succinct word.

Two gilded frames now hung empty, giant square eyes on the wall.

Instinctively, Reggie reached for the light switch. At the same time, a shadow suddenly rose from behind the wing chair and tossed an object high in the air.

"Look out!" Reggie cried, firing on instinct. Immediately the tear gas exploded, releasing its vicious fumes into the air.

Momentarily covered by the mist, the shadowy figure leapt for the door, a gunshot suddenly blasting the silence.

Reggie dropped to one knee instinctively, turned to fire and registered the gun leveled at her chest. Simultaneously Jake dived for her, crashing them both to the floor as three quick shots sliced the air.

They landed hard, gasping for breath, then choked as the tear gas stung their eyes and throat.

"The door," Reggie croaked, struggling forward despite the horrible burning. Squeezing her eyes shut and holding her breath, she blindly crawled forward in search of the door frame with one hand.

She felt Jake's fingers wrap around her ankle, and knew he was trusting her to lead them out. She scrambled faster, her fingers finding a wall and searching for an exit.

Just as her lungs felt as if they would spontaneously combust in her chest, her fingers touched the sweet emptiness of the doorway. She struggled forward, tumbling them both into the hallway where they flattened to the floor and gasped like hooked fish.

In the distance, Reggie heard the sound of a car engine starting. She raised her head, hardly able to see through the tears in her eyes. She had to get outside.

Still choking and gasping, she heaved herself up and surged ahead on legs that wobbled like a newborn colt's. She clutched the front doorframe for support, emerging on the front yard in time to see a car whiz by her, cutting through the crisp night air.

Momentarily, her eyes cleared, pinpointing the speeding sedan with its D.C. license plate. Her eyes widened at the sight, and with a small thud she fell to her knees on the grass.

It couldn't be, it just couldn't be.

"Reggie?" It was Jake stumbling onto the lawn beside her. "Reggie, are you all right?"

Dumbly she nodded, her tear-filled eyes finding his in the moonlight.

"That was a Bucar, Jake," she whispered fiercely. "That was a damn Bucar, or I'm a flat-footed rookie!"

He looked at her, clearly not understanding. Then comprehension hit him, and his eyes rounded in the darkness. "Maybe it was just a surveillance vehicle peeling off in pursuit of the real car," he suggested.

She shook her head. "No siren." She shook her head again, staring out into the night and trying to understand. Where the hell *were* the surveillance people, for that matter? What had just happened?

She suddenly felt very, very scared.

She took a deep breath, letting the cool night air clean out her lungs and clear her burning eyes. She was the FBI agent in charge. She needed her composure. She would show calm, cool capability.

"We should go back and check out the room," she said levelly.

Behind her, Jake nodded, still on all fours as he struggled to clear his own lungs. "The tear gas?" he rasped.

"Only one canister, and in an open area. Most of it has probably disseminated up the foyer by now. If your eyes start to burn, lower your head to the floor. You'll be all right."

He nodded, and wordlessly followed her back into the house. But now, lights blazed and Kendall stood shocked and dazed in the middle of the foyer. He took one look at Reggie and Jake, dressed all in black, and he paled. Reggie did the only thing she could think of: She held her 9-mm to the side in a neutral position and introduced herself.

"It's all right, Mr. Kendall," she said calmly. "I'm FBI Special Agent Regina O'Doul. I came here to guard the house against a suspected break-in by the Highwayman. I'm afraid I was a little too late."

Kendall nodded, but his eyes were still round with the shock. Slowly he looked at Jake.

Jake shrugged, his lips twisting wryly. "She's the brains," he quipped, "I'm just the beauty."

Reggie scowled at him, then turned her attention back to Kendall. "If you'll come with me, sir, I'd like to assess the damages. Other agents should be arriving momentarily, and you can be sure we will do everything in our power to locate your missing items."

Kendall nodded, taking a deep breath. Straightening his shoulders, he seemed to regain his composure and turned at last to his guests who were slowly gathering at the second floor railing. He asked them to please go back to bed, then he followed Jake and Reggie into the library.

Both of the John Waterhouse paintings were gone. Plus, the bullets had destroyed five first edition texts and scorched the priceless tapestry rug.

While dialing Buchanan on the phone, Reggie examined the single red rose that had been left on the mantel. Beside it rested the edition of *Catch-22* that Jake had been reading. She flipped open the cover and found a dramatically scrawled verse: "Seeketh me in ice, findeth me in fire. If you want to catch me, you will have to look much higher."

Reggie gritted her teeth. To add insult to injury, the man was a bad poet.

Reggie was still fuming when Buchanan's sleepy voice finally came on the line.

"What happened to my backup?" she demanded immediately.

"Reggie? Where are you?"

"The Kendall estate, of course. Where the Highwayman just swiped two Waterhouse paintings from beneath my nose, and my backup is nowhere to be found. What the hell happened?" Her voice was so low, so angry she barely recognized it.

After five minutes of terse discussion, they determined that there had been a mix-up in the address. And at that very moment, the three cars pulled up, having heard reports of gunfire on the radio.

The wrong address? Reggie had never heard of anything so stupid, which she proceeded to tell Buchanan in no uncertain terms. Not until she hung up, did she realize she'd forgotten to mention that the Highwayman drove off in a Bucar. She picked up the phone again, then slowly returned the receiver to its cradle. Instinct told her to keep the information to herself until she understood more. The Bucar suggested that the Highwayman was an agent. But why would a corrupt agent drive off in an agency car? It smacked of blatant stupidity, and the Highwayman was never stupid.

She felt chills again.

She put the late-arriving agents to work dusting for prints, picking up the remains of the tear gas canister and analyzing the tire tracks of the car that had sped away.

At 4:00 a.m., Kendall retired upstairs for much-needed sleep. With most of the preliminary investigation done, the other agents also began packing up.

Jake found Reggie in the middle of the foyer. Lightly he touched her shoulder. She jumped immediately, wound tighter than he'd ever seen her.

"You should get some rest, too," he said quietly.

She wearily shook her head.

"You'll think better," he continued levelly. "And you can be sure the Highwayman is curled up somewhere right now getting his *Z*'s. Soon, he'll be refreshed and ready for another round. You'll want to be prepared." He took her hand, and when her shoulders suddenly slumped forward, he guided her upstairs.

"Just a couple of hours," he assured her as he took off her shoes and tucked her into bed fully clothed. He took off his own shoes, then crawled in with her.

He curled her up in his arms, resting his cheek against the top of her head.

"Sleep, darlin'," he ordered.

She did, falling asleep to the steady rhythm of his heartbeat in her ear.

Chapter 11

Three hours later, Reggie woke up as Jake crawled out of bed. She waited until he disappeared into the bathroom, then she sat up. The faint sound of running water filled the silence.

They both needed to pack and get on their way. Certainly they'd overstayed their welcome at Kendall's house. And then what? she asked herself.

She took her clothes out of the closet, laying them on the bed, and knew she already possessed the answer: Jake had done his part, and was no longer a suspect. He would return to his civilian life, and she would continue to track down the real Highwayman.

Hopefully lab tests on the gathered evidence would be available by early afternoon.

As always, they was plenty to be done.

She found herself folding her clothes slowly, however. Her hands were trembling. Her stomach felt achy and empty. She hadn't felt this way since the day she'd kissed Brian on the cheek, wished him the best and driven away forever.

Her eyes burned. She hated that. O'Douls didn't cry.

Right, Dad? *Right, Dad?*

She found herself sitting on the edge of the bed, her hands shaking uncontrollably. She forced herself to take two deep gulps of air. Focus, Reggie, focus. All you ever wanted to be was an agent, right? You're living your dream, right? Don't lose sight of it now. Don't get soft now.

O'Douls were tough.

She stood back up and finished packing.

Moving in short, choppy motions, she picked up the phone and dialed the office while zipping up her bag. The secretary didn't usually get in until eight, but she could check her electronic messages. The recording told her she had three new messages. Two were questions about last night's episode. The third, however, made her tighten her grip on the phone and brought her to complete attention.

It was a man's voice, raspy and unrecognizable. The words, however, were stated with a mocking slowness. "Regina O'Doul, the cop's little girl. Have you forgiven him yet, Reggie? Your father would be so proud...."

The electronic beep sounded, ending the message and leaving her breathless and clammy. Moving on autopilot, she saved the message so the voice could be analyzed. Then very slowly she placed the phone on the hook.

"Your father would be so proud...."

The fear was back, tight and suffocating. For a panicked moment, she couldn't breathe from the sense of violation. Who would have left such a message? What did they mean?

All of a sudden, the last piece of the puzzle clicked into place, and finally she understood. She understood why the Highwayman had driven off in a Bucar, why her backup wasn't available and why the Highwayman always seemed one step ahead. Worse, she understood why the rookie agent from the administrative side of the Bureau had been allowed to take a lead role in a major case.

Hands still trembling, she retrieved her wallet and dialed the 800 number for her bank. Using the automated system, she selected account balance information from the main menu and punched in her account number. "Sixty-five thousand, four hundred thirty-four dollars and twenty-six cents," the automated voice told her pleasantly. "Please press star to return to main menu."

Reggie hung up, placed her head between her knees and concentrated on breathing.

Jake had been right all along—the Highwayman wanted to retire and was looking for a patsy. But Reggie—persistent, eager Reggie—had identified the photos as fakes, contacted Mrs. Ivansson on her own and had been present last night when the *real* Highwayman had tried to kill both her and Jake.

In short, she'd cleared Jake's name.

Unless her own credibility was questioned.

Reggie, the rookie field agent in over her head. Reggie, the female agent seduced by womanizing Jake. Reggie, the corrupt cop's daughter who had an extra fifty thousand dollars in her bank account.

God, she'd been set up as well. The victim of a tidy back-up plan in case the investigation got too close to the real thief.

And who knew everything—her father's record, Jake's background, their schedule, their plan to ambush the Highwayman at the Kendall estate?

Buchanan. Good old Buchanan. The real mastermind behind the thefts.

God, she'd been so naive.

Her green eyes hardened and her spine stiffened. If Buchanan thought she would simply roll over and play dead, he had another thing coming. She knew what the hell was going on now. She was not going down as the corrupt agent who'd been bribed by the Highwayman.

If she confronted Buchanan...? No, he had the upper hand; she was the one in the vulnerable situation.

She would have to catch the real Highwayman and get him to admit everything. But who was the thief? Buchanan had been home when she'd called right after the break-in of the Kendall estate. She still thought he was the only one with access to all the information, which made him the mastermind. So who was doing the real dirty work? Another FBI agent? What about a technical services guy, a professional break-in man?

Suddenly all sorts of possibilities entered her mind.

The door clicked open, and Jake reentered the room, drying his hair with a hand towel while a bath towel adorned his hips. His gaze fell immediately to her packed bag.

"I see you're not wasting any time," he remarked dryly. Then he glanced at her pale face and frowned. "What's wrong?"

"Nothing," she lied immediately, offering him a faint smile. "I'm just tired, that's all."

He nodded, but his sharp brown eyes fell to the phone, her open wallet and the bank card she still held in her hand.

"All right," he said sharply, sitting down on the edge of the bed and pinning her with a hard look, "start talking."

She tried to stand, but he promptly grabbed her wrist. Her eyes narrowed dangerously, her gaze falling to his fingers.

"Let go of my hand," she ordered coldly.

"No," he replied levelly. "Not until you tell me what's going on."

"Your role is over, Jake. Thanks for all your help. You can go back to your business now. Got it?"

"Didn't we have this conversation yesterday?"

"Sometimes, it takes a few tries to get through your thick skull, Guiness."

"Well then you're going to have to keep repeating it, because it's still not sinking in."

Her jaw tightened and abruptly she pivoted sideways, delivering a sharp chopping blow to his forearm, yanking her hand free.

"I warned you," she said in a low voice.

He shook his head, rubbing his forearm while something dark and dangerous shifted in his eyes. "Well, that'll teach me to keep trying to help you, won't it, Reggie?"

"I don't need you," she stated stubbornly, her chin lifting defiantly.

"Yeah, that's right, Reggie. You don't need anyone. Of course, I thought we had that conversation last night as well. Or do you need me to show you once more just how much you do need me?"

Instantly she took a wary step back, then berated herself for the movement. "Jake, you're making this much too personal. I'm an agent. It's my job to go after the Highwayman, and that's what I'm going to do now. Your involvement has ended. After last night, it's clear that you're not the Highwayman. You've been more than cooperative, and I apologize for all the inconvenience. You can now return to your everyday life—"

"Clear to whom, Reggie?" he asked softly from the bed.

Her gaze fell, giving him her answer.

"How much money was in your account, Reggie? Ten thousand more? Twenty thousand? A hundred thousand?"

She paled, her green eyes becoming luminous. "How did you know?"

Jake swore softly and ran a hand through his wet hair. "I didn't," he admitted, "though the possibility had occurred to me once I learned about your father."

She blanched even whiter, and he immediately reached for her. She stepped back too quickly, his fingers capturing only empty air. "I know you didn't do it," he said forcefully, his brown eyes level. "Even when I learned about your father, Reggie, I never doubted you. I only got to thinking about it because of the Thompson case from fifteen years back. You know, when the FBI's best break-in man turned thief."

"What about Thompson?" she asked warily.

"Think about it, Reggie. The FBI's best break-in man gets caught breaking into the FBI's Credit Union safe. They discover he's stolen all sorts of stuff, gems, artwork, cash. That *was* what they'd trained him to do. He simply used those skills to enhance his personal life as well. Now think of your profile, Reggie. You said it would be someone close to law enforcement, someone who follows it. Why not another agent, Reggie? Surely the Highwayman is the best of the best. Now where do you suppose he learned so much?''

She nodded numbly at his words, wondering how he could lay it out so logically when it had taken her until five minutes before to put the pieces together. She'd been so arrogant from the very start to think she could catch the thief. All along, that arrogance had been played against her.

She walked to her bag, resting at the foot of the bed, and zipped it shut. She sat down hard, her lips twisting in frustration. ''So here we are,'' she said softly. ''The one and only Highwayman and his corrupt accomplice.'' She ran her hand through her hair. ''How is it we started the week as Nancy Drew and Frank Hardy, and ended as Bonnie and Clyde?''

''What do you think will happen next?''

She was silent for a moment. ''I believe they'll try to arrest us first chance they get. We're too big a liability to be running around loose.''

''And what will happen if they arrest us?'' Jake asked quietly, slipping on his boxers.

Reggie took a deep breath and ran a hand through her short-cropped hair. ''We'll say we're innocent, and they'll ask us to take a polygraph. We can then point a finger at Buchanan and whoever we think might be the thief. Most likely, they'll agree to take a polygraph test, too. But even if we pass and they fail, polygraph results aren't enough to prove a case. The case agents will then look for physical and circumstantial evidence, of which we have plenty and Buchanan and company has none.''

''Then we have to find solid proof of Buchanan's involvement,'' Jake said. He tossed his clothes into the garment bag, zipping it closed. ''You must have some idea who in the Bureau would make a good thief.''

''Yeah,'' she admitted, ''I was actually considering the possibilities right before you entered the room.'' She hesitated, then looked up at him with serious eyes. ''Maybe you should find someplace to hole up for a bit, until this is over.''

"I'm coming with you."

"Jake, you're not trained in these matters. I am."

"You need me, Reggie."

Her chin came up, and he could already see defiant words forming on her lips. For one moment, he felt a surge of frustration bolt through him. Why was it so hard for her to admit to such a simple, basic thing? When would she really trust him?

But now was not the time to push it. He gave her a careless shrug and a small, knowing wink. "I have the computer," he announced shrewdly.

Her eyes opened wide, a reluctant smile stealing across her lips. He could have sworn he saw relief in her eyes.

"Do you have a modem?"

"Of course."

Her lips curved beautifully. "Then we can log into the Bureau's database using remote access. I know the passwords. If we can just find an out-of-the-way hotel with phone lines, we should be able to access all the information we need."

"Sounds simple enough."

"Yeah, it does."

"Shall we sneak down to my Porsche and make a run for it?"

Her smiled broadened grimly, her green eyes abruptly blazing. "Let's," she said fiercely.

God, he loved her spirit. Jake picked up his bag. "Ready, dear Bonnie?"

"After you, Clyde."

They snuck out of the room and down the stairs. Reggie spotted two surveillance vehicles parked on the street, each pointed in a different direction. She motioned to Jake that they should walk out to the car casually.

He'd just raised the hood and placed their bags inside when the first car door opened and an agent got out.

"Start the car," Reggie whispered to Jake. Out of the corner of her eye, she saw the door of the second car open. The first agent raised a hand to catch her attention. As the wind caught his jacket, she could see the 9-mm strapped in its shoulder harness. Both agents began their approach, their faces sober and serious.

Yeah, Buchanan, you figured they could arrest me before I had any clue what was going on.

She smiled at both men, waved and watched them relax their steps.

"Now," she yelled and leapt for the passenger side door.

Jake gunned the sports car backward, catching both agents off guard. Reggie heard their startled shouts, and saw the first man reach for his gun. She was just reaching for hers when Jake threw the car into a quick one-eighty and floored it toward the nearest agent. Agent number one jumped for safety as agent number two began firing.

A taillight shattered, as they rocketed out of reach. "Where do we go?" Jake asked grimly, swerving them around a sharp corner. River Road cut through a residential area making it poor getaway material.

Reggie directed him onto the first major road, then through a dizzying array of side streets. After fifteen minutes without any dark sedans pulling in behind them, she allowed herself to sink back against the seat.

"It's begun," she said softly.

Jake just looked over at her and grinned.

They ditched the Porsche by parking it in a seedy side street with the keys still in the ignition. Jake gave his car one last caress, his brown eyes forlorn.

"A loyal steed," he declared.

Reggie patted his arm in comfort. "I'm sure whoever steals it will say the same. Hopefully they'll drive it far in the opposite direction before being picked up by the cops."

Jake nodded, but continued to glance back at his toy as she led him away. Reggie flagged down a cab, and they took it to the train station, paying cash. Next they took the train to New Haven, not that far away, but hopefully far enough.

"I don't suppose you ever saw your life coming to this?" Reggie asked as they finally checked into a roadside motel as Mr. and Mrs. Barrow, paying cash.

Jake looked around the tiny room, noting brown carpet, crimson bedspread, and orange curtains. He shook his head. "Mitch warned me, though," he confessed. "The day he found out I'd convinced Liz and Cage to trade me their nickels for pennies, he told me such behavior would lead to no good."

"You got your brother and sister to give you their nickels for pennies?"

He shrugged. "It wasn't too hard really. All coins are silver but pennies. I told them it was because copper was rare and precious. Could I help it if they then wanted to trade?"

"You're a devious man, Jake," she told him, but she was smiling.

Abruptly he brushed his thumb down her cheek. "I like it when you smile," he said softly. "You have beautiful lips."

She simply looked at him, suddenly feeling breathless and needy. Her gaze fell to the lone king-size bed and her stomach tightened.

"We should...we should access the database," she murmured, looking at the floor. If he so much as brushed her shoulder, she would throw herself into his arms.

Jake nodded, his warm gaze caressing her skin. He liked the way her pulse pounded faintly at the base of her throat. He wanted to brush that spot with his mouth, to feel her butterfly pulse against his lips.

"What do you want to know?" he asked huskily.

She swallowed. "Names of agents who work for the Technical Services Division. Any recent cases they've worked on with Buchanan. Anyone who may have recently left the Bureau. We should be able to pare down a list through process of elimination."

"Sounds like a good plan," Jake said. The computer still dangled from his hands.

"We should turn the computer on," she suggested.

"We should," he concurred. Slowly he set down the case, then reached for her.

"Is this really such a good idea?" she asked, her green eyes pleading.

"We'll live dangerously," he whispered, already tipping his head.

"They could find us at anytime!"

He stopped, looking up to find her gaze with his steady brown eyes. "It's okay, Reggie. We paid cash. There's nothing to lead them here. Besides, we're in this together now. And I'm still standing guard."

Her control snapped, her eyes overflowing with the tears O'Douls never shed. She reached for him desperately, her trembling lips finding his with urgent need. He crushed her close, absorbing her tremors, soaking up her tears.

He kissed her passionately, hungrily, sweetly. He gave to her completely, showing her with his lips, his hands, just what she meant to him. She sagged against him, and he lifted her into his arms, carrying her to the bed where he removed her clothes with hands that had removed dozens of women's shirts but only now had learned how to tremble.

He bent low, kissing her throat while her hands tangled in his hair. He unbuttoned his own shirt, wanting the feel of her bare skin against his. No barriers, no words. Just the honesty of touch, taste and feel.

He pulled off her clothes and joined her on the bed. She pulled him, her hips already arching with the force of her need. But he merely stroked her skin, marveling at the softness.

Her body was long and supple, curved and toned from jogging and weights. When she clutched his arm, her fingers were strong and demanding. He respected her strength, he loved her intelligence, he understood her drive.

He combed his hand through her curly nest of hair and listened to her sigh. He knew a lot about laughter, a lot about easy warmth, great friendships and warm sharing. But it had taken him until this moment to understand love and the perfect beauty of the one person you were meant to be with forever.

He suddenly didn't know where to begin.

He kissed her again, feeling his stomach tighten with the emotions. She tasted like tears, but her arms around his neck were certain. He covered her body, suckling her breasts, listening to her sighs.

He parted her legs, and she whispered his name as if it were a prayer.

His brown eyes dark and open, he met her luminous gaze and eased into her.

Her green eyes darkened, forests of need with black, aching fire. He lost himself in those depths, feeling his body tense as he thrust deeply. His neck corded, his hands clenched on the bed. Still she looked at him, her eyes guileless and needy.

She wrapped her lean legs around his waist, arched her hips and drew him deeper than he'd ever been. When he thought he could stand no more, she rotated her hips sinuously, and the passion ripped through his gut like a knife.

He arched his neck, clenched his teeth and felt the climax tear through his body. Beneath him, Reggie cried out, and in her voice he found ecstasy.

He collapsed on top of her, sweaty and barely able to remember his own name. He could only hold her close and bury his face against her sweet neck.

When he finally rolled to the side, she was still trembling in his arms. He cradled her close, gently stroking her back.

It took minutes for either of them to speak.

"Tired?" he asked.

She shook her head against his shoulder.

"Hungry?"

She considered this question a bit longer. "Not really."

"I'm always hungry after making love," he confessed. "I love cookies."

He could feel her cheek curving against his arm as she smiled. "If you had a chocolate sundae in front of you right now," he continued, "surely you wouldn't say no."

She smiled even broader. "I suppose not. But then, all we have is a computer."

"Actually, my dear, we have room service." He tilted up her face, looking at her with sparkling eyes. "What do you say? Two huge banana splits with all the toppings?"

"It's only ten-thirty," she protested.

"Better," he assured her. "Everything tastes best when you're not supposed to be eating it."

She couldn't find fault with that statement. "I suppose we could eat and work."

He brushed his hand down her cheek and smiled so warmly she felt her insides melt. What she would give to hold on to this moment forever.

Abruptly her eyes clouded over, reality settling in. He wasn't really hers. He was Jake Guiness, a man who honestly enjoyed women and life and jokes. He probably meant whatever he said when she was in his arms, and he probably would say those things just as easily to the next woman who would lie there.

"Hey," he whispered softly. "Why so glum? Thinking of the 'bribe' again?"

Deciding that subject was comparatively safer, she nodded.

"It must have been hard having your father arrested like that," he said at last, his gaze serious.

She laughed against his chest, but it wasn't a pleasant sound. "You have no idea."

"Did he really do it, Reggie?"

"Yes."

"Did you ever understand?"

"No."

He stroked her back some more, unconsciously holding her closer. "A father is a father," he said at last.

"I know," she told him. "And I loved him, Jake, even when he pleaded guilty, I loved him. It took me a long time to understand that I couldn't give him whatever he wanted in life. He was such a proud man, such a hungry man. He needed the most beautiful wife, the most successful son, the most money. Whatever he had was never enough.''

She turned in his arms, suddenly restless.

''Are you still trying to make him proud, Reggie?'' Jake asked softly.

She smiled, bitter and resigned. ''Of course. My mother died trying to make him proud, Jake. I just hope I manage a little better than that.''

Instantly his hand stilled. ''I don't understand.''

She turned, looking up until she met his gaze with hard green eyes. ''When my mother died, I was too young to understand. But when I was older, I overhead my aunts talking. About how difficult it was for her to get pregnant with me. About the three miscarriages afterward. The doctors wanted her to stop trying to have children, but Frank wanted a son. Frank had to have a son. So she got pregnant again, miscarried at five months and hemorrhaged to death. In the end, all Frank got was me.''

''Oh God,'' he whispered, his eyes shocked.

She simply waved away his expression. ''It's old news, Jake. I learned about it when I was twelve, and I really hated my father for a bit. We went through our screaming matches. I stopped going to church to punish him. He stopped talking to me in retaliation. But then I started playing basketball, and we had something neutral to talk about. We got along by the time I went to college. We just never mentioned Mom.''

''You miss him, don't you?''

She smiled, and suddenly the bitterness was gone. ''All the time. I can still see him cheering in the front row at graduation. Still see him screaming for the Celtics in the Garden. God, do I miss him. I really wish he could have been happy. Just once, I wish he could have been happy with me.''

He pulled her against him, pressing his cheek against her hair and rocking her naked body against his.

Eventually she squirmed in his grasp, and he reluctantly let her go. He expected to see more tears in her eyes, but instead she was remarkably composed.

"We should start working," she said, her expression serious.

"Yeah," he said. "Yeah."

"I'll order the sundaes," she offered.

"Ah, the pure decadence." He grinned at her and suddenly, out of the blue, she reached over and squeezed his hand.

She still didn't say anything, but he squeezed her hand back with understanding. Slowly she untangled her fingers.

"Chocolate," she said.

"Chocolate," he agreed, and smiled softly as she picked up the phone.

Chapter 12

Hours later, Reggie sat in the middle of the bed, scrolling through a list of agent names on the laptop computer. She wore Jake's shirt, the green jersey bunched at the top of her thighs. An empty sundae dish sat forgotten on the bedside table. From time to time she frowned and jotted down a name on a piece of paper.

Behind her, Jake paced the room wearing his jeans, top button still undone. He was reciting the verse the Highwayman had left at the crime scene, as if it would somehow unlock the keys of the universe.

"Why the verse?" he asked abruptly, stopping on the brown carpet to run a hand through his hair.

Reggie glanced up, blinking twice as her eyes adjusted. "Ego," she said at last. "Dramatic flair. The verses add to his romantic mystique, while emphasizing that he is so good, he even has time to write poetry at the scene of his crimes."

Jake shook his head. "But you can't honestly believe he's leaving just random prose. That makes no sense."

Reggie sighed. "I know. We analyzed the lines from the past break-ins. They really don't seem to mean much. We even ran them through decoding programs. Nothing."

"I don't think it's code," Jake agreed. "I think he's dropping little clues to make the game more interesting."

"How so?"

"Think about the message he left at Kendall's, Reggie. 'If you want to catch me, you will have to look much higher.' Think about Buchanan. He's your superior, higher up in the Bureau."

"That's stretching it," she said skeptically. "For that matter, he could've meant he was escaping by helicopter."

"No, he escaped in a Bucar, one more hint. Boy, the guy has an ego."

"And the pot calls the kettle black," she murmured.

"Hey! At least I'm using my *healthy* and *natural* level of self-confidence to simply take over the world market. That's a bit more respectable than murder and mayhem."

"He's a thief, not a murderer," she corrected absently, still scrolling down the screen. Jake remained silent, and after a moment she glanced up.

He simply looked at her, his brown eyes hard and sober.

"No," she protested immediately. "Buchanan was my mentor. He . . . he even warned me about staking out the library."

"And the thief came armed with tear gas to disorient us and a gun to shoot," Jake replied evenly. "What would have happened if we'd been shot in the library, Reggie? We're both dressed in black. You have fifty thousand dollars in your checking account, and I'm the prime suspect. Twenty-to-one, the real thief rips off his mask, produces his FBI credentials, and says he was sent as backup and caught us stealing the paintings. Dead men can't claim innocence, Reggie. Dead men can't pass polygraph tests and put a wrinkle into things. Dead men can't even say they saw the thief drive away in a Bucar, Reggie. Can't you see how perfect it is?

''We die as criminals. Buchanan and his associate get away with millions of dollars of artwork, scot-free. The unrecovered paintings will appear on 'Unsolved Mysteries,' and life will go on. You gotta admit, it's a great plan.''

She could only stare at him, her breath labored and tight in her throat. She'd thought she'd been angry this morning when she'd realized the depths of Buchanan's betrayal, but that didn't begin to compare with the horror she felt now. He'd been her mentor, her advisor.

And he'd devised a plot to frame and murder her!

She suddenly wanted to laugh. Why should she be surprised? After all, Buchanan had been like a father to her.

Her head bowed, the bitterness tasting harsh and rusty in her mouth. No one could play the fool the way she could play the fool. She felt the bed sag as Jake climbed onto the mattress.

''Come here,'' he whispered and drew her into his arms. He rested her head against his bare shoulder, stroking her hair. ''It's okay, Reggie,'' he told her. ''Buchanan made his mistake when he threw us together. We make a great team, you and I. We're going to find that artwork and blow this thing sky-high.''

She trembled in his arms, closing her eyes as the emotions warred within her. She wanted to push him away, to block him out. How could she trust him, when the person she'd most trusted had been a criminal? How could she turn away, when he represented the only true strength she'd ever known?

Leaning against his shoulder, his strong arms around her, it was easiest to believe in his words. And the need, the pure need to believe in him terrified her.

She straightened, struggling with the doubts that preyed on her like an army of red ants. She needed air. She needed to escape. She needed time to think, free of this man's mesmerizing presence.

''I'm going to scope out the area,'' she whispered abruptly.

''Reggie—''

"Please. It's my job, Jake. We need to find out how close we are to a bank, train station, electronics store—anything that would be useful." She stood, already pulling on her jeans and automatically tucking her 9-mm in the back. "I just want to do the preliminary scope. I'll be back in no time."

"I'll go with you," he said abruptly.

She immediately shook her head.

"Reggie—"

She held up a final, silencing hand. "I'm just scoping the area," she insisted stubbornly. "I'll be back in fifteen minutes."

He nodded, though he understood completely that she was running from him once more. The minute he thought he was getting somewhere with her, she had a tendency to push him back. It was like an elaborate dance—one step forward, two steps back. He was tired of dancing.

"Fine," he said curtly, realizing the more he pushed, the deeper she would dig in her heels. "I'll hold down the fort."

She nodded, buttoning up her canvas jacket and locating her shoes. She didn't look at him, just tied her sneakers and left.

The minute the door closed behind her, Jake lay back on the bed and cursed vehemently.

She walked for twenty minutes, casing a wide perimeter and absently noting a strip mall with a bank and department store, while her thoughts whirled a mile a minute.

She was tired of trying to prove herself, of wanting to make her father proud, of wanting to fulfill Buchanan's expectations. She'd spent so much of her life trying to please other people, and what had she gotten from it? She'd turned into a person as hungry and driven as her father, always wanting, wanting, wanting.

She envied Jake's easy grin and casual demeanor. She envied how everything seemed entertaining for him, how he saw all things as adventures waiting to happen, games waiting to be played. She never thought of the process, only whether she could win or not. O'Douls weren't supposed to lose.

She shook her head, disgusted with her father for being so unrelenting, angry at her mother for getting pregnant against the doctor's orders and furious with herself for having both their weaknesses. Children should learn from their parents' mistakes, not perpetuate them.

She pivoted sharply and walked around another corner. She wanted Jake. She wanted to believe he was warm and easy and flirtatious, and the one person in all the world she could trust. Surely she couldn't be wrong about everyone.

Surely Jake was real.

He'd held her so close, stroked her hair so softly. He was patient with her, tolerant of her temper, respectful of her intelligence. He seemed to genuinely like her just the way she was. No one else had ever offered her that great a gift.

She started back to the hotel. She wanted to curl up in Jake's arms. If she held him close enough, maybe he could teach her how to grin like him. If she held him long enough, maybe he would help her understand happiness.

Walking back up to the second level of the strip motel, she was surprised to see the door of their room open. And then the first ripple of unease shuddered up her spine. Her footsteps slowed. She pulled out her gun and removed the safety.

She peered cautiously into the room.

The computer lay smashed to bits on the floor, and the TV was cracked. Their bags had been ripped to shreds, and the bedside table had been toppled. The analytical, FBI side of her mind registered that there had been a struggle. She walked through the debris, gun poised. Three people she suspected, one having put up a good fight.

Jake...

She kept looking, already knowing what she would find. This time, it was scrawled on the bathroom mirror with her own crimson lipstick.

"The Lord giveth, the Lord taketh away."

She gasped in outrage at the cold arrogant mockery. Her grip on her gun tightened enough to whiten her knuckles. That bastard.

The meaning was all too clear. The Highwayman had gotten Jake involved by faking the photographs, "giving" him to Reggie. And now...now the Highwayman and Buchanan would finish what they'd hoped to do last night at the Kendall estate—kill Jake and leave him to be found guilty postmortem.

She squeezed her eyes shut, took two deep breaths and straightened her shoulders.

She needed to get out of the room, she instructed herself. There was no telling when they would come back. Someone was probably watching the place right now. Move, Reggie, move!

She would find a safe place to think. They hadn't killed Jake yet, she was sure of that. They'd taken him somewhere. But why had they taken him? And where had they taken him?

His Newport home, she thought abruptly.

Gripping her gun tight, she began to run.

The first lookout spotted her as she crossed the motel parking lot. She felt eyes upon her, then heard the rumbling purr of a car engine. She didn't bother to look, and she didn't try to play cool.

She bolted and ran like hell.

Behind her, thin shouts cut through the air. "Halt. FBI. Stop or I'll shoot."

She kept running, tearing around a corner, understanding that she was now fully committed. And she'd never been more aware that FBI agents were authorized to shoot to kill.

She raced across a side street, spotted the thin alley that led to the strip mall and sprinted toward it. Her legs ate up the distance as if they were fear-propelled rockets, but she could hear the car creeping up behind her.

She knew she couldn't outrun a car. They would drive her down in a matter of minutes. Or worse, corner her and open fire.

Her only hope was making it to the mall.

Bursting out of the alley, she spotted the small strip mall across from the four-lane street and ran.

Cars honked and squealed as she ruthlessly dodged four lanes of traffic. Behind her, she heard a long pealing wail of a horn, then the high-pitched crunch of metal. Please don't let anyone be hurt, she thought. Please let everyone be all right.

She raced across the parking lot and bolted through the automatic doors. Coming to a grinding halt, she quickly looked at her store selection, realizing she was in a low-priced department store. She wove in and out of the aisles until she was tucked back in housewares, the department farthest from the door.

Safe for the moment, she collapsed against a display of sofa cushions and caught her breath. A woman walked by with a shopping cart, looked at Reggie curiously, then hurried on.

Think, damn it, think, she chided herself. And for the first time, she didn't picture her father yelling at her, or some college basketball game she didn't win. She didn't even think of the FBI Academy's Hogan's Alley. She just thought of Jake and how much he needed her.

She would not fail him.

In the discount store she purchased a Celtic's cap, a bulky coat and dark sunglasses. Using her FBI badge as leverage, she got the bank in the strip mall to okay a six-thousand-dollar deduction from her savings account. She took grim satisfaction in not touching a penny of the bribe money.

She snuck out of the mall and flagged down a cab. For a thousand dollars cash, the cabby agreed to take her to Newport. He even agreed to radio home base that he'd picked up a lone woman at the mall and was taking her to

the New Haven train station. That would give her followers
something to consider.

On the road again, temporarily free from pursuit, she
pulled the cap down low and closed her hand over the reassuring shape of her gun.

She could do this, she told herself. This was what she'd
been trained for. Fidelity, bravery, integrity.

And Jake.

She rested in the back of the cab, preparing for the moments to come.

She directed the cabdriver to pull over four blocks from
Jake's Newport home. She paid the driver his cash, receiving his assurance that he'd tell no one. Then he was gone,
leaving her alone in the growing gloom.

She pulled the bulky blue jacket tighter around her,
yanked her green Celtics cap lower and shivered in the falling light. She'd gambled that they'd brought him here based
on the fact Buchanan had left the Newport home information out of Jake's file. There had to be a reason for the
omission, and the only one Reggie could think of was that
Buchanan had wanted to keep the investigating agents away
from the house.

She was willing to bet that the real Highwayman was
storing the stolen artwork here. After all, Jake had been out
of the country. Should anything be discovered, Jake would
have just looked guilty, and Buchanan and the real Highwayman would have been safe.

With her and Jake running around like loose cannons,
they'd probably had to adjust their plans. Shooting Jake in
a hotel room would arouse suspicion, and given who Jake's
oldest brother was, that wouldn't have been a good idea. On
the other hand, shooting Jake in possession of a stolen
painting in his own home would build a much stronger case.
They could say they surprised the Highwayman with his
booty, shooting him in self-defense. Sacrificing one mas-
terpiece would be a small price for escaping with the rest,
which they could simply say they never found.

Neat and tidy. Especially once they killed her as a fugitive from the law.

Reggie fought the urge to laugh hysterically and walked along the winding road toward Jake's house. It was a beach home off scenic Ridge Road, isolated from the main stretch of mansions and overlooking Narragansett Bay. At this location the houses were farther apart, some huge and modern, some cute and rustic. Between them all, the sand rose in gentle dunes, beach grass straggling up and flattening from the wind.

She could taste the salt on her tongue and huddled in her jacket for warmth as a biting breeze swept across the road. This time of year, the majority of the houses were boarded up for winter, giving the beach a lonely, desolate feel, punctuated by the wailing cries of circling sea gulls.

Out here, she didn't think anyone would hear a gunshot.

She pulled her cap lower and began to lightly jog toward the house. Please don't let her be too late. Please, please, don't let her be too late. Just this once, she needed everything to go perfectly. She swore never to care whether she won or lost again, if only she could win this time.

If only she could keep Jake.

She crouched low against the sand as she spotted the parked car in the driveway. The Lincoln sedan had black tinted windows, obscuring her view. She crept around it slowly, memorizing the license plate for future reference. Squatting behind it, she checked out the house.

Knowing Jake, he had a security system of some kind. Would it be dismantled already, or would she have to break into the house to break him back out? She found herself giggling at the thought and had to bat down hysteria.

The security system had to be turned off, she told herself forcefully. They'd probably had Jake shut it off when they arrived.

She crept forward to the darkened cabin, which was two stories high, a simple V-frame construction. The front, facing the beach, was a virtual wall of windows and sported a nice deck. She would bet the living room was vaulted, perhaps with an attached dining room. Maybe there was a small study on the lower floor as well, then a couple of bedrooms upstairs. The house wasn't big enough for much more.

She walked around the side, searching for a window. Standing on her tiptoes, she tried to peer in one small window, but the angle of the light only allowed her to see her own reflection.

She gave up casing the house and went to work picking the front door lock. She heard the lock click into place, then took a deep, bracing breath.

Pressing her ear against the cold wood of the door, she strained to hear any sounds from the interior of the house.

Maybe they'd gone out. Maybe they were asleep. She glanced at her watch, registering eight-thirty, and began to feel uneasy. Who would be asleep at eight-thirty? And who would go out but leave their car in the driveway?

Her stomach knotted painfully with the tension. Very slowly, gun in her right hand, she opened the door.

Nothing moved in the entryway, the pale moonlight shimmering through the wall of windows to cast the whole open expanse into a silvery light. It was eerie and beautiful, a still, vaulted room wrapped in shadows.

She moved cautiously into the house, quietly closing and locking the door behind her. She didn't want anyone approaching the front door and noticing something wrong.

She crept through the silent surroundings, wincing as the first floorboard creaked.

She stilled, but nothing moved. She took another careful step, and the moonbeam followed her.

Downstairs, she found an empty bathroom, a den and a door leading down to a basement or cellar. Below, all appeared dark, not a single tone of gray breaking the inky black pool.

She decided to head upstairs first. At the top of the landing, she came to a tiny loft with a bar. She crept to one side, discovering a tiny guest bedroom. A board creaked nearby, and she whirled instantly. Nothing moved save the moonlight and the harsh pounding of her own heart.

She closed the door slowly. She heard another floor-board creak.

This time she froze, taking a deep breath. It was no longer her imagination. Someone was in the house. Someone was in the room behind that door. She crept up next to the doorway, flattening herself against the wall.

What to do, what to do?

She heard another creaking board and the low whisper of someone muttering under his breath. Her hands felt clammy on the gun.

She took another steadying breath and suddenly her hands became calm. This was what she'd trained for. She could do this. She could save Jake.

Her eyes latched on to the bar, and she had an idea. Crossing quickly, she retrieved a glass from the counter. Then she walked to the loft railing and dropped the tumbler down.

It shattered, loud and beautiful, on the hardwood floors.

Immediately, she whipped off her hat and flattened herself against the wall, holding her 9-mm in front of her with both hands. She heard the faint click of the doorknob turning.

Slowly the door cracked open, and she could hear the harsh breathing of a nervous man. The dark barrel of a 10-mm appeared next to her right shoulder.

"Lionel?" he called out gruffly. "Buchanan?"

Patiently, the tension screaming in her shoulders, she waited. The whole gun appeared, followed by a hand.

The shadowed man stepped forward. She slammed the hilt of her gun into his face with all the strength she could muster. With a low cry, the man dropped his gun, bringing his hands instinctively to his mangled face. She delivered two short, sharp uppercuts, and he crumpled at her feet.

Veins overloaded with adrenaline, she found the hand-cuffs tucked at his waist and secured both his hands behind his back. At the bar, she grabbed a towel and tied it around his mouth as a gag, then used another to hog-tie his ankles

behind him. She recovered the 10-mm from the floor and
tucked it into the waistband of her jeans.

Then she stepped back, face sweating, chest heaving and
peered into the darkened room.

The moonlight poured into the space, illuminating a lone,
shirtless figure tied to a chair, head slumped forward. She
fell to her knees before him, looking at Jake's bruised and
battered face.

"No," she breathed, "no, no, no."

She dropped her gun, her trembling hands searching
frantically for a pulse at the base of his neck. For a heart-
stopping moment, she couldn't find it. Then, her shaking
hands made out the feeble beat.

With a low cry, she cradled his head against her chest,
rocking him against her. She pressed her pale cheek against
his matted hair, whispering his name.

His eyes fluttered open. "Hiya, sweetheart," he muttered, and beautiful as ever he grinned.

She stared at him for a breathless moment, and then she
began to weep.

Chapter 13

"Are you all right?" Reggie whispered. Frantically her hands searched his battered head, finding multiple lumps, a half-swollen eye and a lacerated cheek. Wicked scratches zigzagged along his lean ribs, while bruises darkened and swelled on his torso. His skin felt cold and clammy.

Quickly she reached behind him and began tugging on the knotted rope that bound his hands behind the chair.

He moaned against her neck. "I've gotta learn to lay off the rum," he mumbled, squinting his eyes against the pain.

Reggie finished with the stubborn rope, then straightened enough to peel off her large, bulky jacket. She wrapped it around him, rubbing his arms to warm him and ward off the impending shock. Still massaging briskly, she peered down into his one, unswollen eye.

"Tell me your name," she commanded.

"Dogmeat," he replied dryly.

"Seriously," she hissed lowly. "Tell me your name and phone number so I can be sure they haven't beat all the sense out of you."

He winced again. "And you phrased that so delicately, Reggie, my dear. Brings back fond memories, let me tell you. Now are you happy to see me, or simply jealous you didn't get to beat me up first?"

She scowled at him, then abruptly held him close as another surge of protectiveness rushed through her.

"I thought you were dead," she said quietly.

He laid his head against her shoulder, absorbing the softness of her concern. Carefully she stroked his hair, and he thought he might suffer another beating just to get her to hold him this way.

"I knew you would come," he said at last. He raised his head enough to give her a crooked grin. "Now be kind to a battered man and tell me you raced to my side because of my good looks and Southern charm."

"No," she told him, but she smiled softly. "I did it for your money."

He tried to laugh, but the effort made his head pound a little too much. "Get me out of this, Reggie darlin', and all that's mine is yours." Why not? He'd already given her his heart.

She sobered a bit, and he could see the worry in her eyes.

"Do you think you can walk?" she asked quietly.

"Do you think I have a choice?" he countered levelly. But his hands and feet were already tingling unbearably as blood rushed to the ragged, blood-starved nerve endings. He tried to flex his hands and found his fingers nearly incapable of moving. He was a mess.

"How many men?" she asked at last.

He shook his head, struggling to keep his grip on lucidity. "Not sure. It was all kind of a blur." He squinted. "Two men, I think. A big lug who was guarding me and did such nice work on my face, and a smaller, wiry guy with a strange sense of humor. Lionel, I think. I haven't seen Buchanan yet."

"Lionel Henrys," Reggie whispered. "His name was on the list of Tech Services guys. I bet he's the thief." She frowned, her face setting in the dim light. "Why didn't they just kill you, Jake? Surely they've risked more holding you hostage in your own home."

He grinned at her, his smile crooked and sweet. "They know my charm, dear. I'm afraid my reputation has preceded me."

She simply stared at him.

"Bait, darlin'. They've been keeping me to lure you here."

She nodded, not really surprised. Unconsciously she reached up and gently touched his cheek. Immediately he pressed his raspy beard against her hand, half closing his eyes. She leaned forward and kissed his swollen lips.

"I'll get you out of here," she promised, her green eyes as serious as the day she first took the FBI oath to defend and protect.

"Of course," he told her. He grinned once more. "Can I have another kiss for luck?"

She readily complied, fighting the urge to wrap her arms around him and hold him tight.

The sound of a car engine penetrated the silence. Immediately Reggie stood and rushed to the window. Looking out, she saw two headlights approaching the house. Abruptly they swept by, continuing down the winding road. Her breath came out as a tight gasp.

"Time to get moving," she said, her jaw setting.

She turned sharply this time, squatting before him and picking up his hands. Briskly she rubbed circulation through the rope-burned wrists into his cold, slightly blue fingers. He winced, but didn't protest. He rolled his ankles and neck, shaking out his arms.

"Ready to move?" she said at last.

"Darlin', I can always move."

She stood and offered him her hand, her shoulders braced. He allowed her to help him up, placing more weight upon her than he would have liked. The first step made him draw in his breath sharply.

"Ribs," he hissed.

"We'll take it slow," she promised.

He nodded, jaw clenching as he used her to limp from the room. In the loft, they discovered that the big Lug's eyes were open and wary, but the gag kept him quiet in his corner. For a moment, Jake stared down at the larger man while Reggie looked at him with uncertain eyes.

"Take that," Jake said finally, his voice dry. His arm tightened around Reggie, and he looked at the oversize muscle man one last time. "Told you my woman would come."

Reggie tugged gently at Jake's hand, and moving silently, she led him to the stairs. He waved merrily at Lug as they disappeared from sight, but she could see the grim set of his jaw. She swallowed and said nothing.

Downstairs, the moon still poured through the huge expanse of windows, bathing the room in a quiet, blue-toned darkness. They paused in the kitchen long enough for Jake to drink a glass of water. They stood there in shadows, wondering what to do next.

The house was so still, the danger close.

"Reggie," Jake whispered quietly in the moonlit kitchen. "Reggie, come here."

She stepped willingly into his arms, and he rested his battered head against hers, his arms wrapped tightly around her shoulders.

For one, shuddering moment, they held on to each other desperately, as if they were two young kids suddenly alone against the world. In the soft glow of the moonlight, they found strength in their embrace, his cheek pressed against her hair, his arms strong around her body.

The sound of another car engine cut through the silence. Immediately Reggie pulled back, wiping the moisture once more staining her cheeks. Without a word, she cocked her head toward the back sliding-glass door.

Jake nodded, zipped up the thick blue coat and followed her movement.

The car engine cut as Reggie unlocked the door and slid it open. Her stomach cramped in the silence, her heart thudding ominously. At the last minute, she pulled the 10-mm from her waist and handed it to Jake.

He looked at it for a full second, the sound of crashing waves washing over them, then accepted the gun.

"Have you ever shot anyone?" he whispered as he followed her out onto the windy, salt-sprayed deck. She shook her head. "Neither have I," he said. "I think we ought to keep it that way."

Reggie smiled somewhat cynically and led him along the side of the house. The sand was soft and loose beneath their feet, cushioning any noise. Reggie peered around the corner of the house in time to see the car door open. Quickly she flattened herself against the wall, Jake following suit.

Peering carefully from her vantage point, she saw a dark-suited man emerge from the car. Buchanan. He seemed to look around for a minute, cocking his head to the side as if he already knew something was wrong. Her heartbeat accelerated, and she forced herself to remain calm. He couldn't know, damn it. He was just a corrupt man, not a preternatural force. After a minute, he turned and headed for the front door.

They probably had ninety seconds before he knew something was wrong. Sweat trickled down her neck, dried instantly from the cold, coastal winds.

"Now," she whispered. Jake didn't ask, simply followed, once more leaning heavily against her shoulder.

She acted on instinct, not having enough time to plan. She couldn't hot-wire a car fast enough, and Jake was in no condition to run. She opened the unlocked driver-side door and popped the trunk. Her hands trembled now, her insides shaking from the gamble she was about to take.

"Lie down," she ordered, pushing two rifles out of the way. Jake crawled into the sedan's trunk with a small wince, curling up like a child. She had one last glimpse of his somber brown eyes, then closed the trunk.

She heard a small shout from inside the house and shut the driver's side door. Opening the rear door, she dived into the back seat, shutting the car door behind her. Flattening herself against the floor, she untucked her 9-mm, flipped off the safety, and hoped the tinted windows and darkened night helped to hide her.

Minute after minute dragged by. Buchanan was obviously searching the beaches, looking for signs they'd gone along the coast, she told herself. Anytime now, he would return to the car. Her hands grew clammy, and her breathing sounded loud to her ears. Another long minute ticked off.

She thought she heard a low, muffled moan from the trunk, and squeezed her eyes against the building tension. Remain calm, Reggie. Remain calm. You can do this.

Air. What if Jake was suffocating right now in the trunk? What if she'd screwed this up from the very beginning? Anytime now, Buchanan would notice the footprints in the sand, leading around the side of the house to the cars. He would yank open the door and point his 9-mm inside. Two sharp popping noises, and she wouldn't have anything to fear anymore. Then he would turn to the trunk . . .

The car door flew open, and she almost cried out before she realized it was the driver's door. A loud jangle sounded as Buchanan angrily thrust his keys into the ignition. She could hear him swearing under his breath.

The engine roared to life, and with a quick glance in the rearview mirror, Buchanan slammed the car into Reverse and tore out onto Ridge Road.

In the back seat, Reggie held her breath and counseled patience. The roads were winding here. If she sprung too soon, she could kill them all.

She pressed herself flatter against the floor, listening to the rumble of the engine and the sound of passing asphalt. He wasn't driving too fast, probably searching the beaches, the dunes, the parks as he drove.

He slowed for a corner. Was he now looking out at the sand? Was his attention now diverted?

Her muscles screamed with the tension, and the sweat rolled like tears down her face. All right, Reggie. Roll of the dice. Winner takes all.

She jerked up in the back seat and pressed the gun hard against Buchanan's ear.

"One sudden move, and you're dead," she announced coldly. She was rewarded with his eyes widening immediately in the rearview mirror. Her hands stayed remarkably level, and she felt a small flare of triumph.

"Reggie," Buchanan said. She watched him pale, then swallow, and she could practically hear the wheels turning in his mind.

"Reggie," he said again. Then suddenly he gushed out, "I've been looking everywhere for you, O'Doul. I'm so happy to see that you're alive. I've been so worried! My God, O'Doul, do you know what's happened?" He tried to bend forward, and she immediately pressed the gun harder against his ear.

"Don't even try it," she said, her voice harder than steel. "I know exactly what's happened. Now I want you to slow the car down nice and easy. You're going to pull over to the side of the road, and then you're going to get out of the car. Do you remember my marksmanship, Buchanan? Sharpshooter, wasn't it?"

"Let's not do anything brash," he said slowly.

"I'm way beyond brash, Buchanan. I'm a fugitive with nothing to lose."

His foot eased off the gas, and she saw his eyes dart to the side mirror. Still, he made no move to pull over. She felt the tension build once more.

"Buchanan," she warned.

He glanced back at her, but his eyes weren't fearful. "One sharp turn of this wheel, and I could kill us both," he said pointedly. "Plunge us right into the ocean."

She met his gaze in the mirror. "Why would you do that, Buchanan? You're the one with a chance to live. Myself on the other hand . . ."

"What about Jake?" he countered.

She smiled coldly. "Ask Lug what he thinks of his 10-mm now," she said, bluffing.

Buchanan's eyes widened, and he swore under his breath. She continued to smile, wanting him to believe there was no chance of reinforcements arriving. No doubt, after freeing the heavyset man, Buchanan had directed Lug to drive in the other direction to look for them. Sooner or later, Lug would turn around and drive back toward them. So why not let Buchanan believe Jake had control of that vehicle?

"Pull over," she said again. "Real slow, Buchanan. My nerves aren't what they used to be, and this trigger can be very sensitive." The drive was lasting too long. How was Jake in the trunk? What about the carbon monoxide?

She fought to maintain her composure. Finally, with another low curse, Buchanan eased the car over.

"What are you going to do now, Reggie?" he challenged. "Drive to the authorities? Who's gonna believe Frank's kid, Reggie? Ever think of that?"

Yes, she had, and she had no idea what to do next. At this point, she would be happy to survive the next five minutes. The knotted muscles in her neck were cramping from the strain.

"Lower the windows in the car," she ordered, "then turn off the ignition, but leave the lights on." When he didn't immediately comply, she dug the barrel of the gun into the soft spot behind his ear. He lowered the electric windows and killed the ignition. "Keys on the passenger seat," she instructed. "Slow and easy, Buchanan. That's right." Keeping the 9-mm focused on him, she eased open the passenger seat and carefully stepped out. She kept him in sight through the open windows. She rounded the car, then ordered him to open the driver's side door and step out.

Slowly he complied, joining her in the thick darkness. "Now pop open the trunk," she instructed. He did, and she walked close enough to spare a quick glance at Jake. He pushed the lid open awkwardly, and Buchanan took an immediate step toward her.

Reggie dodged him easily. "Remember," she told him with a steely voice, "I have nothing to lose."

Jake crawled out of the trunk, weaving a little on his feet. For the first time, Reggie hesitated. Now, she no longer knew what to do. They had a car and they had a hostage. But Jake needed immediate medical attention and she didn't know if she could keep track of both men.

Jake could hold a gun on Buchanan while she drove, but what if he passed out? She could have Jake drive, but again, what if he passed out?

She stood there, her gun on Buchanan, Jake walking toward her and doubts plaguing her. Then she heard the sound of an approaching car. Lug. Or Lionel.

She turned immediately, shooting on instinct at the headlights. Four quick shots, and the sound of an exploding tire cut the night air. The car squealed, the headlights swerving abruptly for the side of the road. She heard two more shots and braced for impact. But instead, Buchanan uttered a low cry and gripped his left shoulder as his gun fell from his fingers. He started running toward the headlights of the other sedan.

Reggie turned to see Jake's shadowed form lowering his recently fired gun while he leaned heavily against the car.

"I should finish off the bastard, but I can't shoot a man in the back," he said softly, then grimaced at himself. "What a damnable trait."

"It doesn't matter," she said immediately, grateful to see him still lucid and standing. She jerked her head toward Buchanan's car. "Quickly."

He didn't need any other encouragement, wobbling around to the passenger's side. She spared a last glance at Buchanan, who disappeared around the other side of the disabled sedan. The trunk opened and she realized he must be going after rifles. He wouldn't hesitate to use them, either.

She raced to the driver's seat, grabbing the keys from the passenger's side.

"On the road again," Jake whispered, when he'd settled himself in. She smiled starkly, started the engine, and whipped the car on the road as the first rifle shot crackled through the air. She veered the car around a sharp corner, tires squealing slightly, then flattened out in time for another turn. Behind them, another sharp shot cracked the air.

Her foot flattened on the gas, rocketing them down a short straight stretch. A corner hit, and her wiry arms bulged as they fought to keep control of the wheel. The car seemed to bow with the force, and her teeth clenched.

They screeched out of the turn, hitting another small straightaway, then another sharp, hair-raising turn. She couldn't seem to let up on the gas and at any minute she expected another sharp crack of the rifle. The back window would burst, the glass spraying them with wicked shards. Maybe a tire would explode, careening them off the road into cold, icy waters.

"Easy," Jake cautioned. "Their car is disabled, remember?"

She nodded, forcing her foot off the gas as her breath tumbled out in one long gasp. Suddenly she shook all over. Jake reached over and covered her hand. She clung to his grip as if it was the last anchor in an overwhelming ocean.

"I know," he said quietly. "I know."

She shuddered and thought she might be violently ill.

"Pull over," Jake said. "Just for a minute."

Trembling too much to argue, she complied, ducking them into a darkened patch of sea grass and killing the lights. Almost immediately, she threw herself into his arms. He winced slightly as the pain spiked through his ribs like a hot lance. But his arms wrapped tightly around her, his bruised lips finding hers immediately, claiming all her fears and adrenaline and tension.

She tasted savage and raw, needy and fearful. She tasted unbearably hungry and unbearably lost, and he claimed it all because he needed to. He slanted back her neck, plunged his tongue deep into her mouth and ravaged her even as she pressed tightly against him, demanding more. He clutched her face, feeling the warm salt of her tears streak down his cut hands.

"We're alive," he whispered against her mouth. "We're alive, we're alive, we're alive."

For her answer, she kissed him more deeply, raking her tongue across his teeth, biting his lower lip. She cried harder, and he held her even closer, his hand plunging through her hair. She trembled so hard he feared she might break.

With one large hand, he pressed her face against his neck. With the other, he cupped her breast, rubbing his thumb over the rigid nipple through the soft material of her shirt. He kissed her again, more softly this time, teasing the corners of her mouth.

"I love you," he whispered against her lips. "I love you."

While she trembled in his embrace, he reached down and caressed her intimately through her jeans until she bowed like a supple willow in his arms. Her eyes widened with shock, then wonder, and all of a sudden, with one last shuddering gasp, she climaxed.

She collapsed against him, the tension leaving her in an unexpected rush until she was pliable and weak and weary. She folded herself against him, her face pressed against his neck while he continued to stroke her hair.

More tears streaked down her cheeks, but now she no longer knew why she was crying and found herself too tired to care. He cradled her cheek tenderly as another tear escaped.

He brushed it away.

"My sweet Reggie," he whispered and kissed the top of her hair.

She rubbed her cheek against his shoulder.

"We have to keep moving," he whispered against the top of her head.

She nodded, but couldn't meet his eyes. She'd never fallen apart like that. And she'd never been put back together so completely. Deep within herself, she felt a raw, tender place she hadn't known she had.

"Reggie, darlin'," he whispered, brushing her cheek. "Sweetheart, we gotta keep moving."

He felt her stiffen by degrees and wanted to pull her back into his embrace. But his ribs ached, his head swam and he knew he had to keep them moving. And he knew his Reggie well enough to understand that for her, awkwardness always followed these moments. If he gave her something to focus on, it would be easier for her.

Reggie could level a gun at a man, but he knew the three words he'd whispered might be too much for her. Later, he would push her on it. Later, he would make her say those words back to him.

Slowly she eased away. As he'd suspected, she looked at everything but him.

"Where should we go?" she whispered quietly as she reached for the keys in the ignition.

"I don't know," he told her. He shifted slightly, wincing but getting more comfortable.

"I'm sorry," she said immediately. "I've hurt you worse."

He grinned, his teeth a flash of whiteness in the dark. "Honey, there are kinds of pain a man doesn't mind."

"I should have been more considerate," she said softly, steering them onto the road.

"Shut up, Reggie," he told her.

He thought he might have seen her smile.

They drove for another fifteen minutes on the scenic drive, waves pounding outside, darkness pursuing them.

"Maddensfield," Jake said at last. He felt, more than saw, Reggie nod beside him.

"You need medical attention."

"Dr. Jacobs can patch up a crash test dummy," Jake informed her. "Hell, I think he did as much with Garret. Better yet, he won't say a word."

"We have to sleep," Reggie said finally. "After everything we've been through, I don't think I can make it driving all night long."

"Find a roadside motel, if you've got the cash."

She nodded, worrying her lower lip. "The car," she said at last. "They can find us through the car."

"It'll take time," Jake said with a sigh.

She smiled at him dimly in the darkness. "Then it's just a matter of who is most lucky."

His lips twisted smugly. "I've always liked Lady Luck. She's good to me."

Reggie sighed and raked a hand through her hair. "Good, because I think she hates me, Jake. I really think she does."

He reached over and took her hand again. She squeezed his tightly, not saying anything more.

They drove into the night.

Chapter 14

Two hours later, Reggie checked them into a roadside motel, paying cash.

Jake leaned against her heavily as they made it up the stairs to their room. Sitting in the car had stiffened his bruised body, and now he winced with every step. When she finally sat him down on the edge of the bed, he sighed with relief. Reggie disappeared down the hall and returned with a bucket full of ice.

"For your eye," she told him, pouring half the cubes into a towel. "Now lie back and hold it steady. I'll be back in a minute."

Jake nodded obediently, too tired to argue.

Reggie spared him one last glance, worry clutching her stomach with gnarled, insistent fingers. He looked dear to her, his face swollen and bruised and needy. He'd done so much for her, and she wanted desperately to get him to safety. To just this once, get everything right.

In the car, he'd said he loved her. She didn't know whether she believed him or not. He was injured and groggy and only semiconscious. Plus, all law enforcement personnel understood that traumatic events could lead to an artificial sense of closeness. When this was all over, when he was healed and could go back to his adventuresome ways, who knew what he would feel about her?

But, she thought fiercely, she had this moment. Right now, he was hers.

She left, and pushing herself beyond her limits, she drove the car to the furthest of the five available hotels and parked it in the back. Hopefully that would prevent the car from giving them away. She drew a deep breath and ran the three miles back to their facility.

By the time she arrived at their motel, she'd stopped feeling her muscles. She existed in that virtual world of total exhaustion, where there was no sensation, just the robotic compulsion to move, sit, stand, do.

She entered the room to discover that Jake had fallen asleep. The towel full of half-melted ice had slid from his face to the dark blue-and-gold bedspread where it was creating a slow-spreading puddle. Reggie locked the dead bolt and put on the chain. Then she checked the second-story window in case an escape route was needed.

Finally, knowing there was nothing more she could do, she carried the towel and ice to the sink. Moving carefully, she unzipped the oversize jacket covering Jake's inert form. He groaned once, but did not open his eyes. She eased out his arms, then rolled him to his side and pulled the jacket free.

Seeing his upper torso under the full glare of lights made her wince. His entire left side was a giant, purple-green-yellow bruise.

If she saw Lug again, Reggie decided, she would shoot the man.

She shook Jake's shoulder until his eyes finally opened.

"Tell me your name," she commanded softly.

"You need sleep, too," he said quite clearly, then his eyes drifted shut.

She smiled at him softly, bending down and lightly kissing his lips. She shook his shoulder again.

"Your name," she said more forcefully.

He peered at her with glassy eyes, and she suffered a pang of fear. Then he sighed, a deeply weary sound, and his face cracked into the merest of grins. "Dogmeat," he told her. "Still."

She smiled down at him and felt her eyes sting.

"Go to sleep, Dogmeat," she whispered.

He looked at her with tired brown eyes a moment longer. "Still standing guard?" he whispered between cracked lips.

Her heart contracted in her chest and suddenly she could see her dad, uniformed and larger than life, eyes crinkling with his smile as he stood in her doorway to turn out the light. "Still standing guard," she said.

With trembling hands, she tugged the edges of the bed-spread, wrapping it around them as a protective cocoon. Then, with great care, she curled up spoon-fashion next to his side.

Within seconds, both were sound asleep.

"Yow!"

"Well it's supposed to be tight!"

"Honey, breathing is good. Ease up a bit. I'm not as tough as I look."

She arched a skeptical brow. "At this point, you look so tough a brisk wind could blow you over." She did, however, ease up a bit on the strips of sheet she was wrapping around his ribs.

He glared at her halfheartedly. "Good thing I'm natu-rally arrogant," he said with an indignant sniff, "or my ego might actually be affected by your comments."

She smiled grimly and tied off the first strip. Then, with a wicked wiggle of her eyebrows, she picked up the second. He groaned.

It was 9:00 a.m., and they should have been on the road by now. But sleep had restored some of their energy, though Jake's bruises only looked more colorful with the passage of time. They'd already iced his eye again, succeeding in keeping some of the swelling down, though he now looked somewhat lopsided.

She finished wrapping a second strip around his ribs, standing back to inspect her work. God, the man looked like a walking Picasso, all bright colors and disjointed body parts.

She held up three fingers. "How many?" she asked.

He looked at her fingers hard, then shook his head a few times. "Too many," he groaned at last. He squeezed his eyes shut and fell back on the bed.

Wordlessly she regarded him. "We should be in Maddensfield by end of day," she said at last.

She reached down to help him up, but he simply wrapped his hand around her wrist and pulled her down beside him on the bed. She followed the silent command of his hand, resting her head carefully on his chest while he curved his arm around her, holding her close. In silence, he ran his hand through her soft, short hair.

"We're on the defensive," he said quietly.

She shook her head mutely against his chest.

"We can't win, running for our lives," he continued. "If they catch up with us, and we shoot them in self-defense, how will it look? They're the upstanding FBI agents. We're fugitives. Chances are, we'll go from suspected thieves to suspected murderers. It's a lose-lose proposition."

Reggie nodded yet again. She'd figured that out last night. The only real question was what to do. She had some ideas along those lines, but first, she wanted to get Jake safely to Maddensfield. Then, she would personally hunt down Buchanan and set the record straight.

"Surveillance devices," Jake declared, interrupting her thoughts. She tilted her head back, peering at him through narrowed eyes.

"Surveillance devices?"

"Yeah," he said with a long sigh. He rubbed his temples with his right hand, and she could see the tension around his eyes. "Tape recorder, camera, walkie-talkie, that sort of thing. If we can record anything he says, then we'll have backup for our testimony. And, well...." He paused for a moment, then swallowed somberly. "And if anything does go wrong, a tape will give my family a starting point. Mitch will know what to do, and Garret and Cagney will make sure it gets done.''

"My uncles," Reggie whispered softly, "my uncles would help them."

Jake looked at her seriously, then brushed her cheek. "It won't come to that," he said, but she understood he was only saying that to ease her mind.

She pushed herself away, sitting up straight. She brushed a lock of his dark hair from his forehead simply because she wanted to touch him. She followed her fingers with her lips, registering three soft kisses on his battered brow while her breast brushed his cheek.

"Time to hit the road," she said at last. "I parked the car down the street."

"How far?"

"Three miles or so."

He grimaced again, and she knew he was wondering if he could walk that far. "I'll get it," she said. "Then I'll drive up and meet you downstairs."

"They know to look for that vehicle."

"Then we'll just have to move faster. I can switch license plates with another parked car, but this place doesn't have any car rentals."

"I'll go with you," he said and stiffly pulled himself upright.

"Don't be ridiculous," she said immediately. He simply held up his hand.

"Moving will loosen things up, Reggie. Besides, there's strength in numbers. Look what happened last time we separated."

She opened her mouth to argue, but he simply placed his finger over it, lightly outlining her lips. "I gotta save my strength for moving, darlin'," he whispered softly. "So let's not waste it arguing."

She tightened her jaw, then abruptly gave in with a lowering of her eyes. "I don't think men with concussions are supposed to be that logical," she told him.

He managed his familiar grin, and for a moment, some of the old fire returned to his tired eyes. "Guinesses have hard heads. It makes it easier to survive the women they choose. Or men, I suppose, in my sister's case.''

Her chin trembled for a minute, and she brought it up stubbornly. "So did you choose me?" She forced out the question.

For his reply, he bent down and brushed his lips across hers. "Ab-so-lute-ly."

"Good," she whispered fiercely. His eyes held hers for a moment, challenging. But she couldn't bring herself to say the words, so she finally looked away.

"We need to leave," she said. His eyes remained boring into hers. She didn't turn around. "We should buy you a shirt as well," she continued as she picked up the coat. "Maybe we should make a list."

He took the coat from her. "Anything you say, Reggie," he whispered.

She nodded and picked up the pad of paper with a hand that trembled slightly. He stopped her with a hand on her arm. Slowly she turned to find him looking at her with those intense, brooding brown eyes. Her throat went dry, her breath catching in her throat.

"You're very stubborn," he said at last.

"I know," she whispered weakly.

He remained looking at her, as if the force of his gaze could drag the three words he wanted from her throat. Her gaze dropped down to the floor, and he abruptly sighed, a sharp, tired sound.

He turned away. For just one moment, she reached out to him, but she couldn't say the words. They would commit her as surely as steel bars. Her hand fell to her side, and she balled it into a fist.

Jake opened the door and she followed him out.

After consulting the map, they devised their plan of attack. They got back on the highway for two more exits, then turned off to a small town. There, they found an electronics store and purchased a small tape recorder. Reggie drove them to the local post office, while Jake began dictating into the tape recorder.

They'd purchased two tapes, one for Jake to describe events thus far, the other to use when they encountered Buchanan again. The first tape they mailed to Jake's sister, Liz, who Jake thought had the least chance of being under FBI surveillance. If the tape got through, and something did happen to Reggie and him, at least their families would know their side of the story.

They'd debated calling Maddensfield, but Reggie was ninety-eight percent sure all the phone lines for Jake's family were bugged and monitored. If the call was traced back, she and Jake could be caught unawares.

They were going to try to sneak to Dr. Jacobs instead.

Turning onto the local routes, Reggie thought she could get them to Maddensfield by evening.

Once in Virginia, they paused at a trucker's diner for lunch and coffee, because Reggie had begun to fall asleep at the wheel. As soon as they were done eating, however, she felt jittery again. Was a dark sedan already driving by, spotting the Lincoln in the parking lot? Were they just about to turn onto a monitored road? What about the next exit? And the one after that?

They had a new license plate on the car, having swapped with another vehicle in the hotel parking lot. But even then, she felt unbearably conspicuous in the large, dark Town-car.

They drove on, sticking primarily to smaller roads. Finally they had no choice but to pick up the Interstate. They were exposed now for any State police or local FBI agent to spot. They made it through the first ten miles, then the second.

Finally, hours passing into hours, she turned onto 421 West. Another hour or so, and they would be all right. She would wake Jake then, and he could direct them to the doctor's office.

Dusk turned to darkness and the rain began to fall. She drove smoothly along the dark highway, the quiet rhythm of the windshield wipers filling her ears. Forty more minutes, maybe fifty.

They were so close.

She concentrated on the soothing sound of the wind-shield wipers and kept driving.

They made it to Maddensfield without incident.

She woke Jake with a light touch, noticed his glassy eyes and realized a moment of panic. But with a small shake of his head, he cleared his gaze and was able to direct her to Dr. Jacobs's office. It was after eight now, and when they finally pulled up to the tiny brick office all the windows were dark.

Reggie picked the lock on the front door and offered Jake support as she led him inside.

She closed the door quietly behind them, peering out to the dark, rainy street. For the first time, she allowed herself to relax.

"Sit down on the couch," she instructed, helping Jake to the small, leather sofa. "I'll find Dr. Jacobs's home phone number."

Moving to the small desk in front of the door, she snapped on the desk light, searching for the secretary's Rolodex.

And suddenly found herself staring at the chrome metal of a 9-mm. She followed the barrel back to find Buchanan's grinning face.

Her eyes rounded and without thinking, she took a step back. Immediately he leveled the gun.

"Don't be a fool," he told her calmly, his blue eyes hard. He motioned with the gun, pushing her back toward Jake. Reggie took her eyes off the barrel long enough to see that Jake was still awake, his eyes unflinching on the gun. He had the tape recorder, but had he turned it on?

"How did you know?" Jake asked calmly, his brown eyes meeting Buchanan's blue gaze with the composure of a seasoned poker player. Buchanan had a white bandage on his left shoulder, evidence that Jake knew how to fire a gun. The wound, however, could not have been serious, for Buchanan wielded the 9-mm now without the slightest sign of weakness.

"Educated guess. When your brother Garret was hurt and on the run, he also came straight to Maddensfield and Dr.

Jacobs." Buchanan shook his head, clicking his tongue chidingly. "Just to be thorough, I sent Lionel and our assistant to watch Mitch's house. Really, Guiness, you're not as smart as you think."

Jake simply nodded, his eyes never leaving Buchanan's face. Beside him, Reggie felt her hand begin to itch. If she could just reach back for her gun. Maybe a casual stretch... One shot would do it. Even if he fired back, it would give Jake a chance.

The twitch in her fingers became unbearable.

"I'll take your weapon now," Buchanan said, as if reading her mind. "Letting me keep mine when we were in the car was a mistake, you know, Reggie. The kind of rookie mistake that might be made by an agent new to the field. On the other hand, I've been in the field for nearly as long as you've been alive. Whatever you're thinking, I've done it, and I'm faster, smarter and steadier than you are, O'Doul."

She glared at him helplessly, her green eyes spitting dark, frustrated fire. "Well if you're so damn good," she snarled at last, "then how do you explain how Jake and I figured out what you were doing? If you're so damn good, Buchanan, why are we still alive and you're caught having to dispose of us in Jake's hometown?"

Buchanan's eyes darkened, his hand trembling dangerously on the trigger. "Lionel always had a flare for dramatics," he growled. "Damn fool nearly blew it all with his verses and phone messages and theatrics." He pulled back the trigger to within a hairbreadth of firing, and Reggie felt all the blood drain from her face. He looked like a man carved from stone, no longer her fatherly mentor, but someone who was indeed smarter, faster and steadier than she ever would be. "The gun, O'Doul. Now!"

Very slowly, she reached for the weapon in the small of her back and pulled it out with the grip pointed toward him.

"It doesn't matter," she whispered. "It's too messy now. You shoot us here, in Jake's brother's jurisdiction, you'll never be able to cover it up. His family will look into things. My uncles will look into things. Plus we left documentation, Buchanan. Shoot us, and all you've done is exchange theft charges for murder."

Buchanan merely looked at her with his hard blue eyes. He shook his head disdainfully. "You can't bluff worth a damn, O'Doul."

"But I can," Jake said clearly, forcing Buchanan's gaze from Reggie to him.

Reggie didn't hesitate for a moment. She acted on instinct, tossing her gun at Buchanan. His hand jerked automatically toward the silvery sheen, and she used the opportunity to rush him. She caught him around the waist with her head ducked low, using her momentum to plow them both to the ground.

At the same moment he fired, and the sharp blast rang through her ears with stunning fury. She felt a pain, sharp, hot and distant, slice through her shoulder.

Far away, she heard Jake calling her name.

Buchanan's hand lodged under her chin as they tumbled to the floor, the heel of his palm forcing her head back. Lying on top of him, both of her arms were pinned between them, leaving her vulnerable.

Abruptly she rolled to the side, having seen his right hand come up with the gun. She kicked out sharply, once, twice, and the gun went flying. Jake shouted something to her, but her ears still rang from the gunshot.

Buchanan lashed out, catching her squarely in the side with his booted foot. She rolled again, her mind registering more pain and the distant thought that she'd lost control of the fight.

She came up flat against the wall and knew a moment of panic. She arched back to jump to her feet, and pain lanced through her shoulder, sharp and unexpected. She staggered, barely regaining her balance, and rose with more of a drunken stagger than fluid grace.

Buchanan was already crawling toward his gun where it lay beneath the secretary's desk.

"Don't move," Jake said clearly, his voice sharp and remarkably calm. Both Buchanan and Reggie turned to see him level Reggie's gun at Buchanan's head. For a long minute, both simply stared at him.

"You don't have it in you," Buchanan said abruptly. "You're just an overpaid playboy, Guiness. You can't shoot an unarmed man."

Buchanan glanced up, and with one last look at Jake, reached for his gun lying an arm's length away on the floor.

Jake didn't even blink. He simply fired, and the hardwood floor above Buchanan's hand exploded into splinters. Buchanan immediately yelped. "Son of a—!"

Jake fired again, and the floor by Buchanan's ribs exploded. Sharp wooden slivers sprayed the man's side, and he rolled away from the gun, covering his head with his arms.

Jake followed the man with the gun, his grip never wavering. Leaning against the wall, Reggie felt herself smile even as blood trickled down her shoulder.

"Care to try again?" Jake asked Buchanan quite coolly.

Buchanan uncovered his head long enough to look at Jake with naked hatred. "I won't go to jail," he swore darkly, "and you don't have the guts to kill a man."

"I don't have to kill you, Buchanan. A kneecap or elbow will do just fine."

Buchanan flushed crimson with frustration, but Jake could see the beads of sweat rolling down his face. Abruptly the man's eyes went behind him, rounding at some sight behind Jake's shoulder.

"I'll be damned," Buchanan said abruptly. "I did shoot her."

Jake heard a small thud, and without looking knew that Reggie had hit the floor. A black film suddenly covered his eyes, and the cerebral Guiness brother felt the hot fuel of pure rage boil through his veins.

His face turned white beneath his bruises, his jaw tightening. He looked Buchanan straight in the eye and had the satisfaction of seeing the older man suddenly pale.

"No," Buchanan said, raising a hand. He made a sudden desperate lunge.

Jake pulled the trigger.

Epilogue

Reggie stood in the deserted cemetery for a long while.

Her face expressionless, she knelt down and laid the three red carnations on her parents' graves. Then she simply sat in silence in front of Frank O'Doul's headstone. Neither of them had ever been any good with words.

She didn't know why she had come, and so maybe that's why she didn't know the words to say. The FBI questioning had finally ended this morning, and she'd been released from custody to fly up to Boston. She'd passed the lie detector test, and had finally gotten Special Agent in Charge Stan Leonard to admit than Buchanan and Lionel had failed. Stan had also mentioned that the tape recording had helped, but he'd refused to elaborate. Overall, they were keeping her in the dark while they determined if she was an accessory to the thefts or just a victim. She hadn't even been allowed to speak to Jake.

When Reggie had woken up in the hospital, Special Agent Leonard had simply told her Jake was all right and receiving medical attention as well. Buchanan, who'd suffered gunshot wounds to his left shoulder and right hand, was receiving treatment at a separate facility. Then the questioning and true examination of events had begun.

She'd understood the procedure. She'd even understood that she was kept separate from Jake so that they would not have the opportunity to compare notes and prepare a joint story. Their answers needed to be independent and similar to prove their innocence. But they'd taken even the gold *claddagh* from her, leaving her hands as bare and defenseless as the rest of her felt.

She'd woken up alone in the hospital, and there were times when she'd wondered if all those moments with Jake might have been just a dream.

After two weeks of relentless questioning, they'd finally let her go this morning. Stan had shaken her hand and said he looked forward to working with her in the future.

The facts, including Jake's beaten body, the polygraph results and a tape recording of Buchanan's incriminating comments had revealed the true nature of Buchanan and Lionel's actions. Also, the man Reggie mentally called Lug had agreed to testify against them.

It appeared that Lionel had used his breaking-and-entering skills to rob the Isabella Stewart Gardner Museum. Buchanan, who'd been part of the FBI's investigation team for the Gardner thefts, had caught on to Lionel's involvement. Rather than turn in the man, he'd proposed a more elaborate scheme to steal prime pieces from private collectors and sell them to other "underground" collectors. But Buchanan hadn't been able to reign in Lionel's arrogance and increasing need for recognition. Lionel had created the Highwayman persona, leaving flowery prose with various levels of clues. He'd also left Reggie the voicemail, wanting to gloat. The egomaniac liked the chase, the challenge, the chance to prove again and again that he was the best there ever was.

Reggie and Jake had proved otherwise.

The bad guys were now caught, the artwork recovered from Jake's Newport home and Reggie's record cleared. She might even come out ahead for having kept Jake and herself alive. Not bad work for a rookie field agent.

And now? Now she stood alone.

She stared at her father's grave, and the cold November wind whispered through her short auburn hair.

She wasn't Frank O'Doul's kid anymore. She'd proven her fidelity, bravery and integrity by living up to the shield she carried.

Now she was just Regina O'Doul, and all of a sudden, she didn't know what to do. The sharp edge was gone, the overwhelming burden suddenly dissolved. She sat, lost and alone, missing her father more than ever.

I made it, Dad, but you weren't here to see. Two seconds on the clock, and I scored the winning point at last. So where were you, Dad? Why can't I hear you screaming, "That's my girl!"

She picked up one the carnations, then arranged it lovingly on the grave. Her shoulder still ached, but the injury wasn't serious.

And Jake?

His absence hurt more than she'd ever imagined. As if someone had shown her the magic of sparks, then run away with the fire.

Life went on, though. She had her job, right? Wasn't that what she'd always wanted?

She stood, her left hand resting for a moment on the cold granite of the modest tombstone.

"I love you, Dad," she whispered at last, but it still didn't ease the emptiness in her belly. She paused before her mother's grave, seeing her quiet beauty one last time in her mind.

Then Reggie turned and walked down the hillside to the gates. She was halfway down when she saw him.

He leaned against his red Porsche, both hands tucked into the pockets of his jeans. He wore a chocolate suede blazer over a white oxford, the throat unbuttoned enough to reveal a light smattering of brown chest hair.

He looked good. Really, really, damn good.

She stilled for a moment, watching him across a sea of crisp fall grass and half-naked trees. She began to walk and fought the impulse to run.

She knew the minute he spotted her because his face broke into a grin.

She didn't say anything at the bottom of the hill, simply walked within six inches of him and kept staring at him with dark green eyes.

"Hi there, good-lookin'," he drawled at last. He smiled at her dearly, then reached out to trace her cheek. She closed her eyes and marveled at the feel of his fingertips against her skin.

"I figured I might find you here," he said at last.

She opened her eyes. "He was my father," she whispered hoarsely.

He nodded, his brown eyes understanding. "Blood is thicker than water," he agreed.

"I miss him. I miss them both."

He drew her into his arms, one large palm cradling the back of her head as she pressed her cheek against his shoulder. He held her tightly, and she breathed in the rich scent of raw suede and spicy soap.

She wept because she understood now that sometimes even O'Douls need to cry. And laugh. And fall in love. She wrapped her arms around Jake's neck and clung to him while the brisk fall wind whipped around them.

"There now," he said at last, stroking her short, silky hair. "It's all over now, Reggie. I'm sure your father is proud."

She nodded against his jacket, still not letting him go.

"Your shoulder all right?" he asked.

She nodded again, her fingers finding the edges of his dark brown hair and flicking through the thick strands.

"And you?" she asked at last, her voice unusually husky.

"Fine and dandy. I understand from Agent Leonard, however, that Buchanan and Lionel will be moving to a new neighborhood soon. One with lots of bars."

"We did well," she said at last, her voice still muffled against his coat. The suede felt soft and warm against her cheek, his arms hard and real around her shoulders.

She wanted to stand here in the circle of his arms forever, her cheek pressed against his hard shoulder. The sheer need frightened her. The thought of stepping back frightened her more.

Unconsciously her hands tightened on his neck. He stroked her hair.

"Feel up to a little drive?" he asked. She stiffened in confusion, but didn't pull away. He took that as a sign of encouragement. He had to clear his throat twice to get the words out. "I'm, uh, well I find myself in need of a date, you see. My family is having this get-together for my parents' forty-fifth wedding anniversary. As half their entertainment is seeing who I'll bring with me, I'd hate to disappoint them and go solo."

She still didn't say anything, and he felt the first hot jab of insecurity. It had been two weeks. But he'd seen that look on her face when she'd glanced down the hillside and spotted him. Felt the way she'd walked into his arms. Surely she wasn't indifferent.

"So you always bring a date to these things?" she said finally, her voice soft but clear against his chest. He traced his hand down her back, marveling at the sinuous suppleness of her body.

"Yep," he said, purposefully keeping his voice light. "I've brought poets and actresses and models. Never anyone licensed to kill, though. I think this brings my dating standards to a whole new level."

She stepped back, but he wouldn't relinquish his hold.

"So you need a date?"

"Yeah. Will you come along? I promise no one will shoot at us this time."

"I don't know. Could be rather boring then." Her own voice was remarkably level. She had no idea where it was coming from.

"Darlin', you don't know my family if you think that." He rubbed his hands up and down her arms. "Come on. If we leave now, we can be at the Logan airport in time to catch a flight to Winston-Salem. We'll be there by nightfall."

She found herself nodding, though she'd only flown into Boston about an hour ago herself. She'd meant to spend a few days resting at her aunt Helen's, but now that Jake was here before her, she couldn't imagine going anyplace else. He led her to the passenger side of his car, and she followed wordlessly.

A date? It wasn't what she'd imagined, but at least he'd come to find her. She couldn't discount that. But if he had his Porsche, he must have driven up, meaning he'd gotten out at least a day before her. What had he done first? Had he thought of her at all during that first moment of freedom?

He opened the door, and she saw two wrapped presents sitting on the passenger's side. She glanced at him questioningly.

"Open them," he told her, his face smiling easily, but perhaps with a trace of nervousness.

As he drove, she picked up the presents.

The first present was a decent-size square box. She unwrapped it to reveal a basketball. In spite of herself, she smiled. Then she turned it over and saw a blue scrawl across the rough orange surface: Larry Bird.

Her eyes widened a fraction. "Very nice," she said at last, other words failing her.

"I've never tried shopping for someone who saved my life before," he told her modestly from the wheel of his Porsche. "I hope I did okay."

"You did fine," she said finally, turning to the second package. Someone who saved his life? Was that her official positioning then? What about those words of love? Had the sentiment faded with the adrenaline, leaving only his grinning charm and easy friendliness? She needed so much more than that.

The second package revealed catnip. She stared at it in open puzzlement.

"For Tom," Jake explained. "I thought it might soften him up a bit."

"Soften him up for what?"

"We'll just have to see."

She didn't know how to reply to that.

"You didn't have to do any of this," she said at last. They turned into the airport.

"I did," Jake said. "I truly did."

He bought two first-class tickets for them, but she didn't notice the luxury. Instead she leaned against his shoulder, and before the plane even left the runway, fell asleep. He leaned his own head on top of hers and joined her.

Dusk had fallen by the time they arrived at the lighted ranch house.

Reggie felt a moment of self-consciousness. She was dressed simply in jeans and an old gray Bureau sweatshirt. Her short hair was flat from sleeping, her light makeup smudged. She looked like a kid, certainly nothing like Jake's usual dates. But he didn't seem to notice as he kissed her lightly on the lips and rang the doorbell.

She heard several exclamations, then the sharp sound of footprints approaching the door. Immediately it was thrown open by an older woman with fading brown hair and warm brown eyes. The minute she saw Jake, her eyes crinkled with her smile.

"Jake! I'm so glad you are here!"

The woman, not giving Jake time to answer, swept immediately to Reggie, hugging her warmly. "You must be that Agent Regina O'Doul," the woman told her with a brilliant smile. "I'm Jake's mother Dotti, and I would like to personally thank you for all the help you gave my son. Mitch has told me all about it, and I'm just so happy you could join us."

She squeezed Reggie's hand in genuine gratitude, and Reggie could only nod in dazed silence. Beside her, Jake whispered in her ear, "Yes, they're all this overwhelming. But they are kind, and they do mean it."

She summoned a smile for him and managed to retain the smile through the haze of introductions. There was his sister Liz with his mother's rich hair but her own midnight eyes. She sat with her handsome husband, Richard, a dark, impressive man who smiled at Reggie with sympathetic understanding. Sitting by the fire, their oldest son Andrew was reading Winnie the Pooh to his baby sister, Melinda.

On the couch, the tall, handsome Mitch Guiness rose to greet her with his absolutely stunning wife, Jessica. It seemed Jessica had been a model, but was now preparing to teach grade school once their twin boys had turned one.

Sitting at the dining room table, Garret, the second oldest, now lounged comfortably with his arm around a soft, beautiful woman named Suzanne. She was Maddensfield's kindergarten teacher and would marry Garret in just a month. Every time someone mentioned it, her face glowed a little bit more. The two seemed to always be touching, a casual caress here, holding hands there.

Nearly as bad was the youngest Guiness brother, Cagney, who had the steadiest gray eyes Reggie had ever seen. His fiancé, Marina, had striking violet eyes, combined with a wild mane of black hair. They were discussing their upcoming May nuptials, while Henry Guiness sat at the head of the table and beamed as if all this good grace was purely of his making.

In the middle of all the laughter and discussion, Reggie stood with Jake's hand on her shoulder. Liz brought her a glass of white wine and chatted with her before a buzzer in the kitchen called her away.

On cue, Mitch and Cagney added the leaf to a new-looking dining room table, apparently made by Garret and Henry. Jessica and Suzanne set up a card table for the food to sit upon.

Jake and Reggie were put in charge of setting the table while Garret poured drinks. The next thing Reggie knew, she was seated beside Jake, looking at a plate heaped with ham, sweet potatoes, green beans and salad. Mitch, the oldest, said a small grace, then raised his glass for a toast.

"To Mom and Dad," he said clearly, "who married forty-five years ago today, after knowing each other for only four days. Which just goes to prove that insanity does run in the family, and that by God, they did it right. Thank you, both of you, for forty-five years of love and teaching your kids what it ought to be. I think we learned the lesson well."

Everyone concurred with soft "hear, hears," and everyone drank.

Wineglasses were set down and forks picked up when Jake abruptly tapped his glass with his fork. Everyone obligingly stopped eating, waiting for his toast.

For the first time, Reggie noticed that his hand trembled.

"Well now," he started to say, then cleared his throat. "I know popular belief in this family is that I will never settle down. But just to prove that an old dog can learn new tricks—and that I paid attention all those years at home—I think, if Reggie's willing, I'd like to give it a try."

Reggie felt the blood drain from her face while ten pairs of eyes abruptly fastened onto her. Jake turned and pulled out a familiar blue velvet box from his inside jacket pocket. He opened it and revealed the gold *claddagh* he'd given to her weeks before. He picked it up from its blue bed, fingering it for a moment as his family watched.

"When I originally gave this to you," he said quietly, "I said I could take it back if I had to. I suppose that's still true, except that I don't want to have to." He took a deep breath, then slid the ring back onto her finger, crown down. "I hold your heart in my hands," he recited softly, using the traditional Irish words that referred to the ring's emblem of hands holding a heart with a crown, "and I crown it with my love. Will you marry me, Reggie?"

Her lips parted, her eyes suddenly moist and her throat tight. For an awful moment, she thought she wouldn't be able to get the words out, and she would simply die a thousand quiet deaths at this table.

"I love you," she whispered at last through thick lips. The entire table cheered. "I love you," she whispered again and threw herself into his embrace.

"Yes, yes," she told him, kissing his face while the first tears of joy tracked down her cheeks. "Of course, of course."

He kissed her deeply, not caring if his whole family was watching. She was his, and he couldn't be happier.

Finally, they pulled away long enough to look at each other with soft, delighted eyes. For a moment, the whole table was respectfully quiet.

Then nine-year-old Andy spoke up through the hush. "That was gross," he said quite clearly.

And they all started to laugh.

As everyone picked up their silverware, filling the air with the comforting clatter of china and utensils, Henry Guiness looked across the table to his bride of forty-five years. She smiled at him as lovely now as she'd been that first night so many decades ago. Tomorrow, they would fly out to Las Vegas, courtesy of their children, and spend one week alone in the city that had given them so much—each other.

Silently Dotti mouthed "I love you," and in reply, Henry raised his wineglass and toasted the woman he loved more than life itself.

Around them, their children and grandchildren laughed and chattered and loved.

*   *   *   *   *

The first book in the exciting new
Fortune's Children series is

HIRED HUSBAND

by *New York Times* bestselling writer
Rebecca Brandewyne

Beginning in July 1996
Only from Silhouette Books

Here's an exciting sneak preview....

Minneapolis, Minnesota

As Caroline Fortune wheeled her dark blue Volvo into the underground parking lot of the towering, glass-and-steel structure that housed the global headquarters of Fortune Cosmetics, she glanced anxiously at her gold Piaget wristwatch. An accident on the snowy freeway had caused rush-hour traffic to be a nightmare this morning. As a result, she was running late for her 9:00 a.m. meeting—and if there was one thing her grandmother, Kate Winfield Fortune, simply couldn't abide, it was slack, unprofessional behavior on the job. And lateness was the sign of a sloppy, disorganized schedule.

Involuntarily, Caroline shuddered at the thought of her grandmother's infamous wrath being unleashed upon her. The stern rebuke would be precise, apropos, scathing and delivered with coolly raised, condemnatory eyebrows and in icy tones of haughty grandeur that had in the past reduced many an executive—even the male ones—at Fortune Cosmetics not only to obsequious apologies, but even to tears. Caroline had seen it happen on more than one occasion, although, much to her gratitude and relief, she herself was seldom a target of her grandmother's anger. And she wouldn't be this morning, either, not if she could help it. That would be a disastrous way to start out the new year.

Grabbing her Louis Vuitton totebag and her black leather portfolio from the front passenger seat, Caroline stepped gracefully from the Volvo and slammed the door. The heels of her Maud Frizon pumps clicked briskly on the concrete floor as she hurried toward the bank of elevators that would take her up into the skyscraper owned by her family. As the elevator doors slid open, she rushed down the long, plushly carpeted corridors of one of the hushed upper floors toward the conference room.

By now Caroline had her portfolio open and was leafing through it as she hastened along, reviewing her notes she had prepared for her presentation. So she didn't see Dr. Nicolai Valkov until she literally ran right into him. Like her, he had his head bent over his own portfolio, not watching where he was going. As the two of them collided, both their portfolios and the papers inside went flying. At the unexpected impact, Caroline lost her balance, stumbled, and would have fallen had not Nick's strong, sure hands abruptly shot out, grabbing hold of her and pulling her to him to steady her. She gasped, startled and stricken, as she came up hard against his broad chest, lean hips and corded thighs, her face just inches from his own—as though they were lovers about to kiss.

Caroline had never been so close to Nick Valkov before, and, in that instant, she was acutely aware of him—not just as a fellow employee of Fortune Cosmetics but also as a man. Of how tall and ruggedly handsome he was, dressed in an elegant, pin-striped black suit cut in the European fashion, a crisp white shirt, a foulard tie and a pair of Cole Haan loafers. Of how dark his thick, glossy hair and his deep-set eyes framed by raven-wing brows were—so dark that they were almost black, despite the bright, fluorescent lights that blazed overhead. Of the whiteness of his straight teeth against his bronzed skin as a brazen, mocking grin slowly curved his wide, sensual mouth.

"Actually, I *was* hoping for a sweet roll this morning— but I daresay you would prove even tastier, Ms. Fortune," Nick drawled impertinently, his low, silky voice tinged with a faint accent born of the fact that Russian, not English, was his native language.

At his words, Caroline flushed painfully, embarrassed and annoyed. If there was one person she always attempted to avoid at Fortune Cosmetics, it was Nick Valkov. Following the breakup of the Soviet Union, he had emigrated to the

United States, where her grandmother had hired him to direct the company's research and development department. Since that time, Nick had constantly demonstrated marked, traditional, Old World tendencies that had led Caroline to believe he not only had no use for equal rights but also would actually have been more than happy to turn back the clock several centuries where females were concerned. She thought his remark was typical of his attitude toward women: insolent, arrogant and domineering. Really, the man was simply insufferable!

Caroline couldn't imagine what had ever prompted her grandmother to hire him—and at a highly generous salary, too—except that Nick Valkov was considered one of the foremost chemists anywhere on the planet. Deep down inside Caroline knew that no matter how he behaved, Fortune Cosmetics was extremely lucky to have him. Still, that didn't give him the right to manhandle and insult her!

"I assure you that you would find me more bitter than a cup of the strongest black coffee, Dr. Valkov," she insisted, attempting without success to free her trembling body from his steely grip, while he continued to hold her so near that she could feel his heart beating steadily in his chest—and knew he must be equally able to feel the erratic hammering of her own.

"Oh, I'm willing to wager there's more sugar and cream to you than you let on, Ms. Fortune." To her utter mortification and outrage, she felt one of Nick's hands slide insidiously up her back and nape to her luxuriant mass of sable hair, done up in a stylish French twist.

"You know so much about fashion," he murmured, eyeing her assessingly, pointedly ignoring her indignation and efforts to escape from him. "So why do you always wear your hair like this...so tightly wrapped and severe? I've never seen it down. Still, that's the way it needs to be worn, you know...soft, loose, tangled about your face. As it is, your hair fairly cries out for a man to take the pins from it, so he can see how long it is. Does it fall past your shoulders?" He quirked one eyebrow inquisitively, a mocking half smile still twisting his lips, letting her know he was enjoying her obvious discomfiture. "You aren't going to tell me, are you? What a pity. Because my guess is that it does—and I'd like to know if I'm right. And these glasses." He indicated the large, square, tortoiseshell frames perched on her slender, classic nose. "I think you use them to hide behind more than you do to see. I'll bet you don't actually even need them at all."

Caroline felt the blush that had yet to leave her cheeks deepen, its heat seeming to spread throughout her entire quivering body. Damn the man! Why must he be so infuriatingly perceptive?

Because everything that Nick suspected was true.

* * * * *

To read more, don't miss
HIRED HUSBAND
by Rebecca Brandewyne,
Book One in the new
FORTUNE'S CHILDREN series,
beginning this month and available only from
Silhouette Books!

This exciting new cross-line continuity series unites
five of your favorite authors as they weave five
connected novels about love, marriage—and
Daddy's unexpected need for a baby carriage!

Get ready for

THE BABY NOTION by Dixie Browning (SD#1011, 7/96)
Single gal Priscilla Barrington would do anything for a
baby—even visit the local sperm bank. Until cowboy
Jake Spencer set out to convince her to have a family
the natural—and much more exciting—way!

And the romance in New Hope, Texas, continues with:

BABY IN A BASKET
by Helen R. Myers (SR#1169, 8/96)

MARRIED...WITH TWINS!
by Jennifer Mikels (SSE#1054, 9/96)

HOW TO HOOK A HUSBAND (AND A BABY)
by Carolyn Zane (YT#29, 10/96)

DISCOVERED: DADDY
by Marilyn Pappano (IM#746, 11/96)

DADDY KNOWS LAST arrives in July...only from

DKL-D

TRINITY STREET WEST

where danger lies around every corner—and the
biggest danger of all is falling in love.

The new miniseries by

Justine Davis

continues in August 1996 with

LEADER OF THE PACK (IM #728)

Ryan Buckhart needed a place to lie low, to rest his
wounded body, so he went to the only haven he
knew: his ex-wife's home. Lacey was as beautiful as
ever—and still frightened by his dangerous life-style.
Then the *real* trouble began.

Don't miss this new series—only from

New York Times Bestselling Author
REBECCA BRANDEWYNE

Launches a new twelve-book series—FORTUNE'S CHILDREN
beginning in July 1996 with Book One

Hired Husband

Caroline Fortune knew her marriage to Nick Valkov was in
name only. She would help save the family business, Nick
would get a green card, and a paper marriage would suit both
of them. Until Caroline could no longer deny the feelings Nick
stirred in her and the practical union turned passionate.

MEET THE FORTUNES—a family whose legacy is greater than
riches. Because where there's a will...there's a wedding!

Look for Book Two, *The Millionaire and the Cowgirl*,
by Lisa Jackson. Available in August 1996 wherever Silhouette
books are sold.

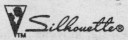